NEW PENGUIN SH
GENERAL EDITOR: T.
ASSOCIATE EDITOR: S

WILLIAM SHAKESPEARE

*

KING HENRY
THE EIGHTH

EDITED BY
A. R. HUMPHREYS

PENGUIN BOOKS

PENGUIN BOOKS

Published by the Penguin Group
Penguin Books Ltd, 27 Wrights Lane, London W8 5TZ, England
Penguin Books USA Inc., 375 Hudson Street, New York, New York 10014, USA
Penguin Books Australia Ltd, Ringwood, Victoria, Australia
Penguin Books Canada Ltd, 10 Alcorn Avenue, Toronto, Ontario, Canada M4V 3B2
Penguin Books (NZ) Ltd, 182–190 Wairau Road, Auckland 10, New Zealand

Penguin Books Ltd, Registered Offices: Harmondsworth, Middlesex, England

This edition first published 1971
7 9 10 8 6

Printed in Great Britain by Antony Rowe Ltd, Chippenham, Wiltshire
Set in Monotype Ehrhardt

CONTENTS

INTRODUCTION

AN early production of *Henry VIII*, on 29 June 1613, sent the Globe Theatre up in flames. The next day Thomas Lorkin wrote to Sir Thomas Puckering – they were both men of affairs about court – and related how, while Burbage's company the King's Men (the leading company of the time) were presenting the play, certain 'chambers' (stage cannon) were fired 'in way of triumph' and set alight the theatre's thatched roof, so that the whole place burnt down in less than two hours. On 2 July Sir Henry Wotton, the diplomat-poet, though he probably had not been present at the performance himself, reported more circumstantially to his nephew Sir Edmund Bacon, and from his account it is clear that the fateful moment was that marked by the stage direction '*Chambers discharged*' (I.4.49). His words throw light on the play's contemporary presentation:

The King's players had a new play, called All is True, *representing some principal pieces of the reign of Henry VIII, which was set forth with many extraordinary circumstances of pomp and majesty, even to the matting of the stage; the Knights of the Order with their Georges and garters, the Guards with their embroidered coats, and the like: sufficient in truth within a while to make greatness very familiar, if not ridiculous. Now, King Henry making a masque at the Cardinal Wolsey's house, and certain chambers being shot off at his entry, some of the paper, or other stuff, wherewith one of them was stopped, did light on the thatch, where being thought at first but an idle smoke, and their eyes more attentive to the show, it kindled inwardly, and ran round like a train [fuse of gunpowder], consuming within less than an hour the whole house to the very grounds. This was the fatal period of that virtuous fabric, wherein yet nothing did perish but wood and straw, and a few forsaken cloaks; only one man had his breeches set on fire, that would perhaps have broiled him, if he had not by the benefit of a provident wit put it out with bottle ale.*

(reprinted in E. K. Chambers, *The Elizabethan Stage*, Volume 2, pages 419–20)

The text as we have it does not exactly bear out this account of Knights of the Garter and a procession of guards, yet the Garter King-of-Arms does appear, and the exceptional degree of ceremonial would justify the version Wotton gives – a degree of ceremonial so realistic as to make him fear that familiarity might breed contempt. The title as Wotton cites it – *All is True* – was perhaps an alternative to that using the King's name, and meant to draw attention, as the Prologue also does, to the play's unusual care to be historically authentic. *Henry VIII* is in fact the only play in the first Folio (1623) to be called a history on its individual title-page – and a 'Famous History' at that (*The Famous History of the Life of King Henry the Eight*): the other histories appear as the 'Tragedy', or 'Life', or 'Life and Death', or 'First Part' (or 'Second' or 'Third Part', as the case may be) of their respective monarchs. A seventeenth-century ballad provides further evidence of the alternative title. It describes the Globe's fate, and each verse bears the refrain 'all this is true'. The second stanza runs as follows (the reference to 'Death' being presumably poetic licence):

All you that please to understand,
Come listen to my story,
To see Death with his raking brand
' Mongst such an auditory;
Regarding neither Cardinal's might,
Nor yet the rugged face of Henry the Eight.
Oh sorrow, pitiful sorrow, and yet all this is true.

*

The play follows its principal sources – Holinshed's *Chronicles* in the second edition (1587) for most of its course, Foxe's *Acts and Monuments* for the Cranmer scenes of Act V – very faithfully indeed, in a scholarly and intelligent way. Often, in fact, it is a close and capable (yet now and then cryptic) versifying of the original prose. The claim that 'all is true', and the Prologue's insistence on historical seriousness, may be reflections on another play at which *Henry VIII* seems often to glance – and to glance not too disapprovingly, though apparently eager to claim more respectful attention for its own superior status. That play is Samuel Rowley's episodic chronicle *When You See Me You Know Me*. This was written for performance at the Fortune Theatre by Prince Henry's Men, the rivals to Shakespeare's company, the King's Men. It was entered on the *Stationers' Register* on 12 February 1605 as 'the enterlude of K. Henry the 8th', and published the same year and again in 1613 (also in 1621 and 1632), with the subtitle *The famous Chronicle History of King Henry the Eighth, with the birth and virtuous life of Edward Prince of Wales*. It is a boisterous affair, fervent with patriotic Protestantism, and enlivened with clown comedy and an impetuous and formidable King.

It offers many parallels to *Henry VIII* and in all probability influenced it. It makes much of ceremonial, state processions, fanfares, and the like. Both plays show Wolsey as the masterful Cardinal, ambitious for supremacy, imperiously free with men's rights and possessions, and alarmed by the spread of Lutheran doctrine (as also is his bigoted follower, Bishop Gardiner). Both plays present Henry himself as bluff, boisterous, and repeatedly bursting out with religious oaths and the expletive 'Ha!' traditionally associated with him (see the note on I.2.186). As Shakespeare's King urgently desires a son, to safeguard a kingdom 'Well worthy the best heir o'th'world' (II.4.195), so likewise Rowley's had done. Rowley's Queen, Jane Seymour, dies in childbirth (as in *Henry VIII* Anne Bullen suffers almost mortally: V.1.18–20, 66–9), and the King cites a verse about the phoenix which dies in producing its offspring (as in *Henry VIII*, V.5.40–42, Princess Elizabeth is to be 'the maiden phoenix' succeeded by 'another heir | As great in admiration as herself'). The Old Lady's entry in *Henry VIII*, to be rewarded for announcing the birth of an heir 'as like you [Henry] | As cherry is to cherry' (V.1.158–70), seems to reflect a scene in Rowley when the King promises to reward whoever brings him similar news, and his court fool adds that the newsbringer must say that the baby is like its father. In both plays the King is given to terrible anger and terrifying glances, and Wolsey falls irretrievably when the King finds out the extent of his exorbitance and ambition. Some of the resemblances between *Henry VIII* and the earlier play go back to common sources in Holinshed and Foxe, but not all.*

Rowley writes entertainingly and presents a lively story

* The following notes in the Commentary point out apparent connexions between the two plays: Prologue, 14–16; I.2.186; II.2.1–8; III.2.99 and 205–6; V.1.43, 69, 86, 153, and 168–70; V.2.21; V.3.30; and V.5.40.

with vigorous feeling. The King, for instance, goes disguised on a night foray to sample the popular life of his capital, finds himself in a sword-and-buckler fight with a robber, and is clapped into gaol by the watch. But the play is a garbled extravaganza on history, and Shakespeare's company at the Globe, representing the highest standards of drama, would presumably wish to show how far, rising to the height of their great argument, they could outdo their competitors in the dignity and distinction with which they would display a king's life.

*

The year *Henry VIII* was first performed, the spectacular nature of the action, and the conclusion in universal rejoicing for a young Princess Elizabeth (daughter of Anne Bullen) suggest an association with a great state occasion, the marriage on 14 February 1613 of Frederick the Elector Palatine and Princess Elizabeth (daughter of Anne of Denmark and James I). Comparisons were common between the Princess and the idolized Queen Elizabeth I, and, as R. A. Foakes points out in the revised Arden edition, Cranmer speaks a language of Biblical blessing, as he baptizes the new-born infant in V.5, which is that too of sermons inspired by the 1613 wedding. The marriage was widely celebrated, and Protestant enthusiasm mounted high over the binding of the religious alliance between England and the Palatinate. No documentary evidence actually connects *Henry VIII* with the wedding; it is not among the entertainments, including six of Shakespeare's plays, recorded as having been offered during the festivities. Yet clearly, though Wotton calls it new, it had been produced before the disastrous performance of 29 June, since he knows about the fourth-act coronation procession, whereas the conflagration occurred in Act I. Lorkin's reference to 'the play of Henry VIII' implies that it was well enough known.

One may assume that, planned when the wedding was arousing keen excitement, and produced in the early months of 1613, the play at least profited by the occasion and made the most of its spectacular opportunities: much of its interest lies in its royal dignities, whether tragic or festive. Holinshed includes elaborate accounts of jousts, masquings, and ceremonies, and these the play amply reflects, while adding to them the spectacle of Katherine's vision (IV.2) to which the chronicles offer no parallel.

*

Holinshed in fact offered a great mass of material; Henry's reign occupies far more space in the *Chronicles* than any other. From this mass, within the scope of the play, certain principal themes stand out: Wolsey's inordinate pride and wealth; the abundance of extravagant pageantry; the dignity of Queen Katherine under the long process of divorce; the splendid and elaborate ceremonies for Anne's coronation; and the high expectations formed of the new-born Elizabeth. These items form a fairly evident framework of dramatic interest within Holinshed's rambling sequence of miscellaneous events.

The play's form is wave-like, with great swells of event bearing the leading figures, under the King, upwards and downwards, to and from high place. These rising and falling movements have suggested to some critics that its scheme relates to the medieval Wheel of Fortune, re-volving from low state to high, high state to low, or to the Morality-play theme of transient earthly glory. Such analogies, however, though in a general sense relevant enough, do not contribute much of value to one's sense of

Henry VIII; they tend to replace the realism of history by the abstraction of didacticism. Three great victims – the Duke of Buckingham, Queen Katherine, and Cardinal Wolsey – fall in turn, and, with moving and dignified resignation, discourse on life's values and changes. But all this remains dramatic and human, not diagrammatic and doctrinaire. Buckingham, having decided to challenge the overweening Wolsey, is arrested before he can take measures either of attack or of defence (I.1). Queen Katherine makes clear her courage and nobility by speaking for him and against Wolsey, but in vain (I.2); Wolsey is still in the ascendant, and Buckingham goes to an execution the rights and wrongs of which remain obscure (II.1). The King, meeting Anne Bullen, shows favour to her and starts her rise to the throne (I.4, II.3); interlinked with this rise there is the movement for Katherine's fall, evident in Wolsey's intrigues, and climaxed in the great divorce trial (II.1–2, II.4), after which she retires to private life and a mournful death (III.1, IV.2). Meanwhile Wolsey himself, having appeared triumphant, is convicted of exorbitant gains and diplomatic duplicity, and falls from the height of power 'Like a bright exhalation in the evening' (III.2.226). But in Acts IV and V a counter-movement to these downward curves enables the play to end in celebration, the foregoing tragedies being distanced by scenes of rejoicing; Anne is crowned, the Princess Elizabeth is born, and Cranmer (saved from his enemies by the King's intervention) secures the acceptance of the new Lutheran doctrines and baptizes the child who will become the great Queen (IV.1, V.1, 3, 5). The kingdom rides on the crest of a wave. This is the only history in the first Folio to treat a peaceful (though partly a tragic) action, the only one save for *Henry V* to show a monarch settled unquestionably on his throne. Celebrating as it does the triumph of Protestantism in England and the baptism of Elizabeth, it makes little of the time's dangers, nothing at all of such future horrors as the executions of More and Anne Bullen, of Cromwell and Cranmer. Clifford Leech has suggested (in 'The Structure of the Last Plays', *Shakespeare Survey 11*, 1958) that Shakespeare's late plays imply cycles of action going on after the plays have ended, that the sense of a conclusion in which nothing is concluded is strongest of all in *Henry VIII*, and that the Jacobean spectators would feel the deep historical irony of the disastrous future lying ahead of those, other than Henry, who when the play finishes are highest in fortune. They might, no doubt: Sir Walter Raleigh, who at the time *Henry VIII* was written had been ten years incarcerated under attainder of high treason, and who five years later was to go to the block, wrote his *History of the World* while in prison, and when in the preface he came to Henry VIII he drew a portrait of unscrupulous tyranny, commenting as he did so, 'If all the pictures and patterns of a merciless prince were lost in the world, they might all again be painted to the life out of the story of this king'.

Yet critical interpretation of *Henry VIII* should not be swayed by what happened afterwards, since the play itself does nothing to realize these fearful ironies. Cranmer's paean on Henry, Elizabeth, and James in the christening scene (V.5.4–62) may sound more than fulsome (and Terence Gray's Cambridge Festival Theatre production in 1931 descended to the vulgarity of treating it as farce), yet the playwright gives no sign of intending anything other than loyal enthusiasm. At the corresponding point in Holinshed the note of Biblically-inspired rejoicing is quite unambiguous (III.787):

God Himself undertaking the tuition of this young princess,
having predestinated her to the accomplishment of His
divine purpose, she prospered under the Lord's hand, as a
chosen plant of His watering, and after the revolution of
certain years with great felicity and joy of all English
hearts attained to the crown of this realm, and now
reigneth over the same; whose heart the Lord direct in His
ways, and long preserve her in life, to His godly will and
pleasure, and the comfort of all true and faithful subjects.

All historical actions involve antecedents and consequen-
ces; they may arise from crimes, and give rise to others.
But *Henry VIII* ends in a flourish of triumph and is
clearly meant to celebrate a reign which, whatever terrors
it involved in reality, is here approved as establishing
Tudor supremacy and Protestant assurance. And indeed,
Professor Leech observes elsewhere (in *Shakespeare: the*
Chronicles) that the play 'makes us for a moment entertain
the fancy that the time was curiously free from tarnish'.
To have dealt too realistically with Henry VIII's reign
would have been highly dangerous. But in any case the
shining prospect of Elizabeth's supremacy was not a thing
to cloud with the tragedies of Henry's later years; and the
whole final cause of the drama might be defined as the
birth of Gloriana.

*

The play has aroused widely differing reactions. Wotton's
letter did not in any way pretend to be serious dramatic
criticism. Yet his phrase, 'some principal pieces of the
reign of Henry VIII', points to what most readers or
spectators feel: that this is a more episodic and scenic
treatment of the subject than Shakespeare's other histories offer, a treatment less organically conceived and less

clearly directed. Pepys, having heard of 'the so much cried-up play of *Henry the Eighth*', went on 1 January 1664 resolved to enjoy a work popular with the King and court, but he came out displeased – 'mightily dissatisfied [with] so simple a thing, made up of a great many patches'; the pageantry alone gave him some satisfaction. Five years later, however, on 30 December 1668, it struck him more favourably: 'my wife and I to the Duke's playhouse, and there did see *King Henry the Eighth*; and was mightily pleased, better than I ever expected, with the history and shows of it'.

Pepys was a shrewd observer, always interesting in his reactions. No more than Wotton was he attempting considered criticism, yet his opposite reactions, of disappointment and enthusiasm, strikingly foreshadow the critical variations the play has provoked, variations such that the range of disagreement throughout its critical history has been unusually wide. Its New Cambridge editor, J. C. Maxwell, finds it less interesting than almost any other of Shakespeare's plays – though in so rating it he still ranks it high among Elizabethan history plays in general, as indeed it is. For Wilson Knight, on the other hand, whose essay in *The Crown of Life* is wholly laudatory, there is no question about its supreme quality; here, it is asserted, is Shakespeare's one 'explicitly Christian play', where his genius attains a spiritual sensitivity, a fine point of Christian penetration, beyond anything he had so far attempted. Buckingham, exploding with anger in Act I, scene 1, by Act II, scene 1, is on his way to execution in a mood of dignified resignation; his parting speeches proceed from 'that deeper, spiritual aristocracy that underlies all Shakespeare's noblest thought'. And Wolsey's 'Farewell, a long farewell' speech (III.2.351–72) is enriched with 'the purest imagery, comparing man's life to the

16

seasonal budding of a tree, its summer blossoming, and final wintry ruin' – and so expresses essentially Shakespeare's profoundest vision of life.

The judicious critic will probably find himself nearer, much nearer, to the former assessment than to the latter. *Henry VIII* is not a deeply rewarding play to criticize (which is doubtless why it has inspired little good criticism) because it does not reveal layers of deep significance, an imaginatively stimulating sense of life, or a poetic style of rich or vivid challenge. In one respect alone does it offer a peculiar incentive to critical attention – that is, in the exercise of critical definition needed to decide how much of it is Shakespeare's. This exercise has its fascination, and the reward of attending to it is not only that of reaching one's own conclusions on a tricky matter but also that of attuning oneself more alertly to modes of poetic composition. But it cannot be said that the play comes out from such scrutiny more integrated, more centrally revealed, more forcefully significant: its inward character remains shadowy. Critics who claim to find strongly organized dramatic or thematic coherence in it produce as their evidence hardly more than its recurrent mood of spiritual resignation. And this, though it is nobly expressed, operates as good doctrine rather than as the soul's – or imagination's – experience. Alternatively, as Wilson Knight does, they discover its inward power by such enthusiastic interpretation as renders it unrecognizable.

At many points the reader who seeks critical guidance finds himself listening to radical disagreements. What to one man is – as it was to Coleridge – 'a sort of historical masque or show-play', eluding analysis of organic form or central idea, will to another – as to Swinburne – disclose 'a singleness of spirit, a general unity or concord of inner tone'. To one notable scholar, Aldis Wright, *Henry VIII* is 'without plot, without development, without any character on which the interest can be concentrated throughout'. To another, David Nichol Smith, it lacks unity of action beyond any other of Shakespeare's plays. To a third, Hardin Craig, however, it is 'consistently planned and well-integrated'. And to a fourth, A. C. Sprague, its unity is 'discovered in variety' – a curious claim, more plausible, perhaps, in R. A. Foakes's argument for a structure based on 'contrasts and oppositions'. One view will take it for a series of lofty but insufficiently dramatized pageants (with, in the New Cambridge editor's words, 'a curious lack of momentousness about the events as they pass before us'). To another, it offers human and gripping significances – the Wheel of Fortune revolves, and the play is a late Morality 'showing the state from which great ones fall'; or worldly power yields before the virtue of Christian resignation, and we become imaginatively aware of life's motives; or Henry emerges from Wolsey's tutelage to become the Great Tudor, the saviour of Cranmer and English Protestantism, and so the nation's life is felt in its heart's core. But such claims, it must be said, are well-meant rather than well-substantiated, if they extend to a claim for organic unity.

*

It is time to broach the vexed question of authorship. This, unfortunately, cannot be dismissed briefly, or relegated to an appendix as a tiresome sideline; it has long been a central puzzle in the play, and indeed the very equipment for reading *Henry VIII* effectively is a sense of poetic style alert enough to perceive how Shakespeare wrote at this stage of his life, with – as it were – what stylistic calligraphy. The discrepant judgements referred to above often go along with differing views on the question of authorship. Critics who contend that Shakespeare wrote the whole play generally find it coherent, organically developed, and thematically rewarding: those who detect a second hand (usually that of John Fletcher, a younger contemporary just reaching his maturity as a playwright) generally discover no more than superficial unity in spirit, themes, structure, or characterization. The present editor holds, with clear conviction, that it does in fact reveal two hands, two poetic temperaments, and two creative procedures.

This conviction arises initially from a judgement about poetic styles, but it coincides with other judgements – that the play lacks integrated character, that, distinguished though it is, it is made up of notable episodes laid in sequence rather than generated dynamically one from another, episodes linked merely by straightforward plot-requirements and the practical connexions which two working dramatists would naturally ensure. (Even so, the management of plot is not entirely happy. Twice, at II.2.16–17 and IV.1.47, there are sardonic references to the King's ambiguous 'conscience' in preferring Anne Bullen to Queen Katherine. These references occur one before and one after the great – and certainly Shakespearian – scene of Queen Katherine's trial, in which Henry passionately insists on his anguish of conscience and his concern to be theologically correct (II.4.167–230). If these sardonic references are Shakespeare's, the King becomes a cynic and hypocrite, and this the play does not at all seem to intend. If they are Fletcher's – and both occur in scenes attributed to him – the explanation is the simple one that, inadequately consulting Shakespeare's intentions, he intruded them from his sense of worldly court gossip and thus confused the rendering of Henry's motives at a time when, one would deduce, Shakespeare meant them to be honest.)

Clearly the authorship question involves more than the mere matter of authenticity; it involves many of the ways in which one interprets the play. Swinburne felt the matter so deeply as to surmise that most serious Shakespearians would rank the search for an acceptable theory about it as the toughest problem the first Folio offers. One need not pitch the matter quite so high, perhaps. Still, to investigate it is to educate oneself in the late Shakespearian instinct for words, and this is an operation of real critical value. The discussion which follows will, therefore, be of some length, but its aim will be to illustrate two different ways in which poetic sensibilities feel for their words in dramatic use. If as a result it becomes apparent that two writers shared the play, then one may content oneself with finding in it the qualities of an impressively devised stage diversion, suitably furnished with splendid acting parts and notable speeches in the presentation of a colourful era of English history, and the prospect of defining some deep symbolical or conceptual unity may be dismissed as a will-o'-the-wisp.

Here and there in the eighteenth century a critic or editor remarked passingly on some curiosities of style in the play, and in the 1821 Variorum edition of Shakespeare's works James Boswell commented on the many feminine endings in Wolsey's charge to Cromwell (quoting III.2.440–42) and observed 'this termination is perpetually to be met with in Fletcher' (I.560). Yet no one questioned Shakespeare's authorship, save perhaps in minor details. But in 1850 two striking arguments appeared almost simultaneously, and independently of each other. Emerson published his lecture 'Shakespeare as a Poet', in which he claimed that the play showed a basic sub-stratum of writing by a 'superior, thoughtful man' with nevertheless 'a vicious ear' (that is, a man who wrote on a fixed 'tune' and with an air of 'pulpit eloquence'); on this Shakespeare had imposed his own work, where 'the thought constructs the tune'. Emerson threw out this startling idea ('vicious ear' has rankled ever since with admirers of Fletcher) almost as an aside and passed on to other matters. But James Spedding, in a *Gentleman's Magazine* article in August 1850 entitled 'Who Wrote Shakspere's *Henry VIII*?', really laid the case forth. Troubled by apparent confusions of plot, such as the inconsistent characterization of Henry, and the contrast between four Acts of tragedy and concluding scenes of festivity, he was prompted by a friend (Tennyson, in fact) to perceive that many passages were 'very much in the manner of Fletcher'.* The first scene, he thought, showed 'the full stamp of Shakspere in his latest manner', being fresh with his 'impatient activity of intellect and fancy'. But when scene 3 was reached the effect was different:

I felt as if I had passed suddenly out of the language of nature into the language of the stage, or of some conventional mode of conversation. The structure of the verse was quite

* In *Personal Reminiscences of Henry Irving* (1906, I.236) Bram Stoker tells the following story, which suggests that Tennyson's dealings with problems of authenticity could now and then smack of the peremptory. Discussing *Henry VIII*, the poet 'mentioned Wolsey's speech, speaking the line: "Cromwell, I charge thee, fling away ambition". Then he added in a very pronounced way: "Shakespeare never wrote that! I know it! I know it! I know it!" As he spoke he smote hard upon the table beside him.' Had Tennyson known that he was to die eleven days later he might have capped this pronouncement with another of the play's 'non-Shakespearian' lines – 'This from a dying man receive as certain'. One may assume, however, that forty years earlier Tennyson had judged the matter on somewhat ampler evidence.

different and full of mannerism. The expression became suddenly diffuse and languid. The wit wanted mirth and character.

Again, comparing Buckingham's impetuous and fiery language in the first Act with the 'languid and mannered cadences' of his farewell scene (II.1) he could only assume a change of authorship. And pursuing the matter further he divided the play between Shakespeare and Fletcher, attributing to Shakespeare Act I, scenes 1 and 2, Act II, scenes 3 and 4, Act III, scene 2 to line 203, Act V, scene 1; and to Fletcher Act I, scenes 3 and 4, Act II, scenes 1 and 2, Act III, scene 1 and scene 2 from line 203, Act IV, scenes 1 and 2, Act V, scenes 2 to 5. He did not comment on the Prologue and Epilogue; these are in fact very much in Fletcher's manner. This division, made on his sense of style, Spedding supported by counts of extra-syllabic (feminine) lines: the proportions of these in the 'Shakespeare' scenes he found to be barely half of what they were in the 'Fletcher', the former approximating to the proportions found in *Cymbeline* and *The Winter's Tale*, the latter to those found in Fletcher's plays written around 1613.

With minor variations Spedding's division has been accepted ever since by those who believe in dual authorship. It is, admittedly, not sacrosanct; some parts of the play he believed to be Fletcher's have a power of composition which, though not as complex and original as one expects from Shakespeare, is not much inferior in spiritedness and might be from Shakespeare writing in a somewhat neutral way – parts, for instance, of Act II, scene 2, of Act III, scene 2 between the King's departure (line 203) and that of the lords (line 349), and of Act V, scenes 2 and 3. Yet these portions are too short of Shakespearian idiosyncrasy really to sound like his work, and even if they were shown to be his they would not carry with them the far more 'Fletcherian' scenes elsewhere. So, given some small uncertainties about the precise shares, Spedding's discriminations stand firm.

The effect of this analysis, on a generation used to prizing the great orations of *Henry VIII* as among Shakespeare's noblest compositions, was startling. Traditionalists, the Shakespeare scholar Halliwell-Phillipps somewhat improbably asserted, were 'literally petrified'. Buckingham's farewell (II.1), Katherine's exchanges with the Cardinals (III.1), her scene with Griffith and Capuchius (IV.2), and Wolsey's speeches after his fall (III.2, from line 203) – these are among the best things in Elizabethan drama; dare anyone rob Shakespeare of them? Yet Spedding fairly soon carried the day, and he remained in command of it until recent decades. His lead was followed, and continues to be followed, by many kinds of supposedly objective metrical, syntactical, grammatical, and other tests, tests tedious to make and not less tedious to read about (they will not be rehearsed here *) but, from their various points of view, strongly supporting Spedding's analysis. Several recent critics have been very sceptical about them, and taken individually they are less than conclusive. But the degree to which they corroborate each other is striking; collectively their evidence is formidable.

Cumulatively indicative though such investigations are when nearly all the different criteria coincide in similar results, what must be the fundamental concern is the sense of style. The great scenes mentioned above, read

---

* They are referred to on pages 52–4 of the Further Reading; the most noteworthy are those mentioned in the entries for Jackson, Law, Maxwell, Oras, Partridge, Thorndike, and particularly Mincoff.

attentively, prove to be eloquent essays on feeling rather than expressions of that original idiom of experience which Shakespeare never misses for more than the briefest of periods. Shakespeare's dialogue lives, in the very minutiae of phrase: Fletcher's, for all its distinction, is talented speech-making. Dryden's lines from his address *To my dear friend Mr Congreve, on his Comedy called 'The Double-Dealer'* make the point aptly:

> *In easy dialogue is Fletcher's praise:*
> *He moved the mind, but had not power to raise.*

However nobly Buckingham departs, however finely Wolsey meets his fall, however movingly Katherine faces the Cardinals or prepares for death, one's response is to murmur, in a grieved and awed emotion, 'How well that is composed!' And that is not one's reaction to Shakespeare. When, for instance, Belarius and his son Arviragus, in *Cymbeline*, lament the supposedly dead Fidele (Imogen), they do so thus:

BELARIUS   *O melancholy!*
 Who ever yet could sound thy bottom? find
 The ooze to show what coast thy sluggish crare*
 Mightst easiliest harbour in? Thou blessèd thing!
 Jove knows what man thou mightst have made; but I,
 Thou diedst, a most rare boy, of melancholy.
 How found you him?
ARVIRAGUS   *Stark, as you see;*
 Thus smiling, as some fly had tickled slumber,
 Not as death's dart, being laughed at; his right cheek
 Reposing on a cushion. . . .

         With fairest flowers,
 Whilst summer lasts and I live here, Fidele,

---

* A kind of inshore vessel.

I'll sweeten thy sad grave. Thou shalt not lack
The flower that's like thy face, pale primrose; nor
The azured harebell, like thy veins; no, nor
The leaf of eglantine, whom not to slander,
Outsweetened not thy breath.

Cymbeline, IV.2.204–13, 219–25

One does not stand back from this, admiring it as a passage of well-turned eloquence. On the contrary, its quickly ranging, quickly varying ideas, moods, syntax, rhythms, and vocabulary engage one to the utmost with a living sense of stimulus and vitality. Unusual words ('crare', 'easiliest'), unexpected phrases of elliptical or eccentric syntax ('thy sluggish crare | Mightst easiliest harbour in'; 'but I, | Thou diedst'; 'whom not to slander, | Outsweetened not thy breath'), the alert shifts of caesura, and the rhythms moving with unpredictable cadences through the lines, and often over their ends – these communicate the freshness and spontaneity of thought itself. The ideas are, indeed, fresh even to strangeness; melancholy appears to be both the muddy water of unknown depth, and the heavy-laden vessel seeking its rest; the contrast between the tickling fly and the dart of death is a shock, accentuated by the immediate return to the laughing sleeper; the play of feeling in 'sweeten thy sad grave' develops delicate conceits comparing flowers and the 'boy' in a way that has all the tenderness of sentimentality yet the precision of justified ingenuity. Such is Shakespeare's characteristic originality in the latest phase of his writing.

*

The basis of this edition, then, is that *Henry VIII* is collaborative, that some of it is in Shakespeare's late style, and that the rest is more like Fletcher's style than anyone else's – so like, indeed, that if it is not his he must have had a dramatic *doppelgänger*. In so far as the 'Fletcher' scenes differ from Fletcher's style when he is writing well in other plays (and the difference is not great), the divergence results from the more consistent dignity, concentration, and seriousness which Holinshed's impressive guidance provided, and doubtless also from the sway of Shakespeare and the decorum proper to an ambitious historical play on the subject of Queen Elizabeth's father. In so far as the 'Shakespeare' scenes show a limpidity unusual in Shakespeare's late plays (and such limpidity is intermittent, certainly not so prevalent as to warrant the claim that he must also have written the limpid 'Fletcher' scenes too), the cause is – once again – fidelity to Holinshed; for instance, Queen Katherine's plea in court (II.4.13–57; see the note thereon) is more lucid than much late Shakespearian writing, simply because it faithfully follows Holinshed's prose. (Her subsequent speeches in the scene are not based on Holinshed and have more inventive vivacity, a vivacity evident also in Hermione's great and comparable defence in *The Winter's Tale*, III.2.21–122.) Yet her mode of expression, relatively lucid though it is, is different from the kind of eloquence heard from Buckingham or Wolsey when they fall, or from Katherine herself in retirement at Kimbolton: it shows itself not as rhetorical stylization, a means of making a noble impression, but as the very movement of mind and psyche working within the intricacies of the problems she faces.

In *Specimens of the English Dramatic Poets*, Charles Lamb recognizes the difference between Shakespeare and Fletcher in another collaboration, *The Two Noble Kinsmen* (written about 1613 *). Fletcher, he remarks,

* In April 1634 this play was registered for publication as being by Fletcher and Shakespeare. It was published the same year, with their

lays line upon line, making up one after the other, adding
image to image so deliberately that we can see where they
join: Shakespeare mingles everything, he runs line into
line, embarrasses sentences and metaphors; before one
idea has burst its shell another is hatched and clamorous for
disclosure.

The difference may be illustrated in various ways – by
inspecting Fletcher himself, by setting beside the results
of this inspection the characteristics of the later Shakespeare, by comparing Fletcher and Shakespeare in *The*
Two Noble Kinsmen, and by juxtaposing material from
different areas of *Henry VIII* itself.

Fletcher's style is fluent in a graceful, or poignant, or
vigorous, fashion but remains a matter of general sentiment, not of original and surprising particularity, the
style of fine talent able to expound emotions but not that
of genius marking their unpredictable complexities in
words which follow their sharpest turns. *A King and No*
King (1611) is close in date to *Henry VIII*, and a passage
such as Gobrias's counsel to Panthea (IV.1.14–26) shows
the qualities which in *Henry VIII* sound un-Shakespearian
– it comes from that part of the play attributed by scholarly
authority to Fletcher, not to Beaumont (see Cyrus Hoy,
Studies in Bibliography, xi, 1958, page 91):

> *You shall feel, if your virtue can induce you*
> *To labour out this tempest – which, I know,*
> *Is but a poor proof 'gainst your patience –*

---

names on the title-page, and it has been very generally accepted as
their joint production. Another play, *Cardenio*, was similarly registered in 1653, but no copy is known to survive, though there is an
eighteenth-century reworking of it by Lewis Theobald, called *The*
Double Falsehood; or, the Distrest Lovers (1728).

All those contents your spirit will arrive at,
Newer and sweeter to you. Your royal brother,
When he shall once collect himself, and see
How far he has been asunder from himself,
What a mere stranger to his golden temper,
Must, from those roots of virtue, never dying,
Though somewhat stopped with humour, shoot again
Into a thousand glories, bearing his fair branches
High as our hopes can look at, straight as justice,
Loaden with ripe contents.

The characteristics here are easy to see (and they are not such as Shakespeare offers) – the decorative exposition, the even rhythms and accomplished lilt on which the words float instead of darting off on swirls and ebulliences of cross-currents, the token-words of emotional and ethical generality ('virtue', 'patience', 'contents', 'golden temper', 'roots of virtue', and the rest), and the images gracefully yet deliberately worked through ('roots of virtue ... never dying ... shoot again ... bearing his fair branches | High ... straight ... Loaden with ripe contents'). Shakespeare does not stand back contemplating his meanings so; but much of *Henry VIII* is written thus lyrically, lucidly, ornately, descriptively.

Or if, in *Bonduca* (probably Fletcher's alone, about 1613), one reads Poenius's farewell, or Caratach's eulogy over his body, the Fletcherian note sounds in the lilting, falling rhythms, in the sentiments, which have a composed and formal air, in the measured cadenced rhetoric of fine feeling. Poenius falls upon his sword and dies thus:

The work's done,
That neither fire, nor age, nor melting envy
Shall ever conquer. Carry my last words

To the great general: kiss his hands, and say,
My soul I give to Heaven, my fault to justice,
Which I have done upon myself; my virtue,
If ever there was any in poor Poenius,
Made more and happier, light on him! – I faint –
And where there is a foe, I wish him fortune. –
I die:
Lie lightly on my ashes, gentle earth!

Bonduca, IV.3.166–76

Antony and Cleopatra presides in the background here, yet there is a great contrast between Shakespeare's unfailing individualization of effect and Fletcher's limpid and proper sentiment, just as behind *All for Love* (despite Dryden's claim to have 'imitated the divine Shakespeare') there lies Fletcher's lilting grace of rhetoric rather than Shakespeare's force. And in *Valentinian* (probably Fletcher's alone, 1614), the long scene of Aëcius's farewells sounds with that well-formulated sad nobility, that distinguished and explanatory pathos, that stylized and self-aware simplicity, which mark the speeches of aristocratic resignation in *Henry VIII*. The note of Buckingham is unmistakable as Aëcius dies:

Dare any man lament I should die nobly?
Am I grown old, to have such enemies?
When I am dead, speak honourably of me,
That is, preserve my memory from dying;
There, if you needs must weep your ruined master,
A tear or two will seem well. This I charge ye –
Because ye say you yet love old Aëcius –
See my poor body burnt, and some to sing
About my pile, and what I have done and suffered,
If Caesar kill not that, too; at your banquets,

29

> *When I am gone, if any chance to number*
> *The times that have been sad and dangerous,*
> *Say how I fell, and 'tis sufficient.*
>
> > *Valentinian*, IV.4.27–39

Much of *Henry VIII* sounds the same note of fluent sentiment, in particular the elegiac scenes in Act II, scene 1, Act III, scene 1, the latter part of Act III, scene 2, and Act IV, scene 2. Even when the 'Fletcher' scenes are more vigorous, less reflective than this, they show the same kind of talent, stating and describing their meanings but not evincing the active Shakespearian pressure.

In Shakespeare one senses infallibly, in Coleridge's phrase, 'a giant power in its strength of vigour and maturity'; the attention is never lulled but is kept alert by concentration and surprise, sharp turns of serious wit, and strange shadowings of sense. *Antony and Cleopatra* is sometimes cited to prove that Shakespeare could sound the same lilting dignity and noble nostalgia as Fletcher and so could have written the most prized speeches of Buckingham, Wolsey, and Katherine; passages like the following may well have influenced Fletcher, as later they influenced Dryden. Yet the central quality is different: however near they seem, superficially, to Fletcher and the elegiac arias of *Henry VIII* they animate and startle the mind rather than soothe or becalm it:

> *I have fled myself, and have instructed cowards*
> *To run and show their shoulders. Friends, be gone;*
> *I have myself resolved upon a course*
> *Which has no need of you; be gone.*
> *My treasure's in the harbour, take it. O,*
> *I followed that I blush to look upon.*
> *My very hairs do mutiny; for the white*
> *Reprove the brown for rashness, and they them*

> *For fear and doting. Friends, be gone ; you shall*
> *Have letters from me to some friends that will*
> *Sweep your way for you. Pray you look not sad,*
> *Nor make replies of loathness ; take the hint*
> *Which my despair proclaims. Let that be left*
> *Which leaves itself.*
>
> Antony and Cleopatra, III.11.7–20

The mood is deeply poignant. Yet the mind moves not through a description of its thoughts but in the very track of them, changing form and direction with the movement of life. Again, when Enobarbus vents his remorse (IV.9.7–23) he does so, according to Wilson Knight, in a fashion fitting the resigned, cause-lost yielding of earthly ambitions – and this is 'precisely the note to be sounded by Shakespeare in Buckingham's farewell speech'. But precisely the note it is not, nor anything really like it. There is in Enobarbus's death-speech (however melancholy the mood) a complexity and surprisingness alien to Buckingham, even a touch of the cryptic and fantastic: Dr Johnson objected, with some reason, against the oddity of the heart thrown against the flint and hardness of its fault:

> *Be witness to me, O thou blessèd moon,*
> *When men revolted shall upon record*
> *Bear hateful memory, poor Enobarbus did*
> *Before thy face repent ! . . .*
> *O sovereign mistress of true melancholy,*
> *The poisonous damp of night disponge upon me,*
> *That life, a very rebel to my will,*
> *May hang no longer on me. Throw my heart*
> *Against the flint and hardness of my fault,*
> *Which, being dried with grief, will break to powder,*
> *And finish all foul thoughts. O Antony,*

31

> *Nobler than my revolt is infamous,*
> *Forgive me in thine own particular,*
> *But let the world rank me in register*
> *A master-leaver and a fugitive!*
> *O Antony! O Antony!*

This is quite different from Buckingham's fine but measured decorum. (Spedding juxtaposed Buckingham's farewell to his friends with Richard II's to his Queen, and remarked that 'Richard's passion makes a new subject of every passing incident and image, and has as many changes as an Aeolian harp'. This is well said.)

In *The Two Noble Kinsmen* Swinburne claimed to see 'to a hair's breadth in a hemistich' how much belonged to Shakespeare, how much to Fletcher. The claim may be hyperbolic, yet the quick ideas and syntax in the early scenes of that play, the rhythms vital yet interrupted and springing, and the originality of idiom, are surely Shakespeare's. There may be conceit or strain, yet the communication is electrical, as in the Third Queen's plea:

> *O, my petition was*
> *Set down in ice, which by hot grief uncandied*
> *Melts into drops: so sorrow wanting form*
> *Is pressed with deeper matter.*
>
> *The Two Noble Kinsmen*, I.1.106–9

With Palamon and Arcite in prison (II.1, from line 59) the style alters, becoming fluently consecutive rather than sharp and instantaneous. Both men discourse beautifully on their plight, with dying falls of double-ended lines (the recognized cadences of pathos) and a liberal sprinkling of elegant key-words ('blessings', 'patience', 'souls', 'noble', 'honour', and so forth). Then in the first scene of Act III Shakespeare reappears, unmistakably, with thought flashing from point to point, and original imagery. Then

Fletcher again, competent, often sprightly, but un-Shakespearian, as when, with lucidly refined sentiments, Arcite opposes himself to Theseus:

> *We seek not*
> *Thy breath of mercy, Theseus: 'tis to me*
> *A thing as soon to die as thee to say it,*
> *And no more moved. Where this man calls me traitor,*
> *Let me say thus much: if in love be treason*
> *In service of so excellent a beauty,*
> *As I love most, and in that faith will perish,*
> *As I have brought my life here to confirm it,*
> *As I have served her truest, worthiest,*
> *As I dare kill this cousin that denies it,*
> *So let me be most traitor, and ye please me.*
>
> The Two Noble Kinsmen, III.6.158–68

Such a well-mannered but not really dramatic style is what caught the nineteenth century's Elizabethanizers, for Fletcher's mode could be imitated, Shakespeare's could not. An interesting exercise would be to compare Emilia's soliloquy about her bewildered feelings (in a Fletcher scene, IV.2.33–54) with her plea to Venus (in a Shakespeare scene, V.1.137–62). Both read well, but the former is a composition about her state of mind; the latter dramatizes thought itself, the words springing from quick eruptive pressures.

*

The strata in *Henry VIII* are not always so clear. Holinshed exerted his centralizing pull and the result is, to quote Sir Edmund Chambers, 'not very characteristic Fletcher' but also 'not very characteristic Shakespeare either'. And *Henry VIII* has a theme whose tragic and dignified pathos was congenial to both playwrights. Yet marked differences remain, of thought processes, rhythmical instincts, and semantic habits. Fletcher can be recognized in his straightforward follow-through of idea (granted the natural recapitulations and qualifications of normal speech), and in orderly evolution of sense and line. A typical example is the passage where Wolsey introduces Campeius to the King (II.2.84–107). These even sequences of idea and heedful definitions of what is meant are very different from the dramatic immediacy of the next scene, with its sudden start, tang of phrase, interweavings of sense, and abrupt syntax, so that one follows fascinated to see whether the mercurial thought will escape – as it triumphantly does – from the embarrassments of its own intricacies:

ANNE
   Not for that neither. Here's the pang that pinches:
   His highness having lived so long with her, and she
   So good a lady that no tongue could ever
   Pronounce dishonour of her – by my life,
   She never knew harm-doing – O, now, after
   So many courses of the sun enthronèd,
   Still growing in a majesty and pomp, the which
   To leave a thousand-fold more bitter than
   'Tis sweet at first t'acquire – after this process,
   To give her the avaunt, it is a pity
   Would move a monster.

OLD LADY   *Hearts of most hard temper*
   Melt and lament for her.

ANNE   *O, God's will! Much better*
   She ne'er had known pomp; though't be temporal,
   Yet, if that quarrel, Fortune, do divorce
   It from the bearer, 'tis a sufferance panging
   As soul and body's severing.   II.3.1–16

34

This is from a minor scene only. Shakespeare is writing with half his mind, writing by routine; yet even that half, that routine, bears the differentia of his style.

*

Other features extend the evidence of shared responsibility. Compared with what one would expect were Shakespeare the sole author, the play's successive moods pay curiously little attention to what has gone before. After the passionate tensions of Act I, scenes 1 and 2, there comes the modish badinage of scenes 3 and 4, and then Buckingham's tragic gravity of Act II, scene 1. Alternating with the King's wandering affections of Act I, scene 4, and Act II, scene 3, there is his earnest concern for his conscience in Act II, scenes 2 and 4. The reflective spirituality of Wolsey's and Katherine's Christian resignation in Act III, scene 2, and Act IV, scene 2, frames the unqualified rejoicing of the coronation procession. And the final celebrations take place as though the preceding tragedies belonged to some other play. Critics have sought to find a meaningful counterpoint among these differing parts, but the argument is unconvincing; the varying moods scarcely if at all recognize each other. 'Contrasts and oppositions' work marvellously for the symphonic unity of *Henry IV*, but no such complementary interaction informs *Henry VIII*. All this is natural if the play is collaborative, curious if it is not.

The plot, it has already been remarked, consists of episodes laid in sequence rather than generated dynamically. This does not necessarily point towards dual authorship, though it would be a probable consequence of it; but leaving the question of authorship on one side one observes it as a matter of fact. The narrative moves forward and each new interest draws a veil over its precursor, just as each new mood does, rather than reciprocating with it some richer charge of meaning.

This is not to say that no care has been taken to inter-link the parts: historical time has been much condensed to bring episodes into interesting relationships (Wolsey's death – 1530 – and Katherine's – 1536 – become nearly simultaneous; this and other reorganizations of chronology are recorded in the Commentary); the oppressive 'commissions' (I.2.20–29, note) are predated to bring Katherine into prominence *vis-à-vis* Wolsey and Buckingham; the King's part is steadily enhanced (I.2.110–28, note); Anne Bullen's introduction to him is anticipated (I.4.53–86 and 75, notes); several references bring Cranmer to our attention before he is seen; Elizabeth's birth is foretold (III.2.50–52, note); Ruthall's inventory is transferred to Wolsey (III.2.124, note); and there are other changes, recorded in the Commentary at I.1.4–5 and 95, and I.3.6. These changes, however, are not more skilful than one would expect of practised professionals – indeed, the early introduction of Anne to Henry is not skilful at all – and no deeply co-ordinating power is evident. The incidents rise to our attention, and fall out of it, fatalistically. And like-wise with the themes – falling greatness, rising authority, spiritual catharsis; none offers a convincing moral 'form'.

The opening scene – Shakespeare's, certainly (the vivid tricky idiom is like the opening of *Cymbeline*) – sounds the note of high-wrought but unstable ostentation, of ex-travagance which under Wolsey's instigation threatens England's very life, of nobles at odds with the overween-ing prelate, and of an anticlericalism which will render welcome the prospect of Protestantism. To have this all mediated through the acrimonious tempers of Wolsey's enemies makes for a finely explosive beginning, and the first two scenes have a dramatic instancy hardly equalled later. Yet Buckingham's immediate capitulation (though historically correct) is an anticlimax, and in the second scene the clash between Wolsey and the Queen (a clash not warranted by history but invented to indicate, thus early, Katherine's courage and humanity) ebbs into a long delation against the absent Buckingham. The major scenes have this curious quality, of surging and ebbing without really generating their successors; they lack the usual dynamic of an onward-pressing action. Buckingham is violently moved against Wolsey: then within thirty lines he has turned into

> *the shadow of poor Buckingham,*
> *Whose figure even this instant cloud puts on*
> *By darkening my clear sun.*   I.1.224–6

The Queen confronts Wolsey over the taxation and the King rebukes him; Wolsey defuses the situation effortlessly (I.2.102–8). Henry, playing an oddly simple-minded part, accepts the proofs of Buckingham's guilt unquestioningly, and merely presides over a long list of charges (I.2.109–214). Two scenes of social banter (Fletcher's) follow, to introduce Anne Bullen (earlier than history authorizes, so making questionable Henry's motives for the divorce: see the note on I.4.75). In II.1 Buckingham's aggressive spirit has given way to measured and dignified resignation, in harmonious Fletcherian cadences. His episode ends on this note of relaxed nobility, and the scene flows on to a foretaste of the looming trial.

Repeatedly the play promises the excitements of political antagonism; repeatedly these are muted as they approach a climax. Norfolk describes Wolsey's machinations with an intensity the Cardinal's own actions on the stage never rival. The King makes a show of exercising authority and ultimately controls events, but his behaviour and utterances cannot be felt as those of an integrated character. The great trial scene is haunted by uncertainties of purpose (traceable, admittedly, to Holinshed); King and Cardinals seem to support each other and all profess religious integrity – yet Wolsey's foxiness is already clear, Henry's infatuation with Anne is already known, and at the end, in an aside, Henry vents his wrath at the 'dilatory sloth and tricks of Rome' (II.4.237). His one truly impressive utterance, that which exonerates Wolsey and describes the storms in the 'wild sea' of his conscience (II.4.155–209), must be meant as genuine (the theme of conscience, with its 'scruple and prick' and the 'spitting power' of its quandaries, is the whole burden of the speech, and the word 'conscience' occurs more often in *Henry VIII* than in any other play of the canon). Yet how does it relate to the King's desire to have Cranmer hasten back to declare the case against Katherine, or to that attachment to Anne vaguely mentioned in Holinshed but in the play clearly presented before our eyes? The claims of integrity, and of faithfulness to 'the good Queen' (II.4.224), must appear dubious; yet Henry seems offered for sympathetic approval.

The characterization likewise fluctuates; Buckingham swings from vehemence to submission, Wolsey from defiant hauteur to forgiving resignation, Henry through a spectrum of credulity, harshness, infatuation, ambiguous fidelity, theological earnestness, and shrewd Machiavellianism, none of which has much to do with the others. And Anne, pert and gay in I.4, is humble and compassionate the next time she appears (II.3), and then supplants her beloved Queen in what the play implies (though she herself is given nothing to say) is a spirit of celebration shared with her subjects. The play holds together as a series of events told responsibly and impressively – its authors' abilities could ensure no less. It does not hold together at the deeper imaginative levels, those of the conceptual force which marks even the early histories of Shakespeare (and *a fortiori* the mature ones), or of the spiritual insight by which even the strange late romances become so inwardly rewarding.

*

It is this kind of moral and temperamental shifting which makes the play a succession of facets rather than a rendering of complete dramatic personalities. R. A. Foakes contrasts it with the earlier histories, which had been strongly concerned with the personality of the king, for he believes that it reflects a later kind of interest; its place, he argues, is not with the other histories but with the other late plays, which treat themes and ideals rather than individual characters. They show 'an abstraction of character from individualization towards an ideal or quality'. Henry, he suggests, is, like Prospero, the controller of the action, and need not be fully 'real'. This is interestingly observed; the romances do concern themselves with conditions of spirit rather than with probable psychology or convincing causality. Imogen's simplemindedness with Iachimo, Posthumus's insane revulsion from her (not to mention those other features of *Cymbeline* which Johnson termed 'unresisting imbecility'), Leontes's avalanche of jealousy, Hermione's sixteen years' patience, Caliban's rapture with music, Prospero's violence with Ariel, and his rapid swing from vengeance to mercy – these are not realistic. They suggest that at this stage Shakespeare was more interested in the essence of feeling than in its naturalistic presentation. Jealousy figures as pure jealousy, anger as pure anger, wickedness as pure wickedness, love as pure love. The devotion of Perdita and

39

Florizel, of Miranda and Ferdinand, has a fairy-tale quality which sets it apart from the passions of earlier lovers.

Yet these considerations do not really work when applied to *Henry VIII*. Not only is an 'ideal or quality' too abstract an organizing factor for a historical play, but the ideals and qualities of the romances are rendered with a vividness not evident in *Henry VIII*. This vividness may not be realism but it strikes us as truth. Caliban, being the creature he is, would be most unlikely to express so magically the island's harmonies. Yet the quality of those harmonies is what counts, not whether Caliban may be credited with a sensitive soul, and that quality comes brilliantly over. To seek, as critics have done, to assimilate the mode of *Henry VIII* to the romances through its spirit of 'regeneration' or 'compassion' (if that is its spirit) is to equate fine statements about peace of mind, and so on, with the imaginative, intimate self-realization (not self-presentation) by which a Leontes or Prospero is regenerate. No such equation will hold. The point may be made by examining Prospero's change of heart when he sees and hears Ariel's compassion for the spellbound Alonso and his accomplices, distracted by magic, with the good old Gonzalo grieving over them; his anger turns to charity in a speech which, brief as it is, discloses a whole inward world of self-redemption:

> *Hast thou, which art but air, a touch, a feeling*
> *Of their afflictions, and shall not myself,*
> *One of their kind, that relish all as sharply*
> *Passion as they, be kindlier moved than thou art?*
> *Though with their high wrongs I am struck to th'quick,*
> *Yet with my nobler reason 'gainst my fury*
> *Do I take part. The rarer action is*

In virtue than in vengeance. They being penitent,
The sole drift of my purpose doth extend
Not a frown further.   *The Tempest*, V.1.21–30

What generally one misses in *Henry VIII* is just this power of realizing emotional essence. Fletcher cannot realize it, good though he is at discoursing about feelings. And Shakespeare, though he gets inside the spirited tensions of Act I, scene 1, and Act III, scene 2, and the impressive manoeuvres of Act I, scene 2, and Act II, scene 4, seems to be writing with less than his full attention. One recognizes some validity in R. A. Foakes's defence of Henry, and admires the persuasiveness with which it is offered, the defence that, 'like Prospero, he has a kind of vagueness, not a lack of solidity, but a lack of definition, as a representative of benevolent power acting upon others'. Yet the play hardly bears convincingly out this idea of providential authority. Henry is too much at the beck and call of events, of the masterfulness which enables Wolsey to rise, the oversight which causes Wolsey to fall, and his own susceptibility to Anne just when his conscience sounds most imperative (and he changes attachment with no real sign of struggle). Against such chances his *deus ex machina* rescue of Cranmer hardly qualifies him as benign presider, nor indeed – though the outlines of such an idea can be glimpsed – as the maturing ruler (when he has already been married 'upward of twenty years' to Katherine) emerging from Wolsey's tutelage to an achieved wisdom.

*

As for the other characters, there is – as has often been observed – a curious lack of salience, save for the fine individualization of Katherine. And even her characterization is a matter of straightforward courage, dignity, and pathos, rather than of creative force. Her part, and Wolsey's (Buckingham's and the King's in lesser measure), have always been famous stage roles; they offer that visible pre-eminence which great performers relish, and their speeches are at once effective with a large and memorable distinction, if without subtlety. While Wolsey is likely nowadays to seem, in a grand way, put together from predictable elements of ecclesiastical grandee and redeemed worldling, both being superbly achieved yet the latter only chancily related to the former, Katherine is finely developed – far more powerfully so than in Holinshed – in her successive aspects of charity, integrity, and spiritual autonomy. But this makes her supersession by Anne, effected with no more ado than a switch from pathos to rejoicing, another sign that the play lacks fundamental articulation. (The fact that Katherine is cast off without Henry's actually appearing to reject her has been offered as 'a remarkable piece of Shakespeare's sleight-of-hand' – but this is special pleading.) The point about all this has been well made by Clifford Leech in *Shakespeare: the Chronicles*:

'There is a structural feature of *Henry VIII* that reminds us of Fletcher. Here we do not have the sense that as the play proceeds we are approaching an increasingly complex view of the characters and situation. ... Rather, we have here a common phenomenon of Fletcher's writing – an adroit change of viewpoint, with a consequent disharmony between the several responses set up by the single play.'

*

Such shortcomings as one notes in reading (and they are shortcomings only by comparison with Shakespeare's own

42

greater plays – which is high praise, indeed) have not militated against it on the stage, where it has appealed by rich production, moving verse, and the notable performance of star parts. Pepys, as has been seen, excepted its shows and processions from his censure, and the production he saw was finely mounted. Thomas Betterton, the leading actor of the time, played the King's part superbly, according to Gerard Langbaine's *Account of the English Dramatic Poets* (1691). John Downes's *Roscius Anglicanus* (1708) relates that Betterton was briefed by Sir William Davenant (who presented the play 'all new clothed and new scenes'), and Davenant drew his ideas from John Lowin the actor, 'that had his instructions from Mr Shakespeare himself'. The new clothes ('proper habits', Downes calls them) may have been an unusual attempt on the Restoration stage to achieve Tudor verisimilitude; the suggestion is made in G. C. D. Odell's *Shakespeare – From Betterton to Irving* (1920; I.204–9). At any rate, despite Pepys's initial displeasure, the production 'continued fifteen days together with general applause' (Downes). The Duke of Buckingham's satire *The Rehearsal* (1672) jests about performers who 'dance worse than the angels in *Harry the Eighth*, or the fat spirits in *The Tempest*'.

The next century saw many productions; *Henry VIII* was the most popular history after *Richard III* and the first part of *Henry IV*, and thirteenth in frequency of all Shakespeare's plays (C. B. Hogan, *Shakespeare in the Theatre, 1701–1800*, 1952 and 1957, II.717). The dramatist-actor-manager Colley Cibber put it on at Drury Lane in October 1727, adding a crowning scene for Anne (not merely the procession) to celebrate George II's coronation. This, he claimed, brought in more money than 'the best play ever writ', and Dr Johnson observed that it drew crowds throughout most of the winter: it was indeed even transferred to other entertainments, and held its place for years. A version of the play done at Drury Lane in 1762 lists about 140 coronation attendants; at Covent Garden, the *Westminster Magazine* of January 1773 reported, George Colman presented it despite an inadequate cast because it 'exhibited the most numerous pageantry'.

Such elaboration marked the play's productions until recently, and to some extent still does; it has always looked handsome. Splendid settings have matched splendid costumes; from the late eighteenth century to the early twentieth it invited designers to extremes of antiquarian zeal. At Drury Lane in 1789 John Philip Kemble lavished his attentions on 'ancient habits and manners ... and the study of the picturesque by which ... Shakespeare transcends all other writers' (James Boaden, *Memoirs ... of John Philip Kemble*, 1825, I.423). Kemble's Covent Garden production in 1811 impressed *The Times* by its architectural scenery, although – the reporter observed – only the sight of well-spread tables, well-lighted chandeliers, and well-rouged maids of honour enabled the spectators to support the accumulated *ennui* the play caused. Charles Kean's renowned production at the Princess's in 1855, Kean claimed, drew on every source illustrating early Tudor habits; the result was described by *The Times* as the most wonderful spectacle ever seen on the London stage, with an elaborate moving panorama of the Lord Mayor's procession from the City to Greenwich. This production ran a hundred nights together and set a standard for spectacle through the rest of the century. Irving's Lyceum revival in 1892, for instance, contained a handsome replica of the King's Stairs, Westminster, for Buckingham to pass on his way to death, a magnificent hall in Blackfriars for Queen Katherine's trial, a 'genuine reproduction of old London . . . with its three-storeyed wooden-beamed houses' for the coronation procession, and a Church of the Grey Friars at Greenwich for the christening, with 'ancient stained glass and time-worn stones' (Odell, II.444-5). And at His Majesty's in 1910 Beerbohm Tree achieved a 'revelation of old-time splendour' (Odell, II.464).

Through the eighteenth and nineteenth centuries the text was heavily cut to let the great roles stand unrivalled and the spectacle unfold; in general, much of the play after Act III was sacrificed. Questionable though this may be, and not to be recommended (since even if the play is episodic much of its interest lies in its variety of tones and manners), one may concede that such treatment gives a magnetism, theatrically successful, in terms of the noble, the moving, and the spectacular, at the expense of portions of text not always distinguished. As in 1765, when Johnson acknowledged that it held the stage by the splendour of its pageantry, *Henry VIII* has lived in terms of great performers and great ceremony, the ceremony of ritual and high bearing. It was the play chosen at Regent's Park to inaugurate the Open-Air Theatre in 1936, and at the Old Vic to mark the coronation of Queen Elizabeth II in 1953. This is what it offers, rather than that psychological originality, that 'great creating nature' inwardly and organically meaningful, which in the mature Shakespeare plays makes the cutting of text so very delicate a matter.

*

What kind of achievement, finally, is it? If its readings of character are relatively superficial, if events rise and fall in chronological sequence with insufficient psychological force, and if the reader's attention, or the spectator's, dwells less on dramatic tensions than on a general elevation of mind (yet counterchanged with a lively variety of social scenes and levels – scheming nobles, commenting gentlemen, stagey plebeians), nevertheless *Henry VIII* offers much that is fine. The writing may be eloquent rather than fully expressive (one critic has sought to claim it all for Shakespeare on the grounds that it *is* prevailingly eloquent – which is precisely not how Shakespeare's style should be described: another, less approvingly, has remarked that 'fluent rhetoric is its lifeblood'). Yet, whether suavely sophisticated or honourably magnanimous, socially brisk or spiritually refined, it keeps up a level of assurance and expertness (and often of memorable fineness) seldom attained by historical drama. The structure may be sequential rather than integrated; yet it brings forward its succession of great tragic figures, before the transmutation to Cranmer and rejoicing, with power enough to make plausible (though not quite finally convincing) the assumption of a guiding idea to which the whole play works – whether the idea be that of the Wheel of Fortune and of mutability in high places (a central Elizabethan preoccupation), or that of pride realizing its vanities, or that of Christian virtue prevailing over the pomp and glory of the world, or that of the Tudor dynasty emerging to evident glory. As controlling ideas these are, in truth, nebulous, likelier to reflect the critic's anxiety to perceive unity and meaning than to show the forms of genuine structure. Yet by the general standards of Elizabethan history plays – indeed, of any history plays – the narrative is clear and powerful, the sequence of interests rich and compulsive, the high seriousness of artistic intention evident. The claims the Prologue makes, of a story 'full of state and woe', of 'noble scenes', 'chosen truth', and

The very persons of our noble story
As they were living . . .

and the pride the Epilogue expresses in having presented a
good woman and avoided satirical levity, are justified.
Henry VIII shows every sign of desiring, ambitiously, to
follow the great events of history in a fully responsible
spirit, and it succeeds well in a risky undertaking.

FURTHER READING

Sources and Historical Background
Henry VIII is so faithful to its sources that editions often include long extracts from Holinshed's *Chronicles* (second edition, 1587) and Foxe's *Acts and Monuments*; see the editions by W. A. Wright (Clarendon, 1895 – including material from George Cavendish's *Negotiations of Thomas Wolsey*, 1641), D. Nichol Smith (Warwick, 1899), C. K. Pooler (Arden, 1915), and S. Schoenbaum (Signet, 1967). Particularly valuable are the extracts given in R. A. Foakes's revised Arden edition (1957), which clearly relates source-episodes to the play's scenes, and in J. C. Maxwell's New Cambridge edition (1962), which presents the relevant chronicle material before the annotations of each scene.

Sources are fully reprinted and analysed in G. Bullough's *Narrative and Dramatic Sources of Shakespeare*, Volume 4 (1962) – this includes extracts from Samuel Rowley's *When You See Me You Know Me* (1605) as well as Holinshed and Foxe. W. G. Boswell-Stone's *Shakespeare's Holinshed* (1896), and *Holinshed's Chronicle as Used in Shakespeare's Plays* (1927), as edited by A. and J. Nicoll in Everyman's Library, are handy sources for the historical material; both italicize the words most closely reproduced, but the most satisfactory modern edition for following Holinshed's narrative is *Shakespeare's Holinshed: An Edition of Holinshed's Chronicles (1587)*, selected, edited, and annotated by Richard Hosley (New York, 1968). There are editions of Rowley's *When You See Me You Know Me* by Karl Elze (1874), with a list of features common to it and *Henry VIII*, and in the Malone Society Reprints by F. P. Wilson and J. Crow (1952).

Texts

The earliest edition is that in the first Folio (1623), of which there are modern facsimiles edited by Sidney Lee (1902), H. Kökeritz and C. T. Prouty (1955), and Charlton Hinman (1969). C. K. Pooler's original Arden edition of *Henry VIII* (1915) abounds in illustrative material; R. A. Foakes's revised Arden (1957) and J. C. Maxwell's New Cambridge (1962) editions are outstanding, with excellent introductions and annotations. Other good modern editions are those by John Munro (London Shakespeare, Volume 4, 1958) and F. D. Hoeniger (*The Complete Pelican Shakespeare*, 1969). The Signet edition by S. Schoenbaum (1967) has a useful introduction source material, and extracts from critical commentaries.

Analyses of textual matters are to be found in E. K. Chambers, *William Shakespeare*, Vol. 1 (Oxford, 1930), W. W. Greg, *The Shakespeare First Folio* (Oxford, 1955), R. A. Foakes, in *Studies in Bibliography*, Vol. 11 (1958), and J. C. Maxwell's edition. The unusually elaborate stage directions are discussed by W. J. Lawrence, in 'The Stage Directions in *King Henry VIII*', *Times Literary Supplement* (18 December 1930), and P. Alexander (*Times Literary Supplement*, 1 January 1931).

Authorship

A balanced and fair account of the arguments for and against dual authorship is given in R. A. Foakes's Arden edition; the conclusion is that Shakespeare was sole author. Equally skilful, but concluding in the opposite sense, is J. C. Maxwell's discussion in the New Cambridge edition. The editions by John Munro and F. D. Hoeniger (see above) have briefer but clear and informative examinations of the problem.

Against collaboration: the following are the more noteworthy arguments against collaboration, set out chronologically.

A. C. Swinburne, *A Study of Shakespeare* (1880), recognizes Fletcherian qualities yet judges the play to be all Shakespeare's, being marked by 'pathos and concentration' beyond Fletcher's powers and by a 'unity or concord of inner tone' which is

Shakespeare's. The essay is readable, but its criticism is not sharp enough to validate its stylistic judgements.

Baldwin Maxwell, 'Fletcher and Shakespeare' (*Manly Anniversary Studies*, 1923; revised in *Studies in Beaumont, Fletcher, and Massinger*, New York, 1939), rejects Fletcher as participant on the grounds that his manner elsewhere shows differences of syntax, metre, and style from his supposed share in *Henry VIII*, and a much looser use of sources.

Peter Alexander, 'Conjectural History, or Shakespeare's *Henry VIII*' (*Essays and Studies of the English Association*, edited by H. J. C. Grierson, Volume 16, 1930), rejects arguments based on the imprecisions of line-counts and similar statistics, and the guesswork of some of Spedding's speculations, and finds throughout the play the 'compassionate spirit of the Fourth Period'. But the argument, briefly resumed in *Shakespeare's Life and Art* (1939), is critically disappointing, and many of the contentions are little more than debating points.

G. Wilson Knight, '*Henry VIII* and the Poetry of Conversion' (*The Crown of Life*, 1947), comes out whole-heartedly against collaboration, asserting that those elements which look Fletcherian are fundamentally related to Shakespeare's poetic, moral, and symbolical procedures throughout his writing life.

Hardin Craig, *An Interpretation of Shakespeare* (1948): the play is 'written throughout ... in the latest variety of Shakespeare's last style', 'consistently well-planned', and 'from the point of view of form ... one of his greatest achievements', and so not collaborative. These contentions are unconvincing, but the account of the play is pleasant and balanced though without special insights; a useful point is made (as against Hazlitt's anti-Henry diatribe) that the Elizabethans viewed Henry, on the whole, favourably.

R. A. Foakes, in a well-conducted argument (Arden edition, 1957), admits the force of claims for collaboration, but concludes that the play shows wide-ranging and single-minded scholarship in its use of source material and that it is allied in spirit and imaginative processes to Shakespeare's other late plays.

G. Bullough, *Narrative and Dramatic Sources of Shakespeare*,

Volume 4 (1962): a single directing mind is indicated by the evidence of coherent controlling intentions, integration of plot, and well-dovetailed use of sources.

Paul Bertram, '*Henry VIII*: the Conscience of the King' (*In Defense of Reading*, edited by R. A. Brower and R. Poirier, New York, 1962), defends the play's unity in terms of the main characters' relations with the King – 'The action . . . shows us a King who reigns becoming a King who rules' – and this unity, as well as the deliberate interconnecting of events, suggests single authorship. In *Shakespeare and 'The Two Noble Kinsmen'* (New Brunswick, 1965), Bertram restates the argument for unity of themes, and includes a long survey of the authorship controversy.

A. C. Sprague, *Shakespeare's Histories: Plays for the Stage* (1964), considers metrical counts unreliable, and collaboration which left the major scenes to the junior partner unlikely. Divided authorship would hardly produce such unifying themes of greatness spiritually redeemed, expressed with integrity of feeling.

For collaboration: the fundamental essay is that of James Spedding, whose 'Who Wrote Shakspere's *Henry VIII*?' appeared in the *Gentleman's Magazine* for August 1850 and was reprinted as 'On the Several Shares of Shakspere and Fletcher in the Play of *Henry VIII*' in *Transactions of the New Shakspere Society* for 1874. Many later commentators either accept Spedding's case as proven or add to it minor (though often useful) corroborative evidence. Independently of Spedding, Ralph Waldo Emerson in a lecture published in *Representative Men* (1850) had announced two styles in the play, the earlier by a thoughtful writer marked by a conscious and artificial eloquence, the later by Shakespeare, spontaneous and original. The following are the more noteworthy later arguments for collaboration, set out chronologically.

Ashley H. Thorndike, *The Influence of Beaumont and Fletcher on Shakespeare* (Worcester, Mass., 1901), detects a marked preponderance of 'them' in the 'Shakespeare' scenes and of ''em' in the 'Fletcher'.

Marjorie Nicolson, 'The Authorship of *Henry VIII*' (*Publications of the Modern Language Association of America*, Volume 37, 1922), speculates that Shakespeare established the themes (mainly the precariousness of high place) and that Fletcher amplified them, worked them through, and provided pathos and social entertainment. The argument is not convincing.

A. C. Partridge, *The Problem of 'Henry VIII' Reopened* (Cambridge, 1949), supports Spedding on grounds of stylistic and syntactical differences, and the differing distributions of the expletive 'do', 'hath'/'has', 'them'/'em', and 'ye'/'you', suggesting also that Shakespeare may have written part of IV.2 (before Katherine's vision) and of Cranmer's eulogy in V.5.

E. M. Waith, *The Pattern of Tragi-Comedy in Beaumont and Fletcher* (New Haven, 1952): *Henry VIII* is accepted as collaborative; the eloquence of the major speeches in Fletcher's share is the kind he uses for his 'biggest effects', and the pageantry is congenial to his procedures.

Ants Oras, '"Extra Monosyllables" in *Henry VIII* and the Problem of Authorship' (*Journal of English and Germanic Philology*, Volume 52, 1953), analyses the different rhythms produced by such extra monosyllables in the 'Shakespeare' and 'Fletcher' scenes. A useful essay, though the sense of rhythm is not impeccable.

W. W. Greg, *The Shakespeare First Folio* (Oxford, 1955): textual matters are the main concern, but joint authorship is accepted as proven.

John Munro, London Shakespeare edition, Volume 4 (1958): the various arguments are defined with care; the conclusion is that Spedding was 'generally right'.

R. A. Law, 'The Double Authorship of *Henry VIII*' (*Studies in Philology*, Volume 56, 1959): this thorough and convincing survey of evidence presents a firm conclusion for joint authorship from the distribution of light/weak endings, endings consisting of verbs and unstressed pronouns, sentence- and syntax-forms, and the dramatic characteristics of the two shares.

Kenneth Muir, *Shakespeare as Collaborator* (1960), does not deal specifically with *Henry VIII* but shares *The Two Noble Kinsmen* between Shakespeare and Fletcher, on grounds of rhythmical habits, style, and image-associations, in a way which throws an interesting light on procedures for studying *Henry VIII*.

Marco Mincoff, '*Henry VIII* and Fletcher' (*Shakespeare Quarterly*, 1961): this admirable analysis subjects the evidence to a most scholarly and critical scrutiny, resulting in the conclusion that 'every single test applied leads to the same clear division into two separate styles, and one of these styles always points to Fletcher. . . . It is not a question of slight, or even of marked, fluctuations with regard to one or two indicators alone, but of two fundamentally different styles'.

J. C. Maxwell, New Cambridge edition (1962), argues cogently against single authorship, taking metrical, prosodic, and grammatical peculiarities to corroborate a division made out clearly on stylistic grounds.

Clifford Leech, *Shakespeare: the Chronicles* (1962): no decisive solution is thought likely, but the play's lack of true structure and development 'reminds us of Fletcher. Here we do not have the sense that as the play proceeds we are approaching an increasingly complex view of the characters and situation'. In *The John Fletcher Plays* (1962) the idea is further discussed that 'at different moments we are offered differing views of the play's events and characters'. This inconsistency is like Fletcher's practice.

M. P. Jackson, 'Affirmative Particles in *Henry VIII*' (*Notes and Queries*, Volume 207, October 1962): the varying uses of 'ay', 'yea', and 'yes' in the two shares of the play correspond to the contrasted practices of Shakespeare and Fletcher elsewhere.

General Criticism

The best criticism is to be found in the introductions to the revised Arden and New Cambridge editions; briefer but very effective commentary is offered by John Munro in the London

Shakespeare edition, Volume 4, by F. D. Hoeniger in *The Complete Pelican Shakespeare*, and by G. Bullough in *Narrative and Dramatic Sources of Shakespeare*, Volume 4.

William Hazlitt, in *Characters of Shakespeare's Plays* (1817), offers little of critical significance, but expresses a characteristically strong objection to the King, as gross, blustering, vulgar, and hypocritical; this may provoke one to a more judicious assessment, prompted less by anti-monarchical fervour and more by recognition of Henry's care for just government and his kingdom's welfare, which the play makes clear. The ambiguity about Henry's 'conscience' is discussed in the Introduction, pages 19 and 38, and the Commentary on I.4.75.

G. Wilson Knight's essay '*Henry VIII* and the Poetry of Conversion' (*The Crown of Life*, 1947) is insufficiently discriminating in collecting and 'comparing' features from the whole body of Shakespeare's work. The analysis of style it offers to prove Shakespeare's sole authorship is too subjectively biased to carry conviction.

J. F. Kermode's 'What is Shakespeare's *Henry VIII* about?' (*Durham University Journal*, N.S. Volume 9, 1948; reprinted in *Shakespeare: the Histories*, edited by E. M. Waith, Englewood Cliffs, New Jersey, 1965, and in *Shakespeare's Histories: An Anthology of Modern Criticism*, edited by William A. Armstrong, Penguin Shakespeare Library, 1972) is a shrewd, interesting essay, arguing that Henry is the play's centre, essential to England's welfare, 'exercising certain God-like functions'; the structure is that of a new kind of *Mirror for Magistrates*, a 'late morality, showing the state from which great ones fall'.

Clifford Leech's comments on the inorganic structure are mentioned on page 42. In 'The Structure of the Last Plays' (*Shakespeare Survey 11*, 1958) he suggests that the last plays (*Henry VIII* most evidently) imply cycles of action larger than the plays' own compass.

J. R. Sutherland's 'The Language of the Last Plays' (*More Talking of Shakespeare*, edited by John Garrett, 1959) comments interestingly on the late plays' supercharged writing and daring stylistic procedures, which threaten to become too complex for drama.

E. M. W. Tillyard, in 'Why did Shakespeare write *Henry VIII*?' (*Critical Quarterly*, Volume 3, 1961), judges it to be written with professional competence but without consistent vitality – a play of 'the Master in his old age' (Shakespeare was forty-nine) – much below *The Winter's Tale* and *Cymbeline* in quality, but revealing 'prodigious skill and experience' in making a well-constructed play from Holinshed's heterogeneous material.

John Wasson's essay 'In Defense of *Henry VIII*' (*Research Studies of Washington University*, Volume 32, Number 3, September 1964) argues that, judged in the terms of a history play – a sequence of events, rather than analysis of character – it is well constructed, with a coherent design, and that 'the theme is the significance of the age of Henry VIII and the relationships among the events of that age'. The succession of falls from high place is not a dramatic weakness but a true account of the course of history, accompanied by the approved moral of noble acquiescence.

Stage History

The stage history is well related by G. C. D. Odell in *Shakespeare – From Betterton to Irving* (two volumes, New York, 1920; reprinted 1966), and C. B. Young in the New Cambridge edition. C. B. Hogan's *Shakespeare in the Theatre, 1701–1800* (two volumes, 1952, 1957) enumerates performances and cast lists. There are shorter but useful discussions by A. C. Sprague in *Shakespeare's Histories: Plays for the Stage* (1964) and R. A. Foakes in the new Arden edition. W. Moelwyn Merchant's *Shakespeare and the Artist* (1959) has interesting pages on some of the scenic effects, and particularly on Queen Katherine's trial scene as presented by J. P. Kemble and some later producers. Muriel St Clare Byrne, writing on 'A Stratford Production: *Henry VIII*' (*Shakespeare Survey 3*, 1950), gives a finely observant account of Tyrone Guthrie's distinguished revival of 1949, stressing the character balances – 'a play for genuine team-work, ... not rival stars ... a play about the Tudor succession by an Elizabethan'. G. Wilson Knight's description, in his *Principles of Shakespearean Production* (1936; revised as *Shakespearian Production*, 1964), of this play as he staged it in 1934 at the Hart House Theatre, Toronto, is a document of truly sympathetic insight.

KING HENRY THE EIGHTH

THE CHARACTERS IN THE PLAY

KING HENRY THE EIGHTH

DUKE OF BUCKINGHAM
DUKE OF NORFOLK
DUKE OF SUFFOLK
EARL OF SURREY
LORD ABERGAVENNY
LORD SANDS (Sir Walter Sands)
LORD CHAMBERLAIN
LORD CHANCELLOR
SIR HENRY GUILFORD
SIR THOMAS LOVELL
SIR NICHOLAS VAUX
SIR ANTHONY DENNY

CARDINAL WOLSEY
THOMAS CROMWELL, in Wolsey's service, afterwards
    in the King's
SECRETARY to Wolsey
SERVANT to Wolsey
CARDINAL CAMPEIUS
CAPUCHIUS, ambassador from the Emperor Charles the
    Fifth
GARDINER, Secretary to the King, afterwards Bishop of
    Winchester
PAGE to Gardiner
BISHOP OF LINCOLN
THOMAS CRANMER, Archbishop of Canterbury

61

BRANDON
SERGEANT-AT-ARMS
SURVEYOR to the Duke of Buckingham
Three GENTLEMEN
SCRIBE
CRIER
MESSENGER to Queen Katherine
KEEPER of the Council Chamber
DOCTOR BUTTS
PORTER
Porter's MAN
GARTER KING-OF-ARMS

QUEEN KATHERINE, wife of King Henry, afterwards
  divorced
GRIFFITH, gentleman usher to Queen Katherine
PATIENCE, Queen Katherine's woman
GENTLEWOMAN⎫
GENTLEMAN ⎭ attending upon Queen Katherine

ANNE BULLEN
OLD LADY, friend of Anne Bullen

Speaker of the PROLOGUE and EPILOGUE

Lords, Ladies, Gentlemen; Bishops, Priests, Vergers;
Judges; Lord Mayor of London, Aldermen, Citizens;
Guards, Tipstaves, Halberdiers; Scribes, Secretaries;
Attendants, Pursuivants, Pages, Choristers, Musicians,
Dancers as spirits appearing to Queen Katherine

I come no more to make you laugh. Things now
That bear a weighty and a serious brow,
Sad, high, and working, full of state and woe,
Such noble scenes as draw the eye to flow,
We now present. Those that can pity here
May, if they think it well, let fall a tear;
The subject will deserve it. Such as give
Their money out of hope they may believe
May here find truth too. Those that come to see
Only a show or two, and so agree   10
The play may pass, if they be still, and willing,
I'll undertake may see away their shilling
Richly in two short hours. Only they
That come to hear a merry, bawdy play,
A noise of targets, or to see a fellow
In a long motley coat guarded with yellow,
Will be deceived; for, gentle hearers, know
To rank our chosen truth with such a show
As fool and fight is, beside forfeiting
Our own brains, and the opinion that we bring   20
To make that only true we now intend,
Will leave us never an understanding friend.
Therefore, for goodness' sake, and as you are known
The first and happiest hearers of the town,
Be sad, as we would make ye. Think ye see
The very persons of our noble story
As they were living; think you see them great,
And followed with the general throng and sweat

Of thousand friends: then, in a moment, see
30 How soon this mightiness meets misery.
And if you can be merry then, I'll say
A man may weep upon his wedding day.

Enter the Duke of Norfolk at one door; at the other,   I.1
the Duke of Buckingham and the Lord Abergavenny

BUCKINGHAM
  Good morrow, and well met. How have ye done
  Since last we saw in France?

NORFOLK   I thank your grace,
  Healthful, and ever since a fresh admirer
  Of what I saw there.

BUCKINGHAM   An untimely ague
  Stayed me a prisoner in my chamber when
  Those suns of glory, those two lights of men,
  Met in the vale of Andren.

NORFOLK   'Twixt Guynes and Arde.
  I was then present, saw them salute on horseback,
  Beheld them when they lighted, how they clung
  In their embracement, as they grew together;   10
  Which had they, what four throned ones could have
     weighed
  Such a compounded one?

BUCKINGHAM   All the whole time
  I was my chamber's prisoner.

NORFOLK   Then you lost
  The view of earthly glory; men might say,
  Till this time pomp was single, but now married
  To one above itself. Each following day
  Became the next day's master, till the last
  Made former wonders its. Today the French,
  All clinquant, all in gold, like heathen gods,

20 Shone down the English; and tomorrow they
Made Britain India; every man that stood
Showed like a mine. Their dwarfish pages were
As cherubins, all gilt; the madams too,
Not used to toil, did almost sweat to bear
The pride upon them, that their very labour
Was to them as a painting. Now this masque
Was cried incomparable; and th'ensuing night
Made it a fool and beggar. The two Kings,
Equal in lustre, were now best, now worst,
30 As presence did present them: him in eye
Still him in praise; and being present both,
'Twas said they saw but one, and no discerner
Durst wag his tongue in censure. When these suns –
For so they phrase 'em – by their heralds challenged
The noble spirits to arms, they did perform
Beyond thought's compass, that former fabulous story,
Being now seen possible enough, got credit,
That Bevis was believed.

BUCKINGHAM   O, you go far!
NORFOLK
As I belong to worship, and affect
40 In honour honesty, the tract of everything
Would by a good discourser lose some life
Which action's self was tongue to. All was royal;
To the disposing of it naught rebelled.
Order gave each thing view; the office did
Distinctly his full function.

BUCKINGHAM   Who did guide –
I mean, who set the body and the limbs
Of this great sport together, as you guess?
NORFOLK
One, certes, that promises no element
In such a business.

66

BUCKINGHAM   I pray you, who, my lord?

NORFOLK

  All this was ordered by the good discretion   50
  Of the right reverend Cardinal of York.

BUCKINGHAM

  The devil speed him! No man's pie is freed
  From his ambitious finger. What had he
  To do in these fierce vanities? I wonder
  That such a keech can with his very bulk
  Take up the rays o'th'beneficial sun,
  And keep it from the earth.

NORFOLK   Surely, sir,
  There's in him stuff that puts him to these ends;
  For, being not propped by ancestry, whose grace
  Chalks successors their way, nor called upon   60
  For high feats done to th'crown, neither allied
  To eminent assistants, but spider-like,
  Out of his self-drawing web, 'a gives us note,
  The force of his own merit makes his way –
  A gift that heaven gives for him, which buys
  A place next to the King.

ABERGAVENNY   I cannot tell
  What heaven hath given him – let some graver eye
  Pierce into that; but I can see his pride
  Peep through each part of him. Whence has he that?
  If not from hell, the devil is a niggard,   70
  Or has given all before, and he begins
  A new hell in himself.

BUCKINGHAM   Why the devil,
  Upon this French going out, took he upon him –
  Without the privity o'th'King – t'appoint
  Who should attend on him? He makes up the file
  Of all the gentry, for the most part such
  To whom as great a charge as little honour

He meant to lay upon; and his own letter,
The honourable board of Council out,
80 Must fetch him in he papers.

ABERGAVENNY   I do know
Kinsmen of mine, three at the least, that have
By this so sickened their estates that never
They shall abound as formerly.

BUCKINGHAM   O, many
Have broke their backs with laying manors on 'em
For this great journey. What did this vanity
But minister communication of
A most poor issue?

NORFOLK   Grievingly I think
The peace between the French and us not values
The cost that did conclude it.

BUCKINGHAM   Every man,
90 After the hideous storm that followed, was
A thing inspired, and, not consulting, broke
Into a general prophecy – that this tempest,
Dashing the garment of this peace, aboded
The sudden breach on't.

NORFOLK   Which is budded out;
For France hath flawed the league, and hath attached
Our merchants' goods at Bordeaux.

ABERGAVENNY   Is it therefore
Th'ambassador is silenced?

NORFOLK   Marry, is't.

ABERGAVENNY
A proper title of a peace, and purchased
At a superfluous rate!

BUCKINGHAM   Why, all this business
100 Our reverend Cardinal carried.

NORFOLK   Like it your grace,
The state takes notice of the private difference

68

Betwixt you and the Cardinal. I advise you –
And take it from a heart that wishes towards you
Honour and plenteous safety – that you read
The Cardinal's malice and his potency
Together; to consider further, that
What his high hatred would effect wants not
A minister in his power. You know his nature,
That he's revengeful; and I know his sword
Hath a sharp edge – it's long, and't may be said   110
It reaches far, and where 'twill not extend,
Thither he darts it. Bosom up my counsel;
You'll find it wholesome. Lo, where comes that rock
That I advise your shunning.

> *Enter Cardinal Wolsey, the purse borne before him,*
> *certain of the guard, and two Secretaries with papers.*
> *The Cardinal in his passage fixeth his eye on Bucking-*
> *ham, and Buckingham on him, both full of disdain*

WOLSEY
The Duke of Buckingham's surveyor, ha?
Where's his examination?

SECRETARY   Here, so please you.

WOLSEY
Is he in person ready?

SECRETARY   Ay, please your grace.

WOLSEY
Well, we shall then know more, and Buckingham
Shall lessen this big look.
> *Exeunt Cardinal and his train*

BUCKINGHAM
This butcher's cur is venom-mouthed, and I   120
Have not the power to muzzle him; therefore best
Not wake him in his slumber. A beggar's book
Outworths a noble's blood.

NORFOLK   What, are you chafed?

69

Ask God for temperance; that's th'appliance only
Which your disease requires.

BUCKINGHAM   I read in's looks
Matter against me, and his eye reviled
Me as his abject object. At this instant
He bores me with some trick. He's gone to th'King.
I'll follow, and outstare him.

NORFOLK   Stay, my lord,
130 And let your reason with your choler question
What 'tis you go about. To climb steep hills
Requires slow pace at first. Anger is like
A full hot horse, who being allowed his way,
Self-mettle tires him. Not a man in England
Can advise me like you: be to yourself
As you would to your friend.

BUCKINGHAM   I'll to the King,
And from a mouth of honour quite cry down
This Ipswich fellow's insolence, or proclaim
There's difference in no persons.

NORFOLK   Be advised:
140 Heat not a furnace for your foe so hot
That it do singe yourself. We may outrun
By violent swiftness that which we run at,
And lose by over-running. Know you not
The fire that mounts the liquor till't run o'er
In seeming to augment it wastes it? Be advised.
I say again there is no English soul
More stronger to direct you than yourself,
If with the sap of reason you would quench
Or but allay the fire of passion.

BUCKINGHAM   Sir,
150 I am thankful to you, and I'll go along
By your prescription; but this top-proud fellow –
Whom from the flow of gall I name not, but

From sincere motions – by intelligence,
And proofs as clear as founts in July when
We see each grain of gravel, I do know
To be corrupt and treasonous.

NORFOLK   Say not treasonous.

BUCKINGHAM
To th'King I'll say't, and make my vouch as strong
As shore of rock. Attend: this holy fox,
Or wolf, or both – for he is equal ravenous
As he is subtle, and as prone to mischief   160
As able to perform't, his mind and place
Infecting one another, yea, reciprocally –
Only to show his pomp, as well in France
As here at home, suggests the King our master
To this last costly treaty, th'interview
That swallowed so much treasure, and like a glass
Did break i'th'wrenching.

NORFOLK   Faith, and so it did.

BUCKINGHAM
Pray give me favour, sir. This cunning Cardinal
The articles o'th'combination drew
As himself pleased; and they were ratified   170
As he cried 'Thus let be', to as much end
As give a crutch to th'dead. But our Count-Cardinal
Has done this, and 'tis well; for worthy Wolsey,
Who cannot err, he did it. Now this follows –
Which, as I take it, is a kind of puppy
To th'old dam, treason – Charles the Emperor,
Under pretence to see the Queen his aunt –
For 'twas indeed his colour, but he came
To whisper Wolsey – here makes visitation.
His fears were that the interview betwixt   180
England and France might through their amity
Breed him some prejudice, for from this league

Peeped harms that menaced him. He privily
Deals with our Cardinal, and, as I trow –
Which I do well, for I am sure the Emperor
Paid ere he promised, whereby his suit was granted
Ere it was asked – but when the way was made,
And paved with gold, the Emperor thus desired
That he would please to alter the King's course
190 And break the foresaid peace. Let the King know,
As soon he shall by me, that thus the Cardinal
Does buy and sell his honour as he pleases,
And for his own advantage.

NORFOLK   I am sorry
To hear this of him, and could wish he were
Something mistaken in't.

BUCKINGHAM   No, not a syllable:
I do pronounce him in that very shape
He shall appear in proof.

> *Enter Brandon, a Sergeant-at-Arms before him, and*
> *two or three of the guard*

BRANDON
Your office, sergeant: execute it.

SERGEANT   Sir,
My lord the Duke of Buckingham, and Earl
200 Of Hereford, Stafford, and Northampton, I
Arrest thee of high treason, in the name
Of our most sovereign King.

BUCKINGHAM   Lo you, my lord,
The net has fall'n upon me! I shall perish
Under device and practice.

BRANDON   I am sorry
To see you ta'en from liberty, to look on
The business present. 'Tis his highness' pleasure
You shall to th'Tower.

BUCKINGHAM   It will help me nothing

To plead mine innocence, for that dye is on me
Which makes my whit'st part black. The will of heaven
Be done in this and all things! I obey.   210
O my Lord Aberga'nny, fare you well!

BRANDON
   Nay, he must bear you company. (*To Abergavenny*) The King
   Is pleased you shall to th'Tower, till you know
   How he determines further.

ABERGAVENNY   As the Duke said,
   The will of heaven be done, and the King's pleasure
   By me obeyed.

BRANDON   Here is a warrant from
   The King, t'attach Lord Montacute, and the bodies
   Of the Duke's confessor, John de la Car,
   One Gilbert Perk, his chancellor –

BUCKINGHAM   So, so;
   These are the limbs o'th'plot: no more, I hope.   220

BRANDON
   A monk o'th'Chartreux.

BUCKINGHAM   O, Nicholas Hopkins?

BRANDON   He.

BUCKINGHAM
   My surveyor is false. The o'er-great Cardinal
   Hath showed him gold. My life is spanned already.
   I am the shadow of poor Buckingham,
   Whose figure even this instant cloud puts on
   By darkening my clear sun. My lord, farewell.   *Exeunt*

Cornets. Enter King Henry, leaning on the Cardinal's I.2
shoulder, the nobles, and Sir Thomas Lovell. The
Cardinal places himself under the King's feet on his
right side. Wolsey's Secretary in attendance

KING HENRY
My life itself, and the best heart of it,
Thanks you for this great care. I stood i'th'level
Of a full-charged confederacy, and give thanks
To you that choked it. Let be called before us
That gentleman of Buckingham's. In person
I'll hear him his confessions justify,
And point by point the treasons of his master
He shall again relate.

A noise within, crying 'Room for the Queen!'
Enter the Queen, ushered by the Dukes of Norfolk
and Suffolk. She kneels. The King riseth from his
state, takes her up, kisses and placeth her by him

QUEEN KATHERINE
Nay, we must longer kneel: I am a suitor.

KING HENRY
10   Arise, and take place by us. Half your suit
Never name to us: you have half our power.
The other moiety ere you ask is given.
Repeat your will, and take it.

QUEEN KATHERINE   Thank your majesty.
That you would love yourself, and in that love
Not unconsiderèd leave your honour nor
The dignity of your office, is the point
Of my petition.

KING HENRY   Lady mine, proceed.

QUEEN KATHERINE
I am solicited, not by a few,
And those of true condition, that your subjects
20   Are in great grievance. There have been commissions
Sent down among 'em which hath flawed the heart
Of all their loyalties; wherein, although,
My good lord Cardinal, they vent reproaches
Most bitterly on you as putter-on

74

Of these exactions, yet the King our master –
Whose honour heaven shield from soil! – even he
    escapes not
Language unmannerly, yea, such which breaks
The sides of loyalty, and almost appears
In loud rebellion.

NORFOLK   Not 'almost appears' –
It doth appear; for, upon these taxations,   30
The clothiers all, not able to maintain
The many to them 'longing, have put off
The spinsters, carders, fullers, weavers, who,
Unfit for other life, compelled by hunger
And lack of other means, in desperate manner
Daring th'event to th'teeth, are all in uproar,
And danger serves among them.

KING HENRY   Taxation?
Wherein? and what taxation? My lord Cardinal,
You that are blamed for it alike with us,
Know you of this taxation?

WOLSEY   Please you, sir,   40
I know but of a single part in aught
Pertains to th'state, and front but in that file
Where others tell steps with me.

QUEEN KATHERINE   No, my lord?
You know no more than others? But you frame
Things that are known alike, which are not wholesome
To those which would not know them, and yet must
Perforce be their acquaintance. These exactions,
Whereof my sovereign would have note, they are
Most pestilent to th'hearing, and to bear 'em
The back is sacrifice to th'load. They say   50
They are devised by you, or else you suffer
Too hard an exclamation.

KING HENRY   Still exaction!

The nature of it? In what kind, let's know,
Is this exaction?

QUEEN KATHERINE I am much too venturous
In tempting of your patience, but am boldened
Under your promised pardon. The subject's grief
Comes through commissions, which compels from each
The sixth part of his substance, to be levied
Without delay; and the pretence for this
60 Is named your wars in France. This makes bold mouths,
Tongues spit their duties out, and cold hearts freeze
Allegiance in them. Their curses now
Live where their prayers did, and it's come to pass
This tractable obedience is a slave
To each incensèd will. I would your highness `
Would give it quick consideration, for
There is no primer business.

KING HENRY   By my life,
This is against our pleasure.

WOLSEY   And for me,
I have no further gone in this than by
70 A single voice, and that not passed me but
By learnèd approbation of the judges. If I am
Traduced by ignorant tongues, which neither know
My faculties nor person, yet will be
The chronicles of my doing, let me say
'Tis but the fate of place, and the rough brake
That virtue must go through. We must not stint
Our necessary actions in the fear
To cope malicious censurers, which ever,
As ravenous fishes, do a vessel follow
80 That is new-trimmed, but benefit no further
Than vainly longing. What we oft do best,
By sick interpreters, once weak ones, is
Not ours, or not allowed; what worst, as oft

Hitting a grosser quality, is cried up
For our best act. If we shall stand still,
In fear our motion will be mocked or carped at,
We should take root here where we sit,
Or sit state-statues only.

KING HENRY   Things done well,
And with a care, exempt themselves from fear;
Things done without example, in their issue   90
Are to be feared. Have you a precedent
Of this commission? I believe, not any.
We must not rend our subjects from our laws,
And stick them in our will. Sixth part of each?
A trembling contribution! Why, we take
From every tree lop, bark, and part o'th'timber,
And though we leave it with a root, thus hacked,
The air will drink the sap. To every county
Where this is questioned send our letters with
Free pardon to each man that has denied   100
The force of this commission. Pray look to't;
I put it to your care.

WOLSEY (*aside to Secretary*) A word with you.
Let there be letters writ to every shire
Of the King's grace and pardon. The grievèd commons
Hardly conceive of me – let it be noised
That through our intercession this revokement
And pardon comes. I shall anon advise you
Further in the proceeding.   *Exit Secretary*
     Enter Surveyor

QUEEN KATHERINE
I am sorry that the Duke of Buckingham
Is run in your displeasure.

KING HENRY   It grieves many.   110
The gentleman is learned, and a most rare speaker,
To nature none more bound; his training such

That he may furnish and instruct great teachers,
And never seek for aid out of himself. Yet see,
When these so noble benefits shall prove
Not well disposed, the mind growing once corrupt,
They turn to vicious forms, ten times more ugly
Than ever they were fair. This man so complete,
Who was enrolled 'mongst wonders, and when we
120   Almost with ravished listening, could not find
His hour of speech a minute – he, my lady,
Hath into monstrous habits put the graces
That once were his, and is become as black
As if besmeared in hell. Sit by us. You shall hear –
This was his gentleman in trust – of him
Things to strike honour sad. Bid him recount
The fore-recited practices, whereof
We cannot feel too little, hear too much.

WOLSEY

Stand forth, and with bold spirit relate what you,
130   Most like a careful subject, have collected
Out of the Duke of Buckingham.

KING HENRY   Speak freely.

SURVEYOR

First, it was usual with him – every day
It would infect his speech – that if the King
Should without issue die, he'll carry it so
To make the sceptre his. These very words
I've heard him utter to his son-in-law,
Lord Aberga'nny, to whom by oath he menaced
Revenge upon the Cardinal.

WOLSEY   Please your highness, note
This dangerous conception in this point:
140   Not friended by his wish to your high person,
His will is most malignant, and it stretches
Beyond you to your friends.

QUEEN KATHERINE   My learned lord Cardinal,
  Deliver all with charity.
KING HENRY   Speak on.
  How grounded he his title to the crown
  Upon our fail? To this point hast thou heard him
  At any time speak aught?
SURVEYOR   He was brought to this
  By a vain prophecy of Nicholas Henton.
KING HENRY
  What was that Henton?
SURVEYOR   Sir, a Chartreux friar,
  His confessor, who fed him every minute
  With words of sovereignty.
KING HENRY   How know'st thou this?   150
SURVEYOR
  Not long before your highness sped to France,
  The Duke being at the Rose, within the parish
  Saint Lawrence Poultney, did of me demand
  What was the speech among the Londoners
  Concerning the French journey. I replied
  Men feared the French would prove perfidious,
  To the King's danger. Presently the Duke
  Said 'twas the fear indeed, and that he doubted
  'Twould prove the verity of certain words
  Spoke by a holy monk, 'that oft', says he,   160
  'Hath sent to me, wishing me to permit
  John de la Car, my chaplain, a choice hour
  To hear from him a matter of some moment;
  Whom after under the confession's seal
  He solemnly had sworn that what he spoke
  My chaplain to no creature living but
  To me should utter, with demure confidence
  This pausingly ensued: "Neither the King nor's heirs,
  Tell you the Duke, shall prosper. Bid him strive

170   To win the love o'th'commonalty. The Duke
     Shall govern England."'

QUEEN KATHERINE   If I know you well,
   You were the Duke's surveyor, and lost your office
   On the complaint o'th'tenants. Take good heed
   You charge not in your spleen a noble person
   And spoil your nobler soul – I say, take heed;
   Yes, heartily beseech you.

KING HENRY   Let him on.
   Go forward.

SURVEYOR   On my soul, I'll speak but truth.
   I told my lord the Duke, by th'devil's illusions
   The monk might be deceived, and that 'twas dangerous
180   For him to ruminate on this so far, until
   It forged him some design, which, being believed,
   It was much like to do. He answered, 'Tush,
   It can do me no damage'; adding further
   That, had the King in his last sickness failed,
   The Cardinal's and Sir Thomas Lovell's heads
   Should have gone off.

KING HENRY   Ha! What, so rank? Ah, ha!
   There's mischief in this man. Canst thou say further?

SURVEYOR
   I can, my liege.

KING HENRY   Proceed.

SURVEYOR   Being at Greenwich,
   After your highness had reproved the Duke
190   About Sir William Bulmer –

KING HENRY   I remember
   Of such a time; being my sworn servant,
   The Duke retained him his. But on; what hence?

SURVEYOR
   'If', quoth he, 'I for this had been committed,
   As to the Tower I thought, I would have played

The part my father meant to act upon
Th'usurper Richard; who, being at Salisbury,
Made suit to come in's presence, which if granted,
As he made semblance of his duty, would
Have put his knife into him.'

KING HENRY   A giant traitor!

WOLSEY

Now, madam, may his highness live in freedom,   200
And this man out of prison?

QUEEN KATHERINE   God mend all!

KING HENRY

There's something more would out of thee: what sayst?

SURVEYOR

After 'the Duke his father', with the 'knife',
He stretched him, and, with one hand on his dagger,
Another spread on's breast, mounting his eyes,
He did discharge a horrible oath, whose tenor
Was, were he evil used, he would outgo
His father by as much as a performance
Does an irresolute purpose.

KING HENRY   There's his period,
To sheathe his knife in us. He is attached;   210
Call him to present trial. If he may
Find mercy in the law, 'tis his; if none,
Let him not seek't of us. By day and night!
He's traitor to th'height!   *Exeunt*

Enter the Lord Chamberlain and Lord Sands   I.3

LORD CHAMBERLAIN

Is't possible the spells of France should juggle
Men into such strange mysteries?

SANDS   New customs,
Though they be never so ridiculous,

Nay, let 'em be unmanly, yet are followed.

LORD CHAMBERLAIN
As far as I see, all the good our English
Have got by the late voyage is but merely
A fit or two o'th'face – but they are shrewd ones;
For when they hold 'em, you would swear directly
Their very noses had been counsellors
10 To Pepin or Clotharius, they keep state so.

SANDS
They have all new legs, and lame ones. One would take it,
That never see 'em pace before, the spavin
Or springhalt reigned among 'em.

LORD CHAMBERLAIN   Death, my lord!
Their clothes are after such a pagan cut to't
That sure they've worn out Christendom.

Enter Sir Thomas Lovell

How now?
What news, Sir Thomas Lovell?

LOVELL   Faith, my lord,
I hear of none but the new proclamation
That's clapped upon the court gate.

LORD CHAMBERLAIN   What is't for?

LOVELL
The reformation of our travelled gallants,
20 That fill the court with quarrels, talk, and tailors.

LORD CHAMBERLAIN
I'm glad 'tis there. Now I would pray our monsieurs
To think an English courtier may be wise,
And never see the Louvre.

LOVELL   They must either,
For so run the conditions, leave those remnants
Of fool and feather that they got in France,
With all their honourable points of ignorance
Pertaining thereunto, as fights and fireworks,

Abusing better men than they can be
Out of a foreign wisdom, renouncing clean
The faith they have in tennis and tall stockings,   30
Short blistered breeches, and those types of travel,
And understand again like honest men,
Or pack to their old playfellows. There, I take it,
They may, *cum privilegio*, 'oui' away
The lag end of their lewdness, and be laughed at.

SANDS
'Tis time to give 'em physic, their diseases
Are grown so catching.

LORD CHAMBERLAIN   What a loss our ladies
Will have of these trim vanities!

LOVELL   Ay, marry,
There will be woe indeed, lords! The sly whoresons
Have got a speeding trick to lay down ladies.   40
A French song and a fiddle has no fellow.

SANDS
The devil fiddle 'em! I am glad they are going,
For sure there's no converting of 'em. Now
An honest country lord, as I am, beaten
A long time out of play, may bring his plainsong,
And have an hour of hearing, and, by'r lady,
Held current music too.

LORD CHAMBERLAIN   Well said, Lord Sands.
Your colt's tooth is not cast yet?

SANDS   No, my lord,
Nor shall not while I have a stump.

LORD CHAMBERLAIN   Sir Thomas,
Whither were you a-going?

LOVELL   To the Cardinal's;   50
Your lordship is a guest too.

LORD CHAMBERLAIN   O, 'tis true.
This night he makes a supper, and a great one,

To many lords and ladies. There will be
The beauty of this kingdom, I'll assure you.

LOVELL
That churchman bears a bounteous mind indeed,
A hand as fruitful as the land that feeds us.
His dews fall everywhere.

LORD CHAMBERLAIN   No doubt he's noble.
He had a black mouth that said other of him.

SANDS
He may, my lord; has wherewithal: in him
60 Sparing would show a worse sin than ill doctrine.
Men of his way should be most liberal;
They are set here for examples.

LORD CHAMBERLAIN   True, they are so;
But few now give so great ones. My barge stays;
Your lordship shall along. Come, good Sir Thomas,
We shall be late else, which I would not be,
For I was spoke to, with Sir Henry Guilford,
This night to be comptrollers.

SANDS   I am your lordship's.

Exeunt

I.4   *Hautboys. A small table under a state for the Cardinal,
         a longer table for the guests. Then enter Anne Bullen
         and divers other ladies and gentlemen as guests, at one
         door; at another door enter Sir Henry Guilford*

GUILFORD
Ladies, a general welcome from his grace
Salutes ye all. This night he dedicates
To fair content, and you. None here, he hopes,
In all this noble bevy, has brought with her
One care abroad. He would have all as merry
As, first, good company, good wine, good welcome

84

Can make good people.

Enter the Lord Chamberlain, Lord Sands, and Sir
Thomas Lovell

O, my lord, you're tardy.
The very thought of this fair company
Clapped wings to me.

LORD CHAMBERLAIN

You are young, Sir Harry Guilford.

SANDS

Sir Thomas Lovell, had the Cardinal   10
But half my lay thoughts in him, some of these
Should find a running banquet, ere they rested,
I think would better please 'em. By my life,
They are a sweet society of fair ones.

LOVELL

O that your lordship were but now confessor
To one or two of these!

SANDS   I would I were;
They should find easy penance.

LOVELL   Faith, how easy?

SANDS

As easy as a down bed would afford it.

LORD CHAMBERLAIN

Sweet ladies, will it please you sit? Sir Harry,
Place you that side; I'll take the charge of this.   20
His grace is entering. – Nay, you must not freeze –
Two women placed together makes cold weather.
My Lord Sands, you are one will keep 'em waking:
Pray sit between these ladies.

SANDS   By my faith,
And thank your lordship. By your leave, sweet ladies.
If I chance to talk a little wild, forgive me;
I had it from my father.

ANNE   Was he mad, sir?

SANDS

    O, very mad, exceeding mad, in love too;
    But he would bite none. Just as I do now,
30   He would kiss you twenty with a breath.
        He kisses her

LORD CHAMBERLAIN   Well said, my lord.
    So, now you're fairly seated. Gentlemen,
    The penance lies on you if these fair ladies
    Pass away frowning.

SANDS   For my little cure,
    Let me alone.
        Hautboys. Enter Cardinal Wolsey and takes his state

WOLSEY

    You're welcome, my fair guests. That noble lady
    Or gentleman that is not freely merry
    Is not my friend. This, to confirm my welcome –
    And to you all, good health!
        He drinks

SANDS   Your grace is noble.
    Let me have such a bowl may hold my thanks,
40   And save me so much talking.

WOLSEY   My Lord Sands,
    I am beholding to you. Cheer your neighbours.
    Ladies, you are not merry! Gentlemen,
    Whose fault is this?

SANDS   The red wine first must rise
    In their fair cheeks, my lord; then we shall have 'em
    Talk us to silence.

ANNE   You are a merry gamester,
    My Lord Sands.

SANDS   Yes, if I make my play.
    Here's to your ladyship; and pledge it, madam,
    For 'tis to such a thing –

ANNE   You cannot show me.

SANDS

   I told your grace they would talk anon.

     Drum and trumpet. Chambers discharged

WOLSEY   What's that?

LORD CHAMBERLAIN

   Look out there, some of ye.   *Exit a Servant*

WOLSEY   What warlike voice,   50

   And to what end, is this? Nay, ladies, fear not;

   By all the laws of war you're privileged.

     Enter Servant

LORD CHAMBERLAIN

   How now, what is't?

SERVANT   A noble troop of strangers,

   For so they seem. They've left their barge and landed,

   And hither make, as great ambassadors

   From foreign princes.

WOLSEY   Good Lord Chamberlain,

   Go, give 'em welcome – you can speak the French

      tongue;

   And pray receive 'em nobly, and conduct 'em

   Into our presence, where this heaven of beauty

   Shall shine at full upon them. Some attend him.   60

          Exit Lord Chamberlain, attended

    All rise, and tables removed

   You have now a broken banquet, but we'll mend it.

   A good digestion to you all; and once more

   I shower a welcome on ye – welcome all!

    Hautboys. Enter the King and others as masquers,
    habited like shepherds, ushered by the Lord Chamber-
    lain. They pass directly before the Cardinal, and
    gracefully salute him

   A noble company! What are their pleasures?

LORD CHAMBERLAIN

   Because they speak no English, thus they prayed

To tell your grace, that, having heard by fame
Of this so noble and so fair assembly
This night to meet here, they could do no less,
Out of the great respect they bear to beauty,
70   But leave their flocks, and, under your fair conduct,
Crave leave to view these ladies, and entreat
An hour of revels with 'em.

WOLSEY   Say, Lord Chamberlain,
They have done my poor house grace; for which I pay
       'em
A thousand thanks, and pray 'em take their pleasures.
     They choose ladies; the King chooses Anne Bullen

KING HENRY
The fairest hand I ever touched! O beauty,
Till now I never knew thee.
     Music. Dance

WOLSEY
My lord!

LORD CHAMBERLAIN
         Your grace?

WOLSEY   Pray tell 'em thus much from me:
There should be one amongst 'em, by his person,
More worthy this place than myself, to whom,
80   If I but knew him, with my love and duty
I would surrender it.

LORD CHAMBERLAIN I will, my lord.
     He whispers with the masquers

WOLSEY
What say they?

LORD CHAMBERLAIN Such a one, they all confess,
There is indeed, which they would have your grace
Find out, and he will take it.

WOLSEY   Let me see then.
     He comes from his state

By all your good leaves, gentlemen; here I'll make
My royal choice.

The King unmasks

KING HENRY   Ye have found him, Cardinal.
You hold a fair assembly; you do well, lord.
You are a churchman, or I'll tell you, Cardinal,
I should judge now unhappily.

WOLSEY   I am glad
Your grace is grown so pleasant.

KING HENRY   My Lord Chamberlain, 90
Prithee come hither: what fair lady's that?

LORD CHAMBERLAIN
An't please your grace, Sir Thomas Bullen's daughter,
The Viscount Rochford, one of her highness' women.

KING HENRY
By heaven, she is a dainty one. Sweetheart,
I were unmannerly to take you out
And not to kiss you. A health, gentlemen!
Let it go round.

WOLSEY
Sir Thomas Lovell, is the banquet ready
I'th'privy chamber?

LOVELL   Yes, my lord.

WOLSEY   Your grace,
I fear, with dancing is a little heated.   100

KING HENRY
I fear, too much.

WOLSEY   There's fresher air, my lord,
In the next chamber.

KING HENRY
Lead in your ladies every one. Sweet partner,
I must not yet forsake you. Let's be merry,
Good my lord Cardinal: I have half a dozen healths
To drink to these fair ladies, and a measure

To lead 'em once again; and then let's dream
Who's best in favour. Let the music knock it.

Exeunt, with trumpets

*

II.1   *Enter two Gentlemen, at several doors*

FIRST GENTLEMAN
Whither away so fast?

SECOND GENTLEMAN O, God save ye!
Even to the Hall, to hear what shall become
Of the great Duke of Buckingham.

FIRST GENTLEMAN   I'll save you
That labour, sir. All's now done but the ceremony
Of bringing back the prisoner.

SECOND GENTLEMAN   Were you there?

FIRST GENTLEMAN
Yes, indeed was I.

SECOND GENTLEMAN Pray speak what has happened.

FIRST GENTLEMAN
You may guess quickly what.

SECOND GENTLEMAN   Is he found guilty?

FIRST GENTLEMAN
Yes, truly is he, and condemned upon't.

SECOND GENTLEMAN
I am sorry for't.

FIRST GENTLEMAN So are a number more.

SECOND GENTLEMAN
10   But pray, how passed it?

FIRST GENTLEMAN
I'll tell you in a little. The great Duke
Came to the bar, where to his accusations
He pleaded still not guilty, and allegèd

Many sharp reasons to defeat the law.
The King's attorney, on the contrary,
Urged on the examinations, proofs, confessions,
Of divers witnesses, which the Duke desired
To have brought *viva voce* to his face;
At which appeared against him his surveyor,
Sir Gilbert Perk his chancellor, and John Car, 20
Confessor to him, with that devil-monk,
Hopkins, that made this mischief.

SECOND GENTLEMAN   That was he
That fed him with his prophecies.

FIRST GENTLEMAN   The same.
All these accused him strongly, which he fain
Would have flung from him; but indeed he could not;
And so his peers, upon this evidence,
Have found him guilty of high treason. Much
He spoke, and learnèdly, for life, but all
Was either pitied in him or forgotten.

SECOND GENTLEMAN
After all this, how did he bear himself? 30

FIRST GENTLEMAN
When he was brought again to th'bar, to hear
His knell rung out, his judgement, he was stirred
With such an agony he sweat extremely,
And something spoke in choler, ill and hasty;
But he fell to himself again, and sweetly
In all the rest showed a most noble patience.

SECOND GENTLEMAN
I do not think he fears death.

FIRST GENTLEMAN   Sure he does not;
He never was so womanish. The cause
He may a little grieve at.

SECOND GENTLEMAN   Certainly
The Cardinal is the end of this.

40 FIRST GENTLEMAN   'Tis likely,
   By all conjectures: first, Kildare's attainder,
   Then deputy of Ireland, who removed,
   Earl Surrey was sent thither, and in haste too,
   Lest he should help his father.
SECOND GENTLEMAN   That trick of state
   Was a deep envious one.
FIRST GENTLEMAN   At his return
   No doubt he will requite it. This is noted,
   And generally: whoever the King favours,
   The Cardinal instantly will find employment,
   And far enough from court too.
SECOND GENTLEMAN   All the commons
50 Hate him perniciously, and, o'my conscience,
   Wish him ten fathom deep This Duke as much
   They love and dote on, call him bounteous Buckingham,
   The mirror of all courtesy –
FIRST GENTLEMAN   Stay there, sir,
   And see the noble ruined man you speak of.

   Enter Buckingham from his arraignment, tipstaves
   before him, the axe with the edge towards him,
   halberds on each side, accompanied with Sir Thomas
   Lovell, Sir Nicholas Vaux, Sir Walter Sands, and
   common people, etc.

SECOND GENTLEMAN
   Let's stand close, and behold him.
BUCKINGHAM   All good people,
   You that thus far have come to pity me,
   Hear what I say, and then go home and lose me.
   I have this day received a traitor's judgement,
   And by that name must die. Yet, heaven bear witness,
60 And if I have a conscience let it sink me,
   Even as the axe falls, if I be not faithful!
   The law I bear no malice for my death:

'T has done, upon the premises, but justice.
But those that sought it I could wish more Christians.
Be what they will, I heartily forgive 'em.
Yet let 'em look they glory not in mischief,
Nor build their evils on the graves of great men,
For then my guiltless blood must cry against 'em.
For further life in this world I ne'er hope,
Nor will I sue, although the King have mercies   70
More than I dare make faults. You few that loved me,
And dare be bold to weep for Buckingham,
His noble friends and fellows, whom to leave
Is only bitter to him, only dying,
Go with me like good angels to my end,
And as the long divorce of steel falls on me
Make of your prayers one sweet sacrifice,
And lift my soul to heaven. Lead on, a God's name!

LOVELL

I do beseech your grace, for charity,
If ever any malice in your heart   80
Were hid against me, now to forgive me frankly.

BUCKINGHAM

Sir Thomas Lovell, I as free forgive you
As I would be forgiven. I forgive all.
There cannot be those numberless offences
'Gainst me that I cannot take peace with. No black envy
Shall mark my grave. Commend me to his grace,
And if he speak of Buckingham, pray tell him
You met him half in heaven. My vows and prayers
Yet are the King's and, till my soul forsake,
Shall cry for blessings on him. May he live   90
Longer than I have time to tell his years;
Ever beloved and loving may his rule be;
And, when old time shall lead him to his end,
Goodness and he fill up one monument!

LOVELL

    To th'waterside I must conduct your grace,
    Then give my charge up to Sir Nicholas Vaux,
    Who undertakes you to your end.

VAUX   **Prepare there;**

    The Duke is coming. See the barge be ready,
    And fit it with such furniture as suits
100   The greatness of his person.

BUCKINGHAM   **Nay, Sir Nicholas,**

    Let it alone; my state now will but mock me.
    When I came hither, I was Lord High Constable
    And Duke of Buckingham; now, poor Edward Bohun.
    Yet I am richer than my base accusers
    That never knew what truth meant. I now seal it,
    And with that blood will make 'em one day groan for't.
    My noble father, Henry of Buckingham,
    Who first raised head against usurping Richard,
    Flying for succour to his servant Banister,
110   Being distressed, was by that wretch betrayed,
    And without trial fell. God's peace be with him!
    Henry the Seventh succeeding, truly pitying
    My father's loss, like a most royal prince
    Restored me to my honours, and out of ruins
    Made my name once more noble. Now his son,
    Henry the Eighth, life, honour, name, and all
    That made me happy, at one stroke has taken
    For ever from the world. I had my trial,
    And must needs say a noble one; which makes me
120   A little happier than my wretched father;
    Yet thus far we are one in fortunes: both
    Fell by our servants, by those men we loved most –
    A most unnatural and faithless service.
    Heaven has an end in all. Yet, you that hear me,
    This from a dying man receive as certain:

Where you are liberal of your loves and counsels
Be sure you be not loose; for those you make friends
And give your hearts to, when they once perceive
The least rub in your fortunes, fall away
Like water from ye, never found again   130
But where they mean to sink ye. All good people,
Pray for me! I must now forsake ye; the last hour
Of my long weary life is come upon me.
Farewell;
And when you would say something that is sad,
Speak how I fell. I have done; and God forgive me.

Exeunt Duke and train

FIRST GENTLEMAN
  O, this is full of pity! Sir, it calls,
  I fear, too many curses on their heads
  That were the authors.
SECOND GENTLEMAN If the Duke be guiltless,
  'Tis full of woe; yet I can give you inkling   140
  Of an ensuing evil, if it fall,
  Greater than this.
FIRST GENTLEMAN Good angels keep it from us!
  What may it be? You do not doubt my faith, sir?
SECOND GENTLEMAN
  This secret is so weighty, 'twill require
  A strong faith to conceal it.
FIRST GENTLEMAN   Let me have it;
  I do not talk much.
SECOND GENTLEMAN I am confident;
  You shall, sir. Did you not of late days hear
  A buzzing of a separation
  Between the King and Katherine?
FIRST GENTLEMAN   Yes, but it held not;
  For when the King once heard it, out of anger   150
  He sent command to the Lord Mayor straight

> To stop the rumour and allay those tongues
> That durst disperse it.

SECOND GENTLEMAN But that slander, sir,
> Is found a truth now, for it grows again
> Fresher than e'er it was, and held for certain
> The King will venture at it. Either the Cardinal
> Or some about him near have, out of malice
> To the good Queen, possessed him with a scruple
> That will undo her. To confirm this too,
160 Cardinal Campeius is arrived, and lately,
> As all think, for this business.

FIRST GENTLEMAN 'Tis the Cardinal;
> And merely to revenge him on the Emperor
> For not bestowing on him at his asking
> The archbishopric of Toledo, this is purposed.

SECOND GENTLEMAN
> I think you have hit the mark; but is't not cruel
> That she should feel the smart of this? The Cardinal
> Will have his will, and she must fall.

FIRST GENTLEMAN 'Tis woeful.
> We are too open here to argue this;
> Let's think in private more. *Exeunt*

II.2 *Enter the Lord Chamberlain, reading this letter*

LORD CHAMBERLAIN *My lord, the horses your lordship*
sent for, with all the care I had I saw well chosen, ridden,
and furnished. They were young and handsome, and of the
best breed in the north. When they were ready to set out for
London, a man of my lord Cardinal's, by commission and
main power, took 'em from me, with this reason: his
master would be served before a subject, if not before the
King; which stopped our mouths, sir.

I fear he will indeed. Well, let him have them.

He will have all, I think.   10
  Enter to the Lord Chamberlain the Dukes of Norfolk
  and Suffolk

NORFOLK
 Well met, my Lord Chamberlain.

LORD CHAMBERLAIN
 Good day to both your graces.

SUFFOLK
 How is the King employed?

LORD CHAMBERLAIN   I left him private,
 Full of sad thoughts and troubles.

NORFOLK   What's the cause?

LORD CHAMBERLAIN
 It seems the marriage with his brother's wife
 Has crept too near his conscience.

SUFFOLK (*aside*)   No, his conscience
 Has crept too near another lady.

NORFOLK   'Tis so;
 This is the Cardinal's doing; the King-Cardinal,
 That blind priest, like the eldest son of fortune,
 Turns what he list. The King will know him one day.   20

SUFFOLK
 Pray God he do! He'll never know himself else.

NORFOLK
 How holily he works in all his business,
 And with what zeal! For, now he has cracked the league
 Between us and the Emperor, the Queen's great nephew,
 He dives into the King's soul and there scatters
 Dangers, doubts, wringing of the conscience,
 Fears, and despairs – and all these for his marriage.
 And out of all these to restore the King,
 He counsels a divorce, a loss of her
 That like a jewel has hung twenty years   30
 About his neck, yet never lost her lustre;

Of her that loves him with that excellence
That angels love good men with; even of her
That, when the greatest stroke of fortune falls,
Will bless the King – and is not this course pious?

LORD CHAMBERLAIN
Heaven keep me from such counsel! 'Tis most true
These news are everywhere, every tongue speaks 'em,
And every true heart weeps for't. All that dare
Look into these affairs see this main end,
The French King's sister. Heaven will one day open
The King's eyes, that so long have slept upon
This bold bad man.

SUFFOLK   And free us from his slavery.

NORFOLK
We had need pray,
And heartily, for our deliverance,
Or this imperious man will work us all
From princes into pages. All men's honours
Lie like one lump before him, to be fashioned
Into what pitch he please.

SUFFOLK   For me, my lords,
I love him not, nor fear him – there's my creed.
As I am made without him, so I'll stand,
If the King please. His curses and his blessings
Touch me alike; they're breath I not believe in.
I knew him, and I know him; so I leave him
To him that made him proud – the Pope.

NORFOLK   Let's in,
And with some other business put the King
From these sad thoughts that work too much upon him.
My lord, you'll bear us company?

LORD CHAMBERLAIN   Excuse me,
The King has sent me otherwhere. Besides,
You'll find a most unfit time to disturb him.

Health to your lordships!

NORFOLK   Thanks, my good Lord Chamberlain.   60

Exit Lord Chamberlain

The King draws the curtain and sits reading pensively

SUFFOLK

How sad he looks; sure he is much afflicted.

KING HENRY

Who's there, ha?

NORFOLK   Pray God he be not angry.

KING HENRY

Who's there, I say? How dare you thrust yourselves

Into my private meditations?

Who am I, ha?

NORFOLK

A gracious king that pardons all offences

Malice ne'er meant. Our breach of duty this way

Is business of estate, in which we come

To know your royal pleasure.

KING HENRY   Ye are too bold.

Go to; I'll make ye know your times of business.   70

Is this an hour for temporal affairs, ha?

Enter Wolsey and Campeius with a commission

Who's there? My good lord Cardinal? O my Wolsey,

The quiet of my wounded conscience,

Thou art a cure fit for a king. (*To Campeius*) You're welcome,

Most learnèd reverend sir, into our kingdom;

Use us, and it. (*To Wolsey*) My good lord, have great care

I be not found a talker.

WOLSEY   Sir, you cannot.

I would your grace would give us but an hour

Of private conference.

KING HENRY (*to Norfolk and Suffolk*) We are busy; go.

NORFOLK (*aside to Suffolk*)
80   This priest has no pride in him!

SUFFOLK (*aside to Norfolk*)   Not to speak of!
    I would not be so sick though for his place.
    But this cannot continue.

NORFOLK (*aside to Suffolk*) If it do,
    I'll venture one have-at-him.

SUFFOLK (*aside to Norfolk*)   I another.
                       Exeunt Norfolk and Suffolk

WOLSEY
    Your grace has given a precedent of wisdom
    Above all princes, in committing freely
    Your scruple to the voice of Christendom.
    Who can be angry now? What envy reach you?
    The Spaniard, tied by blood and favour to her,
    Must now confess, if they have any goodness,
90   The trial just and noble. All the clerks –
    I mean the learnèd ones in Christian kingdoms –
    Have their free voices. Rome, the nurse of judgement,
    Invited by your noble self, hath sent
    One general tongue unto us, this good man,
    This just and learnèd priest, Cardinal Campeius,
    Whom once more I present unto your highness.

KING HENRY
    And once more in mine arms I bid him welcome,
    And thank the holy conclave for their loves.
    They have sent me such a man I would have wished for.

CAMPEIUS
100   Your grace must needs deserve all strangers' loves,
    You are so noble. To your highness' hand
    I tender my commission, by whose virtue,
    The court of Rome commanding, you, my lord
    Cardinal of York, are joined with me their servant

In the unpartial judging of this business.

KING HENRY
Two equal men. The Queen shall be acquainted
Forthwith for what you come. Where's Gardiner?

WOLSEY
I know your majesty has always loved her
So dear in heart not to deny her that
A woman of less place might ask by law –   110
Scholars allowed freely to argue for her.

KING HENRY
Ay, and the best she shall have, and my favour
To him that does best, God forbid else. Cardinal,
Prithee call Gardiner to me, my new secretary;
I find him a fit fellow.   *Exit Wolsey*

        Enter Wolsey with Gardiner

WOLSEY (*aside to Gardiner*)
Give me your hand: much joy and favour to you.
You are the King's now.

GARDINER (*aside to Wolsey*) But to be commanded
For ever by your grace, whose hand has raised me.

KING HENRY
Come hither, Gardiner.
        Walks and whispers

CAMPEIUS
My lord of York, was not one Doctor Pace   120
In this man's place before him?

WOLSEY   Yes, he was.

CAMPEIUS
Was he not held a learnèd man?

WOLSEY   Yes, surely.

CAMPEIUS
Believe me, there's an ill opinion spread then,
Even of yourself, lord Cardinal.

WOLSEY How? Of me?

CAMPEIUS

They will not stick to say you envied him,
And fearing he would rise, he was so virtuous,
Kept him a foreign man still, which so grieved him
That he ran mad and died.

WOLSEY Heaven's peace be with him!
That's Christian care enough. For living murmurers
130   There's places of rebuke. He was a fool,
For he would needs be virtuous. That good fellow,
If I command him, follows my appointment;
I will have none so near else. Learn this, brother,
We live not to be griped by meaner persons.

KING HENRY

Deliver this with modesty to th'Queen.

Exit Gardiner

The most convenient place that I can think of
For such receipt of learning is Blackfriars;
There ye shall meet about this weighty business.
My Wolsey, see it furnished. O, my lord,
140   Would it not grieve an able man to leave
So sweet a bedfellow? But conscience, conscience!
O, 'tis a tender place, and I must leave her. *Exeunt*

II.3   *Enter Anne Bullen and an Old Lady*

ANNE

Not for that neither. Here's the pang that pinches:
His highness having lived so long with her, and she
So good a lady that no tongue could ever
Pronounce dishonour of her – by my life,
She never knew harm-doing – O, now, after
So many courses of the sun enthronèd,
Still growing in a majesty and pomp, the which

To leave a thousand-fold more bitter than
'Tis sweet at first t'acquire – after this process,
To give her the avaunt, it is a pity   10
Would move a monster.

OLD LADY   Hearts of most hard temper
Melt and lament for her.

ANNE   O, God's will! Much better
She ne'er had known pomp; though't be temporal,
Yet, if that quarrel, Fortune, do divorce
It from the bearer, 'tis a sufferance panging
As soul and body's severing.

OLD LADY   Alas, poor lady!
She's a stranger now again.

ANNE   So much the more
Must pity drop upon her. Verily,
I swear, 'tis better to be lowly born,
And range with humble livers in content,   20
Than to be perked up in a glistering grief
And wear a golden sorrow.

OLD LADY   Our content
Is our best having.

ANNE   By my troth and maidenhead,
I would not be a queen.

OLD LADY   Beshrew me, I would,
And venture maidenhead for't; and so would you,
For all this spice of your hypocrisy.
You that have so fair parts of woman on you
Have too a woman's heart, which ever yet
Affected eminence, wealth, sovereignty;
Which, to say sooth, are blessings; and which gifts,   30
Saving your mincing, the capacity
Of your soft cheveril conscience would receive
If you might please to stretch it.

ANNE   Nay, good troth.

OLD LADY

Yes, troth and troth. You would not be a queen?

ANNE

No, not for all the riches under heaven.

OLD LADY

'Tis strange: a threepence bowed would hire me,
Old as I am, to queen it. But, I pray you,
What think you of a duchess? Have you limbs
To bear that load of title?

ANNE   No, in truth.

OLD LADY

40   Then you are weakly made. Pluck off a little;
I would not be a young count in your way
For more than blushing comes to. If your back
Cannot vouchsafe this burden, 'tis too weak
Ever to get a boy.

ANNE   How you do talk!
I swear again, I would not be a queen
For all the world.

OLD LADY   In faith, for little England
You'd venture an emballing. I myself
Would for Caernarvonshire, although there 'longed
No more to th'crown but that. Lo, who comes here?

Enter the Lord Chamberlain

LORD CHAMBERLAIN

50   Good morrow, ladies. What were't worth to know
The secret of your conference?

ANNE   My good lord,
Not your demand; it values not your asking.
Our mistress' sorrows we were pitying.

LORD CHAMBERLAIN

It was a gentle business, and becoming
The action of good women. There is hope
All will be well.

ANNE   Now I pray God, amen!
LORD CHAMBERLAIN
  You bear a gentle mind, and heavenly blessings
  Follow such creatures. That you may, fair lady,
  Perceive I speak sincerely, and high note's
  Ta'en of your many virtues, the King's majesty   60
  Commends his good opinion of you, and
  Does purpose honour to you no less flowing
  Than Marchioness of Pembroke; to which title
  A thousand pound a year, annual support,
  Out of his grace he adds.
ANNE   I do not know
  What kind of my obedience I should tender.
  More than my all is nothing; nor my prayers
  Are not words duly hallowed, nor my wishes
  More worth than empty vanities; yet prayers and wishes
  Are all I can return. Beseech your lordship,   70
  Vouchsafe to speak my thanks and my obedience,
  As from a blushing handmaid, to his highness,
  Whose health and royalty I pray for.
LORD CHAMBERLAIN   Lady,
  I shall not fail t'approve the fair conceit
  The King hath of you. (*Aside*) I have perused her well;
  Beauty and honour in her are so mingled
  That they have caught the King; and who knows yet
  But from this lady may proceed a gem
  To lighten all this isle? (*To them*) I'll to the King,
  And say I spoke with you.
ANNE   My honoured lord!   80
                                Exit Lord Chamberlain

OLD LADY
  Why, this it is: see, see!
  I have been begging sixteen years in court,
  Am yet a courtier beggarly, nor could

Come pat betwixt too early and too late
For any suit of pounds; and you – O fate! –
A very fresh fish here – fie, fie, fie upon
This compelled fortune! – have your mouth filled up
Before you open it.

ANNE   This is strange to me.

OLD LADY
How tastes it? Is it bitter? Forty pence, no.
90   There was a lady once – 'tis an old story –
That would not be a queen, that would she not,
For all the mud in Egypt. Have you heard it?

ANNE
Come, you are pleasant.

OLD LADY   With your theme I could
O'ermount the lark. The Marchioness of Pembroke!
A thousand pounds a year, for pure respect!
No other obligation! By my life,
That promises more thousands: honour's train
Is longer than his foreskirt. By this time
I know your back will bear a duchess. Say,
100   Are you not stronger than you were?

ANNE   Good lady,
Make yourself mirth with your particular fancy,
And leave me out on't. Would I had no being,
If this salute my blood a jot; it faints me
To think what follows.
The Queen is comfortless, and we forgetful
In our long absence. Pray do not deliver
What here you've heard to her.

OLD LADY   What do you think me?

Exeunt

Trumpets, sennet, and cornets. Enter two Vergers, II.4
*with short silver wands; next them two Scribes, in
the habit of doctors; after them, the Archbishop of
Canterbury alone; after him, the Bishops of Lincoln,
Ely, Rochester, and Saint Asaph; next them, with
some small distance, follows a Gentleman bearing the
purse, with the great seal, and a cardinal's hat; then
two Priests bearing each a silver cross; then Griffith,
a Gentleman Usher, bare-headed, accompanied with a
Sergeant-at-Arms bearing a silver mace; then two
Gentlemen bearing two great silver pillars; after
them, side by side, the two Cardinals; two noblemen
with the sword and mace. The King takes place under
the cloth of state. The two Cardinals sit under him as
judges. The Queen takes place some distance from the
King. The Bishops place themselves on each side the
court in manner of a consistory; below them the
Scribes. The Lords sit next the Bishops. The rest of the
attendants stand in convenient order about the stage*

WOLSEY
  Whilst our commission from Rome is read,
  Let silence be commanded.
KING HENRY   What's the need?
  It hath already publicly been read,
  And on all sides th'authority allowed.
  You may then spare that time.
WOLSEY   Be't so, proceed.
SCRIBE Say 'Henry, King of England, come into the
  court'.
CRIER Henry, King of England, come into the court.
KING HENRY Here.
SCRIBE Say 'Katherine, Queen of England, come into the 10
  court'.
CRIER Katherine, Queen of England, come into the court.

*The Queen makes no answer, rises out of her chair,
goes about the court, comes to the King, and kneels at
his feet; then speaks*

QUEEN KATHERINE

Sir, I desire you do me right and justice,
And to bestow your pity on me; for
I am a most poor woman, and a stranger,
Born out of your dominions, having here
No judge indifferent, nor no more assurance
Of equal friendship and proceeding. Alas, sir,
In what have I offended you? What cause
20   Hath my behaviour given to your displeasure
That thus you should proceed to put me off
And take your good grace from me? Heaven witness,
I have been to you a true and humble wife,
At all times to your will conformable,
Ever in fear to kindle your dislike,
Yea, subject to your countenance, glad or sorry
As I saw it inclined. When was the hour
I ever contradicted your desire,
Or made it not mine too? Or which of your friends
30   Have I not strove to love, although I knew
He were mine enemy? What friend of mine
That had to him derived your anger did I
Continue in my liking, nay, gave notice
He was from thence discharged? Sir, call to mind
That I have been your wife in this obedience
Upward of twenty years, and have been blessed
With many children by you. If, in the course
And process of this time, you can report,
And prove it too, against mine honour aught,
40   My bond to wedlock, or my love and duty
Against your sacred person, in God's name
Turn me away, and let the foul'st contempt

Shut door upon me, and so give me up
To the sharp'st kind of justice. Please you, sir,
The King your father was reputed for
A prince most prudent, of an excellent
And unmatched wit and judgement. Ferdinand
My father, King of Spain, was reckoned one
The wisest prince that there had reigned, by many
A year before. It is not to be questioned   50
That they had gathered a wise council to them
Of every realm, that did debate this business,
Who deemed our marriage lawful. Wherefore I humbly
Beseech you, sir, to spare me, till I may
Be by my friends in Spain advised, whose counsel
I will implore. If not, i'th'name of God,
Your pleasure be fulfilled.

WOLSEY   You have here, lady,
And of your choice, these reverend fathers, men
Of singular integrity and learning,
Yea, the elect o'th'land, who are assembled   60
To plead your cause. It shall be therefore bootless
That longer you desire the court, as well
For your own quiet, as to rectify
What is unsettled in the King.

CAMPEIUS   His grace
Hath spoken well and justly. Therefore, madam,
It's fit this royal session do proceed,
And that without delay their arguments
Be now produced and heard.

QUEEN KATHERINE   Lord Cardinal,
To you I speak.

WOLSEY   Your pleasure, madam.

QUEEN KATHERINE   Sir,
I am about to weep; but, thinking that   70
We are a queen, or long have dreamed so, certain

The daughter of a king, my drops of tears
I'll turn to sparks of fire.

WOLSEY   Be patient yet.

QUEEN KATHERINE
I will, when you are humble; nay, before,
Or God will punish me. I do believe,
Induced by potent circumstances, that
You are mine enemy, and make my challenge
You shall not be my judge; for it is you
Have blown this coal betwixt my lord and me –
80 Which God's dew quench! Therefore I say again,
I utterly abhor, yea, from my soul
Refuse you for my judge, whom yet once more
I hold my most malicious foe, and think not
At all a friend to truth.

WOLSEY   I do profess
You speak not like yourself, who ever yet
Have stood to charity and displayed th'effects
Of disposition gentle and of wisdom
O'ertopping woman's power. Madam, you do me
    wrong:
I have no spleen against you, nor injustice
90 For you or any. How far I have proceeded,
Or how far further shall, is warranted
By a commission from the consistory,
Yea, the whole consistory of Rome. You charge me
That I have blown this coal. I do deny it.
The King is present. If it be known to him
That I gainsay my deed, how may he wound,
And worthily, my falsehood – yea, as much
As you have done my truth. If he know
That I am free of your report, he knows
100 I am not of your wrong. Therefore in him
It lies to cure me, and the cure is to

Remove these thoughts from you; the which before
His highness shall speak in, I do beseech
You, gracious madam, to unthink your speaking
And to say so no more.

QUEEN KATHERINE   My lord, my lord,
I am a simple woman, much too weak
T'oppose your cunning. You're meek and humble-
        mouthed;
You sign your place and calling, in full seeming,
With meekness and humility; but your heart
Is crammed with arrogancy, spleen, and pride.   110
You have, by fortune and his highness' favours,
Gone slightly o'er low steps, and now are mounted
Where powers are your retainers, and your words,
Domestics to you, serve your will as't please
Yourself pronounce their office. I must tell you,
You tender more your person's honour than
Your high profession spiritual, that again
I do refuse you for my judge, and here,
Before you all, appeal unto the Pope,
To bring my whole cause 'fore his holiness,   120
And to be judged by him.

She curtsies to the King, and offers to depart

CAMPEIUS   The Queen is obstinate,
Stubborn to justice, apt to accuse it, and
Disdainful to be tried by't; 'tis not well.
She's going away.

KING HENRY Call her again.

CRIER Katherine, Queen of England, come into the court.

GRIFFITH Madam, you are called back.

QUEEN KATHERINE
What need you note it? Pray you keep your way;
When you are called, return. Now the Lord help!
They vex me past my patience. Pray you, pass on.   130

III

I will not tarry; no, nor ever more
Upon this business my appearance make
In any of their courts.

Exeunt Queen and her attendants

KING HENRY   Go thy ways, Kate.
That man i'th'world who shall report he has
A better wife, let him in naught be trusted
For speaking false in that. Thou art alone –
If thy rare qualities, sweet gentleness,
Thy meekness saint-like, wife-like government,
Obeying in commanding, and thy parts
140 Sovereign and pious else, could speak thee out –
The queen of earthly queens. She's noble born,
And like her true nobility she has
Carried herself towards me.

WOLSEY   Most gracious sir,
In humblest manner I require your highness
That it shall please you to declare in hearing
Of all these ears – for where I am robbed and bound,
There must I be unloosed, although not there
At once and fully satisfied – whether ever I
Did broach this business to your highness, or
150 Laid any scruple in your way which might
Induce you to the question on't, or ever
Have to you, but with thanks to God for such
A royal lady, spake one the least word that might
Be to the prejudice of her present state,
Or touch of her good person?

KING HENRY   My lord Cardinal,
I do excuse you; yea, upon mine honour,
I free you from't. You are not to be taught
That you have many enemies that know not
Why they are so, but, like to village curs,
160 Bark when their fellows do. By some of these

The Queen is put in anger. You're excused.
But will you be more justified? You ever
Have wished the sleeping of this business, never
    desired
It to be stirred, but oft have hindered, oft,
The passages made toward it. On my honour,
I speak my good lord Cardinal to this point,
And thus far clear him. Now, what moved me to't,
I will be bold with time and your attention.
Then mark th'inducement. Thus it came – give heed
    to't:
My conscience first received a tenderness,   170
Scruple, and prick, on certain speeches uttered
By th'Bishop of Bayonne, then French ambassador,
Who had been hither sent on the debating
A marriage 'twixt the Duke of Orleans and
Our daughter Mary. I'th'progress of this business,
Ere a determinate resolution, he –
I mean the Bishop – did require a respite,
Wherein he might the King his lord advertise
Whether our daughter were legitimate,
Respecting this our marriage with the dowager,   180
Sometimes our brother's wife. This respite shook
The bosom of my conscience, entered me,
Yea, with a spitting power, and made to tremble
The region of my breast; which forced such way
That many mazed considerings did throng
And pressed in with this caution. First, methought
I stood not in the smile of heaven, who had
Commanded nature that my lady's womb,
If it conceived a male child by me, should
Do no more offices of life to't than   190
The grave does to th'dead; for her male issue
Or died where they were made, or shortly after

This world had aired them. Hence I took a thought
This was a judgement on me, that my kingdom,
Well worthy the best heir o'th'world, should not
Be gladded in't by me. Then follows that
I weighed the danger which my realms stood in
By this my issue's fail, and that gave to me
Many a groaning throe. Thus hulling in
200 The wild sea of my conscience, I did steer
Toward this remedy, whereupon we are
Now present here together; that's to say,
I meant to rectify my conscience, which
I then did feel full sick, and yet not well,
By all the reverend fathers of the land
And doctors learned. First I began in private
With you, my lord of Lincoln. You remember
How under my oppression I did reek
When I first moved you.

LINCOLN   Very well, my liege.

KING HENRY
210 I have spoke long; be pleased yourself to say
How far you satisfied me.

LINCOLN   So please your highness,
The question did at first so stagger me –
Bearing a state of mighty moment in't,
And consequence of dread – that I committed
The daring'st counsel which I had to doubt,
And did entreat your highness to this course
Which you are running here.

KING HENRY   I then moved you,
My lord of Canterbury, and got your leave
To make this present summons. Unsolicited
220 I left no reverend person in this court,
But by particular consent proceeded
Under your hands and seals. Therefore, go on,

For no dislike i'th'world against the person
Of the good Queen, but the sharp thorny points
Of my allegèd reasons, drives this forward.
Prove but our marriage lawful, by my life
And kingly dignity, we are contented
To wear our mortal state to come with her,
Katherine our Queen, before the primest creature
That's paragoned o'th'world.

CAMPEIUS   So please your highness, 230
The Queen being absent, 'tis a needful fitness
That we adjourn this court till further day.
Meanwhile must be an earnest motion
Made to the Queen to call back her appeal
She intends unto his holiness.

KING HENRY (*aside*)   I may perceive
These Cardinals trifle with me. I abhor
This dilatory sloth and tricks of Rome.
My learnèd and well-belovèd servant, Cranmer,
Prithee return. With thy approach I know
My comfort comes along. (*To them*) Break up the court; 240
I say, set on.

                    Exeunt in manner as they entered

*

Enter the Queen and her women, as at work   III.1
QUEEN KATHERINE
Take thy lute, wench. My soul grows sad with troubles;
Sing, and disperse 'em if thou canst. Leave working.
GENTLEWOMAN (*sings*)
            Orpheus with his lute made trees,
            And the mountain tops that freeze,
              Bow themselves when he did sing.

       To his music plants and flowers
       Ever sprung, as sun and showers
         There had made a lasting spring.

       Everything that heard him play,
       Even the billows of the sea,
         Hung their heads, and then lay by.
       In sweet music is such art,
       Killing care and grief of heart
         Fall asleep, or hearing die.

    Enter a Gentleman

QUEEN KATHERINE
  How now?

GENTLEMAN
  An't please your grace, the two great Cardinals
  Wait in the presence.

QUEEN KATHERINE   Would they speak with me?

GENTLEMAN
  They willed me say so, madam.

QUEEN KATHERINE   Pray their graces
  To come near.   *Exit Gentleman*
        What can be their business
  With me, a poor weak woman, fall'n from favour?
  I do not like their coming. Now I think on't,
  They should be good men, their affairs as righteous:
  But all hoods make not monks.

    Enter the two Cardinals, Wolsey and Campeius

WOLSEY   Peace to your highness!

QUEEN KATHERINE
  Your graces find me here part of a housewife –
  I would be all, against the worst may happen.
  What are your pleasures with me, reverend lords?

WOLSEY
  May it please you, noble madam, to withdraw

Into your private chamber, we shall give you
The full cause of our coming.

QUEEN KATHERINE   Speak it here.
There's nothing I have done yet, o'my conscience,   30
Deserves a corner. Would all other women
Could speak this with as free a soul as I do!
My lords, I care not – so much I am happy
Above a number – if my actions
Were tried by every tongue, every eye saw 'em,
Envy and base opinion set against 'em,
I know my life so even. If your business
Seek me out, and that way I am wife in,
Out with it boldly. Truth loves open dealing.

WOLSEY *Tanta est erga te mentis integritas, Regina serenis-*   40
sima –

QUEEN KATHERINE
O, good my lord, no Latin!
I am not such a truant since my coming
As not to know the language I have lived in.
A strange tongue makes my cause more strange, sus-
          picious;
Pray speak in English. Here are some will thank you,
If you speak truth, for their poor mistress' sake.
Believe me, she has had much wrong. Lord Cardinal,
The willing'st sin I ever yet committed
May be absolved in English.

WOLSEY   Noble lady,   50
I am sorry my integrity should breed –
And service to his majesty and you –
So deep suspicion, where all faith was meant.
We come not by the way of accusation,
To taint that honour every good tongue blesses,
Nor to betray you any way to sorrow –
You have too much, good lady – but to know

117

How you stand minded in the weighty difference
Between the King and you, and to deliver,
60 Like free and honest men, our just opinions
And comforts to your cause.

CAMPEIUS   Most honoured madam,
My lord of York, out of his noble nature,
Zeal and obedience he still bore your grace,
Forgetting, like a good man, your late censure
Both of his truth and him – which was too far –
Offers, as I do, in a sign of peace,
His service, and his counsel.

QUEEN KATHERINE (*aside*)   To betray me. –
My lords, I thank you both for your good wills.
Ye speak like honest men – pray God ye prove so!
70 But how to make ye suddenly an answer
In such a point of weight, so near mine honour,
More near my life, I fear, with my weak wit,
And to such men of gravity and learning,
In truth I know not. I was set at work
Among my maids, full little – God knows – looking
Either for such men or such business.
For her sake that I have been – for I feel
The last fit of my greatness – good your graces,
Let me have time and counsel for my cause.
80 Alas, I am a woman friendless, hopeless!

WOLSEY
Madam, you wrong the King's love with these fears;
Your hopes and friends are infinite.

QUEEN KATHERINE   In England
But little for my profit. Can you think, lords,
That any Englishman dare give me counsel,
Or be a known friend, 'gainst his highness' pleasure –
Though he be grown so desperate to be honest –
And live a subject? Nay, forsooth, my friends,

They that must weigh out my afflictions,
They that my trust must grow to, live not here.
They are, as all my other comforts, far hence,   90
In mine own country, lords.

CAMPEIUS   I would your grace
  Would leave your griefs, and take my counsel.

QUEEN KATHERINE   How, sir?

CAMPEIUS
  Put your main cause into the King's protection;
  He's loving and most gracious. 'Twill be much
  Both for your honour better and your cause;
  For if the trial of the law o'ertake ye
  You'll part away disgraced.

WOLSEY   He tells you rightly.

QUEEN KATHERINE
  Ye tell me what ye wish for both – my ruin.
  Is this your Christian counsel? Out upon ye!
  Heaven is above all yet; there sits a judge   100
  That no king can corrupt.

CAMPEIUS   Your rage mistakes us.

QUEEN KATHERINE
  The more shame for ye! Holy men I thought ye,
  Upon my soul, two reverend cardinal virtues;
  But cardinal sins and hollow hearts I fear ye.
  Mend 'em for shame, my lords. Is this your comfort?
  The cordial that ye bring a wretched lady,
  A woman lost among ye, laughed at, scorned?
  I will not wish ye half my miseries;
  I have more charity. But say I warned ye;
  Take heed, for heaven's sake take heed, lest at once   110
  The burden of my sorrows fall upon ye.

WOLSEY
  Madam, this is a mere distraction.
  You turn the good we offer into envy.

QUEEN KATHERINE
>Ye turn me into nothing. Woe upon ye,
>And all such false professors! Would you have me –
>If you have any justice, any pity,
>If ye be anything but churchmen's habits –
>Put my sick cause into his hands that hates me?
>Alas, 'has banished me his bed already,
120>His love too long ago! I am old, my lords,
>And all the fellowship I hold now with him
>Is only my obedience. What can happen
>To me above this wretchedness? All your studies
>Make me a curse like this!

CAMPEIUS   Your fears are worse.

QUEEN KATHERINE
>Have I lived thus long – let me speak myself,
>Since virtue finds no friends – a wife, a true one?
>A woman, I dare say without vainglory,
>Never yet branded with suspicion?
>Have I with all my full affections
130>Still met the King, loved him next heaven, obeyed him,
>Been, out of fondness, superstitious to him,
>Almost forgot my prayers to content him,
>And am I thus rewarded? 'Tis not well, lords.
>Bring me a constant woman to her husband,
>One that ne'er dreamed a joy beyond his pleasure,
>And to that woman, when she has done most,
>Yet will I add an honour – a great patience.

WOLSEY
>Madam, you wander from the good we aim at.

QUEEN KATHERINE
>My lord, I dare not make myself so guilty
140>To give up willingly that noble title
>Your master wed me to. Nothing but death
>Shall e'er divorce my dignities.

WOLSEY   Pray hear me.

QUEEN KATHERINE

Would I had never trod this English earth,
Or felt the flatteries that grow upon it!
Ye have angels' faces, but heaven knows your hearts.
What will become of me now, wretched lady?
I am the most unhappy woman living.

(*To her women*)

Alas, poor wenches, where are now your fortunes?
Shipwrecked upon a kingdom where no pity,
No friends, no hope, no kindred weep for me;   150
Almost no grave allowed me. Like the lily
That once was mistress of the field and flourished,
I'll hang my head, and perish.

WOLSEY   If your grace

Could but be brought to know our ends are honest,
You'd feel more comfort. Why should we, good lady,
Upon what cause, wrong you? Alas, our places,
The way of our profession is against it.
We are to cure such sorrows, not to sow 'em.
For goodness' sake, consider what you do,
How you may hurt yourself, ay, utterly   160
Grow from the King's acquaintance, by this carriage.
The hearts of princes kiss obedience,
So much they love it; but to stubborn spirits
They swell, and grow as terrible as storms.
I know you have a gentle, noble temper,
A soul as even as a calm. Pray think us
Those we profess, peace-makers, friends, and servants.

CAMPEIUS

Madam, you'll find it so. You wrong your virtues
With these weak women's fears. A noble spirit,
As yours was put into you, ever casts   170
Such doubts as false coin from it. The King loves you;

121

Beware you lose it not. For us, if you please
To trust us in your business, we are ready
To use our utmost studies in your service.

QUEEN KATHERINE
Do what ye will, my lords, and pray forgive me
If I have used myself unmannerly.
You know I am a woman, lacking wit
To make a seemly answer to such persons.
Pray do my service to his majesty;
180 He has my heart yet, and shall have my prayers
While I shall have my life. Come, reverend fathers,
Bestow your counsels on me. She now begs
That little thought, when she set footing here,
She should have bought her dignities so dear.

Exeunt

III.2   *Enter the Duke of Norfolk, Duke of Suffolk, Lord*
     Surrey, and the Lord Chamberlain

NORFOLK
If you will now unite in your complaints
And force them with a constancy, the Cardinal
Cannot stand under them. If you omit
The offer of this time, I cannot promise
But that you shall sustain more new disgraces
With these you bear already.

SURREY   I am joyful
To meet the least occasion that may give me
Remembrance of my father-in-law, the Duke,
To be revenged on him.

SUFFOLK   Which of the peers
10 Have uncontemned gone by him, or at least
Strangely neglected? When did he regard

The stamp of nobleness in any person
Out of himself?

LORD CHAMBERLAIN
                    My lords, you speak your pleasures.
What he deserves of you and me I know;
What we can do to him – though now the time
Gives way to us – I much fear. If you cannot
Bar his access to th'King, never attempt
Anything on him, for he hath a witchcraft
Over the King in's tongue.

NORFOLK   O, fear him not;
His spell in that is out. The King hath found   20
Matter against him that for ever mars
The honey of his language. No, he's settled,
Not to come off, in his displeasure.

SURREY   Sir,
I should be glad to hear such news as this
Once every hour.

NORFOLK   Believe it, this is true.
In the divorce his contrary proceedings
Are all unfolded, wherein he appears
As I would wish mine enemy.

SURREY   How came
His practices to light?

SUFFOLK   Most strangely.

SURREY   O, how, how?

SUFFOLK
The Cardinal's letters to the Pope miscarried,   30
And came to th'eye o'th'King, wherein was read
How that the Cardinal did entreat his holiness
To stay the judgement o'th'divorce; for if
It did take place, 'I do' – quoth he – 'perceive
My King is tangled in affection to
A creature of the Queen's, Lady Anne Bullen.'

SURREY
  Has the King this?
SUFFOLK   Believe it.
SURREY   Will this work?
LORD CHAMBERLAIN
  The King in this perceives him how he coasts
  And hedges his own way. But in this point
40 All his tricks founder, and he brings his physic
  After his patient's death: the King already
  Hath married the fair lady.
SURREY   Would he had!
SUFFOLK
  May you be happy in your wish, my lord,
  For I profess you have it.
SURREY   Now all my joy
  Trace the conjunction!
SUFFOLK   My amen to't!
NORFOLK   All men's!
SUFFOLK
  There's order given for her coronation.
  Marry, this is yet but young, and may be left
  To some ears unrecounted. But, my lords,
  She is a gallant creature, and complete
50 In mind and feature. I persuade me, from her
  Will fall some blessing to this land, which shall
  In it be memorized.
SURREY   But will the King
  Digest this letter of the Cardinal's?
  The Lord forbid!
NORFOLK   Marry, amen!
SUFFOLK   No, no.
  There be more wasps that buzz about his nose
  Will make this sting the sooner. Cardinal Campeius
  Is stol'n away to Rome; hath ta'en no leave;

Has left the cause o'th'King unhandled, and
Is posted as the agent of our Cardinal
To second all his plot. I do assure you   60
The King cried 'Ha!' at this.

LORD CHAMBERLAIN   Now God incense him,
And let him cry 'Ha!' louder!

NORFOLK   But, my lord,
When returns Cranmer?

SUFFOLK
He is returned in his opinions, which
Have satisfied the King for his divorce,
Together with all famous colleges
Almost in Christendom. Shortly, I believe,
His second marriage shall be published, and
Her coronation. Katherine no more
Shall be called Queen, but Princess Dowager,   70
And widow to Prince Arthur.

NORFOLK   This same Cranmer's
A worthy fellow, and hath ta'en much pain
In the King's business.

SUFFOLK   He has, and we shall see him
For it an archbishop.

NORFOLK   So I hear.

SUFFOLK   'Tis so.
        Enter Wolsey and Cromwell
The Cardinal!

NORFOLK   Observe, observe, he's moody.

WOLSEY
The packet, Cromwell,
Gave't you the King?

CROMWELL   To his own hand, in's bedchamber.

WOLSEY
Looked he o'th'inside of the paper?

CROMWELL   Presently

125

He did unseal them, and the first he viewed
80 He did it with a serious mind; a heed
Was in his countenance. You he bade
Attend him here this morning.

WOLSEY   Is he ready
To come abroad?

CROMWELL   I think by this he is.

WOLSEY
Leave me awhile.   *Exit Cromwell*
(*Aside*) It shall be to the Duchess of Alençon,
The French King's sister; he shall marry her.
Anne Bullen? No, I'll no Anne Bullens for him;
There's more in't than fair visage. Bullen!
No, we'll no Bullens. Speedily I wish
90 To hear from Rome. The Marchioness of Pembroke?

NORFOLK
He's discontented.

SUFFOLK   Maybe he hears the King
Does whet his anger to him.

SURREY   Sharp enough,
Lord, for Thy justice!

WOLSEY (*aside*)
The late Queen's gentlewoman, a knight's daughter,
To be her mistress' mistress? the Queen's Queen?
This candle burns not clear; 'tis I must snuff it,
Then out it goes. What though I know her virtuous
And well deserving? Yet I know her for
A spleeny Lutheran, and not wholesome to
100 Our cause, that she should lie i'th'bosom of
Our hard-ruled King. Again, there is sprung up
An heretic, an arch-one, Cranmer, one
Hath crawled into the favour of the King,
And is his oracle.

NORFOLK   He is vexed at something.

SURREY

    I would 'twere something that would fret the string,
    The master-cord on's heart!

        Enter the King, reading of a schedule, and Lovell

SUFFOLK   The King, the King!

KING HENRY

    What piles of wealth hath he accumulated
    To his own portion! And what expense by th'hour
    Seems to flow from him! How, i'th'name of thrift,
    Does he rake this together? – Now, my lords,   110
    Saw you the Cardinal?

NORFOLK   My lord, we have
    Stood here observing him. Some strange commotion
    Is in his brain; he bites his lip, and starts,
    Stops on a sudden, looks upon the ground,
    Then lays his finger on his temple; straight
    Springs out into fast gait; then stops again,
    Strikes his breast hard, and anon he casts
    His eye against the moon. In most strange postures
    We have seen him set himself.

KING HENRY   It may well be,
    There is a mutiny in's mind. This morning   120
    Papers of state he sent me to peruse,
    As I required; and wot you what I found
    There, on my conscience, put unwittingly?
    Forsooth, an inventory, thus importing
    The several parcels of his plate, his treasure,
    Rich stuffs, and ornaments of household, which
    I find at such proud rate that it outspeaks
    Possession of a subject.

NORFOLK   It's heaven's will;
    Some spirit put this paper in the packet
    To bless your eye withal.

KING HENRY   If we did think   130

His contemplation were above the earth
And fixed on spiritual object, he should still
Dwell in his musings; but I am afraid
His thinkings are below the moon, not worth
His serious considering.

*The King takes his seat, whispers Lovell, who goes to
the Cardinal*

WOLSEY   Heaven forgive me!
Ever God bless your highness!

KING HENRY   Good my lord,
You are full of heavenly stuff, and bear the inventory
Of your best graces in your mind, the which
You were now running o'er. You have scarce time
To steal from spiritual leisure a brief span
To keep your earthly audit. Sure, in that
I deem you an ill husband, and am glad
To have you therein my companion.

WOLSEY   Sir,
For holy offices I have a time; a time
To think upon the part of business which
I bear i'th'state; and nature does require
Her times of preservation, which perforce
I, her frail son, amongst my brethren mortal,
Must give my tendance to.

KING HENRY   You have said well.

WOLSEY
And ever may your highness yoke together,
As I will lend you cause, my doing well
With my well saying!

KING HENRY   'Tis well said again,
And 'tis a kind of good deed to say well;
And yet words are no deeds. My father loved you;
He said he did, and with his deed did crown
His word upon you. Since I had my office,

I have kept you next my heart, have not alone
Employed you where high profits might come home,
But pared my present havings to bestow
My bounties upon you.

WOLSEY (*aside*)   What should this mean?   160

SURREY (*aside*)
The Lord increase this business!

KING HENRY   Have I not made you
The prime man of the state? I pray you tell me
If what I now pronounce you have found true;
And, if you may confess it, say withal
If you are bound to us or no. What say you?

WOLSEY
My sovereign, I confess your royal graces,
Showered on me daily, have been more than could
My studied purposes requite, which went
Beyond all man's endeavours. My endeavours
Have ever come too short of my desires,   170
Yet filed with my abilities. Mine own ends
Have been mine so that evermore they pointed
To th'good of your most sacred person and
The profit of the state. For your great graces
Heaped upon me, poor undeserver, I
Can nothing render but allegiant thanks,
My prayers to heaven for you, my loyalty,
Which ever has and ever shall be growing,
Till death, that winter, kill it.

KING HENRY   Fairly answered!
A loyal and obedient subject is   180
Therein illustrated. The honour of it
Does pay the act of it, as, i'th'contrary,
The foulness is the punishment. I presume
That as my hand has opened bounty to you,
My heart dropped love, my power rained honour, more

On you than any, so your hand and heart,
Your brain and every function of your power,
Should, notwithstanding that your bond of duty,
As 'twere in love's particular, be more
190   To me, your friend, than any.

WOLSEY   I do profess
That for your highness' good I ever laboured
More than mine own; that am, have, and will be –
Though all the world should crack their duty to you,
And throw it from their soul; though perils did
Abound, as thick as thought could make 'em, and
Appear in forms more horrid – yet my duty,
As doth a rock against the chiding flood,
Should the approach of this wild river break,
And stand unshaken yours.

KING HENRY   'Tis nobly spoken.
200   Take notice, lords, he has a loyal breast,
For you have seen him open't. Read o'er this,
     (he gives him papers)
And after, this; and then to breakfast with
What appetite you have.
     Exit King, frowning upon the Cardinal; the nobles
     throng after him, smiling and whispering

WOLSEY   What should this mean?
What sudden anger's this? How have I reaped it?
He parted frowning from me, as if ruin
Leaped from his eyes. So looks the chafèd lion
Upon the daring huntsman that has galled him,
Then makes him nothing. I must read this paper:
I fear, the story of his anger. 'Tis so;
210   This paper has undone me. 'Tis th'account
Of all that world of wealth I have drawn together
For mine own ends – indeed, to gain the popedom,
And fee my friends in Rome. O negligence,

Fit for a fool to fall by! What cross devil
Made me put this main secret in the packet
I sent the King? Is there no way to cure this?
No new device to beat this from his brains?
I know 'twill stir him strongly; yet I know
A way, if it take right, in spite of fortune
Will bring me off again. What's this? 'To th'Pope'?   220
The letter, as I live, with all the business
I writ to's holiness. Nay then, farewell!
I have touched the highest point of all my greatness,
And from that full meridian of my glory
I haste now to my setting. I shall fall
Like a bright exhalation in the evening,
And no man see me more.

> *Enter to Wolsey the Dukes of Norfolk and Suffolk, the
> Earl of Surrey, and the Lord Chamberlain*

NORFOLK
　Hear the King's pleasure, Cardinal, who commands you
　To render up the great seal presently
　Into our hands, and to confine yourself   230
　To Asher House, my lord of Winchester's,
　Till you hear further from his highness.

WOLSEY   Stay:
　Where's your commission, lords? Words cannot carry
　Authority so weighty.

SUFFOLK   Who dare cross 'em,
　Bearing the King's will from his mouth expressly?

WOLSEY
　Till I find more than will or words to do it –
　I mean your malice – know, officious lords,
　I dare, and must deny it. Now I feel
　Of what coarse metal ye are moulded – envy;
　How eagerly ye follow my disgraces   240
　As if it fed ye! And how sleek and wanton

Ye appear in everything may bring my ruin!
Follow your envious courses, men of malice;
You have Christian warrant for 'em, and no doubt
In time will find their fit rewards. That seal
You ask with such a violence, the King,
Mine and your master, with his own hand gave me;
Bade me enjoy it, with the place and honours,
During my life; and, to confirm his goodness,
250   Tied it by letters patents. Now, who'll take it?

SURREY
The King that gave it.

WOLSEY   It must be himself then.

SURREY
Thou art a proud traitor, priest.

WOLSEY   Proud lord, thou liest.
Within these forty hours Surrey durst better
Have burnt that tongue than said so.

SURREY   Thy ambition,
Thou scarlet sin, robbed this bewailing land
Of noble Buckingham, my father-in-law.
The heads of all thy brother Cardinals,
With thee and all thy best parts bound together,
Weighed not a hair of his. Plague of your policy!
260   You sent me deputy for Ireland,
Far from his succour, from the King, from all
That might have mercy on the fault thou gav'st him;
Whilst your great goodness, out of holy pity,
Absolved him with an axe.

WOLSEY   This, and all else
This talking lord can lay upon my credit,
I answer is most false. The Duke by law
Found his deserts. How innocent I was
From any private malice in his end

His noble jury and foul cause can witness.
If I loved many words, lord, I should tell you   270
You have as little honesty as honour,
That in the way of loyalty and truth
Toward the King, my ever royal master,
Dare mate a sounder man than Surrey can be,
And all that love his follies.

SURREY   By my soul,
Your long coat, priest, protects you; thou shouldst feel
My sword i'th'life-blood of thee else. My lords,
Can ye endure to hear this arrogance,
And from this fellow? If we live thus tamely,
To be thus jaded by a piece of scarlet,   280
Farewell nobility! Let his grace go forward,
And dare us with his cap, like larks.

WOLSEY   All goodness
Is poison to thy stomach.

SURREY   Yes, that goodness
Of gleaning all the land's wealth into one,
Into your own hands, Cardinal, by extortion –
The goodness of your intercepted packets
You writ to th'Pope against the King! Your goodness,
Since you provoke me, shall be most notorious.
My lord of Norfolk, as you are truly noble,
As you respect the common good, the state   290
Of our despised nobility, our issues –
Who, if he live, will scarce be gentlemen –
Produce the grand sum of his sins, the articles
Collected from his life. I'll startle you
Worse than the sacring bell, when the brown wench
Lay kissing in your arms, lord Cardinal.

WOLSEY
How much, methinks, I could despise this man,

But that I am bound in charity against it!

NORFOLK

Those articles, my lord, are in the King's hand;
300   But thus much, they are foul ones.

WOLSEY   So much fairer
And spotless shall mine innocence arise
When the King knows my truth.

SURREY   This cannot save you.
I thank my memory, I yet remember
Some of these articles, and out they shall.
Now, if you can blush and cry 'Guilty', Cardinal,
You'll show a little honesty.

WOLSEY   Speak on, sir;
I dare your worst objections. If I blush,
It is to see a nobleman want manners.

SURREY

I had rather want those than my head. Have at you!
310   First, that without the King's assent or knowledge
You wrought to be a legate, by which power
You maimed the jurisdiction of all bishops.

NORFOLK

Then, that in all you writ to Rome, or else
To foreign princes, '*Ego et Rex meus*'
Was still inscribed; in which you brought the King
To be your servant.

SUFFOLK   Then, that without the knowledge
Either of King or Council, when you went
Ambassador to the Emperor, you made bold
To carry into Flanders the great seal.

SURREY

320   Item, you sent a large commission
To Gregory de Cassado, to conclude,
Without the King's will or the state's allowance,
A league between his highness and Ferrara.

SUFFOLK

That out of mere ambition you have caused
Your holy hat to be stamped on the King's coin.

SURREY

Then, that you have sent innumerable substance –
By what means got I leave to your own conscience –
To furnish Rome, and to prepare the ways
You have for dignities, to the mere undoing
Of all the kingdom. Many more there are,   330
Which since they are of you, and odious,
I will not taint my mouth with.

LORD CHAMBERLAIN   O my lord,

Press not a falling man too far! 'Tis virtue.
His faults lie open to the laws; let them,
Not you, correct him. My heart weeps to see him
So little of his great self.

SURREY   I forgive him.

SUFFOLK

Lord Cardinal, the King's further pleasure is –
Because all those things you have done of late
By your power legatine within this kingdom
Fall into th'compass of a praemunire –   340
That therefore such a writ be sued against you:
To forfeit all your goods, lands, tenements,
Chattels, and whatsoever, and to be
Out of the King's protection. This is my charge.

NORFOLK

And so we'll leave you to your meditations
How to live better. For your stubborn answer
About the giving back the great seal to us,
The King shall know it and, no doubt, shall thank
          you.
So fare you well, my little good lord Cardinal.

Exeunt all but Wolsey

135

WOLSEY

350 So farewell – to the little good you bear me.
Farewell, a long farewell, to all my greatness!
This is the state of man: today he puts forth
The tender leaves of hopes, tomorrow blossoms,
And bears his blushing honours thick upon him.
The third day comes a frost, a killing frost,
And when he thinks, good easy man, full surely
His greatness is a-ripening, nips his root,
And then he falls, as I do. I have ventured,
Like little wanton boys that swim on bladders,
360 This many summers in a sea of glory,
But far beyond my depth. My high-blown pride
At length broke under me, and now has left me
Weary, and old with service, to the mercy
Of a rude stream that must for ever hide me.
Vain pomp and glory of this world, I hate ye.
I feel my heart new opened. O, how wretched
Is that poor man that hangs on princes' favours!
There is betwixt that smile we would aspire to,
That sweet aspect of princes, and their ruin,
370 More pangs and fears than wars or women have;
And when he falls, he falls like Lucifer,
Never to hope again.
      Enter Cromwell, standing amazed
            Why, how now, Cromwell?

CROMWELL
I have no power to speak, sir.

WOLSEY   What, amazed
At my misfortunes? Can thy spirit wonder
A great man should decline? Nay, an you weep
I am fall'n indeed.

CROMWELL   How does your grace?

WOLSEY   Why, well;

Never so truly happy, my good Cromwell.
I know myself now, and I feel within me
A peace above all earthly dignities,
A still and quiet conscience. The King has cured me, 380
I humbly thank his grace, and from these shoulders,
These ruined pillars, out of pity, taken
A load would sink a navy – too much honour.
O, 'tis a burden, Cromwell, 'tis a burden
Too heavy for a man that hopes for heaven!

CROMWELL
I am glad your grace has made that right use of it.

WOLSEY
I hope I have: I am able now, methinks,
Out of a fortitude of soul I feel,
To endure more miseries and greater far
Than my weak-hearted enemies dare offer. 390
What news abroad?

CROMWELL   The heaviest, and the worst,
Is your displeasure with the King.

WOLSEY   God bless him!

CROMWELL
The next is that Sir Thomas More is chosen
Lord Chancellor in your place.

WOLSEY   That's somewhat sudden.
But he's a learnèd man. May he continue
Long in his highness' favour, and do justice
For truth's sake, and his conscience, that his bones,
When he has run his course and sleeps in blessings,
May have a tomb of orphans' tears wept on him.
What more?

CROMWELL   That Cranmer is returned with welcome, 400
Installed lord Archbishop of Canterbury.

WOLSEY
That's news indeed.

CROMWELL   Last, that the Lady Anne,
Whom the King hath in secrecy long married,
This day was viewed in open as his queen,
Going to chapel, and the voice is now
Only about her coronation.

WOLSEY

There was the weight that pulled me down. O Cromwell,
The King has gone beyond me. All my glories
In that one woman I have lost for ever.
410 No sun shall ever usher forth mine honours,
Or gild again the noble troops that waited
Upon my smiles. Go get thee from me, Cromwell;
I am a poor fall'n man, unworthy now
To be thy lord and master. Seek the King –
That sun, I pray, may never set! I have told him
What and how true thou art. He will advance thee;
Some little memory of me will stir him –
I know his noble nature – not to let
Thy hopeful service perish too. Good Cromwell,
420 Neglect him not; make use now, and provide
For thine own future safety.

CROMWELL   O my lord,
Must I then leave you? Must I needs forgo
So good, so noble, and so true a master?
Bear witness, all that have not hearts of iron,
With what a sorrow Cromwell leaves his lord.
The King shall have my service, but my prayers
For ever and for ever shall be yours.

WOLSEY

Cromwell, I did not think to shed a tear
In all my miseries, but thou hast forced me,
430 Out of thy honest truth, to play the woman.
Let's dry our eyes, and thus far hear me, Cromwell,
And when I am forgotten, as I shall be,

138

And sleep in dull cold marble, where no mention
Of me more must be heard of, say I taught thee –
Say Wolsey, that once trod the ways of glory,
And sounded all the depths and shoals of honour,
Found thee a way, out of his wreck, to rise in,
A sure and safe one, though thy master missed it.
Mark but my fall, and that that ruined me.
Cromwell, I charge thee, fling away ambition: 440
By that sin fell the angels. How can man then,
The image of his Maker, hope to win by it?
Love thyself last, cherish those hearts that hate thee;
Corruption wins not more than honesty.
Still in thy right hand carry gentle peace
To silence envious tongues. Be just, and fear not.
Let all the ends thou aim'st at be thy country's,
Thy God's, and truth's. Then if thou fall'st, O Crom-
        well,
Thou fall'st a blessèd martyr. Serve the King;
And prithee, lead me in.   450
There take an inventory of all I have,
To the last penny; 'tis the King's. My robe,
And my integrity to heaven, is all
I dare now call mine own. O Cromwell, Cromwell,
Had I but served my God with half the zeal
I served my King, He would not in mine age
Have left me naked to mine enemies.

CROMWELL
  Good sir, have patience.

WOLSEY   So I have. Farewell,
  The hopes of court! My hopes in heaven do dwell.

                                        Exeunt

✳

Enter two Gentlemen, meeting one another

FIRST GENTLEMAN
  You're well met once again.

SECOND GENTLEMAN   So are you.

FIRST GENTLEMAN
  You come to take your stand here and behold
  The Lady Anne pass from her coronation?

SECOND GENTLEMAN
  'Tis all my business. At our last encounter
  The Duke of Buckingham came from his trial.

FIRST GENTLEMAN
  'Tis very true. But that time offered sorrow,
  This, general joy.

SECOND GENTLEMAN 'Tis well. The citizens,
  I am sure, have shown at full their royal minds –
  As, let 'em have their rights, they are ever forward –
10 In celebration of this day with shows,
  Pageants, and sights of honour.

FIRST GENTLEMAN   Never greater,
  Nor, I'll assure you, better taken, sir.

SECOND GENTLEMAN
  May I be bold to ask what that contains,
  That paper in your hand?

FIRST GENTLEMAN   Yes, 'tis the list
  Of those that claim their offices this day,
  By custom of the coronation.
  The Duke of Suffolk is the first, and claims
  To be High Steward; next, the Duke of Norfolk,
  He to be Earl Marshal. You may read the rest.

SECOND GENTLEMAN
20 I thank you, sir; had I not known those customs,
  I should have been beholding to your paper.
  But I beseech you, what's become of Katherine,
  The Princess Dowager? How goes her business?

FIRST GENTLEMAN
That I can tell you too. The Archbishop
Of Canterbury, accompanied with other
Learnèd and reverend fathers of his order,
Held a late court at Dunstable, six miles off
From Ampthill, where the Princess lay; to which
She was often cited by them, but appeared not.
And, to be short, for not appearance, and   30
The King's late scruple, by the main assent
Of all these learnèd men, she was divorced,
And the late marriage made of none effect;
Since which she was removed to Kimbolton,
Where she remains now sick.

SECOND GENTLEMAN   Alas, good lady!
Trumpets
The trumpets sound. Stand close, the Queen is coming.
Hautboys
The Order of the Coronation:

1.   A lively flourish of trumpets
2.   Then two Judges
3.   Lord Chancellor, with purse and mace before him
4.   Choristers singing
     Music
*5.   Mayor of London, bearing the mace. Then Garter,
in his coat of arms, and on his head he wore a gilt
copper crown*
*6.   Marquis Dorset, bearing a sceptre of gold, on his
head a demi-coronal of gold. With him the Earl of
Surrey, bearing the rod of silver with the dove,
crowned with an earl's coronet. Collars of Esses*
*7.   Duke of Suffolk, in his robe of estate, his coronet
on his head, bearing a long white wand, as High
Steward. With him the Duke of Norfolk, with the rod
of marshalship, a coronet on his head. Collars of Esses*

8. *A canopy borne by four of the Cinque Ports;*
under it the Queen in her robe; in her hair, richly
adorned with pearl, crowned. On each side her the
Bishops of London and Winchester
9. *The old Duchess of Norfolk, in a coronal of gold*
wrought with flowers, bearing the Queen's train
10. *Certain ladies or Countesses, with plain circlets*
of gold without flowers
The procession passes over the stage in order and state

SECOND GENTLEMAN
  A royal train, believe me. These I know.
  Who's that that bears the sceptre?

FIRST GENTLEMAN   Marquis Dorset;
  And that the Earl of Surrey, with the rod.

SECOND GENTLEMAN
40 A bold brave gentleman. That should be
  The Duke of Suffolk?

FIRST GENTLEMAN   'Tis the same: High Steward.

SECOND GENTLEMAN
  And that my Lord of Norfolk?

FIRST GENTLEMAN   Yes.

SECOND GENTLEMAN (*looking at the Queen*)
                    Heaven bless thee!
  Thou hast the sweetest face I ever looked on.
  Sir, as I have a soul, she is an angel;
  Our King has all the Indies in his arms,
  And more, and richer, when he strains that lady.
  I cannot blame his conscience.

FIRST GENTLEMAN   They that bear
  The cloth of honour over her are four barons
  Of the Cinque Ports.

SECOND GENTLEMAN
50 Those men are happy, and so are all are near her.
  I take it, she that carries up the train

Is that old noble lady, Duchess of Norfolk.

FIRST GENTLEMAN

It is, and all the rest are countesses.

SECOND GENTLEMAN

Their coronets say so. These are stars indeed –

FIRST GENTLEMAN

And sometimes falling ones.

SECOND GENTLEMAN   No more of that.

*The end of the procession leaves; and then a great
flourish of trumpets
Enter a third Gentleman*

FIRST GENTLEMAN

God save you, sir! Where have you been broiling?

THIRD GENTLEMAN

Among the crowd i'th'Abbey, where a finger
Could not be wedged in more; I am stifled
With the mere rankness of their joy.

SECOND GENTLEMAN   You saw
The ceremony?

THIRD GENTLEMAN That I did.

FIRST GENTLEMAN   How was it?   60

THIRD GENTLEMAN

Well worth the seeing.

SECOND GENTLEMAN Good sir, speak it to us.

THIRD GENTLEMAN

As well as I am able. The rich stream
Of lords and ladies, having brought the Queen
To a prepared place in the choir, fell off
A distance from her, while her grace sat down
To rest awhile, some half an hour or so,
In a rich chair of state, opposing freely
The beauty of her person to the people.
Believe me, sir, she is the goodliest woman
That ever lay by man; which when the people   70

Had the full view of, such a noise arose
As the shrouds make at sea in a stiff tempest,
As loud, and to as many tunes. Hats, cloaks –
Doublets, I think – flew up, and had their faces
Been loose, this day they had been lost. Such joy
I never saw before. Great-bellied women,
That had not half a week to go, like rams
In the old time of war, would shake the press,
And make 'em reel before 'em. No man living
80   Could say 'This is my wife' there, all were woven
So strangely in one piece.

SECOND GENTLEMAN   But what followed?

THIRD GENTLEMAN
At length her grace rose, and with modest paces
Came to the altar, where she kneeled, and saint-like
Cast her fair eyes to heaven, and prayed devoutly,
Then rose again, and bowed her to the people;
When by the Archbishop of Canterbury
She had all the royal makings of a queen,
As holy oil, Edward Confessor's crown,
The rod, and bird of peace, and all such emblems
90   Laid nobly on her: which performed, the choir,
With all the choicest music of the kingdom,
Together sung *Te Deum*. So she parted,
And with the same full state paced back again
To York Place, where the feast is held.

FIRST GENTLEMAN   Sir,
You must no more call it York Place; that's past,
For since the Cardinal fell that title's lost:
'Tis now the King's, and called Whitehall.

THIRD GENTLEMAN   I know it,
But 'tis so lately altered that the old name
Is fresh about me.

SECOND GENTLEMAN What two reverend bishops

144

Were those that went on each side of the Queen?　　100
THIRD GENTLEMAN
　Stokesley and Gardiner, the one of Winchester,
　Newly preferred from the King's secretary,
　The other, London.
SECOND GENTLEMAN　He of Winchester
　Is held no great good lover of the Archbishop's,
　The virtuous Cranmer.
THIRD GENTLEMAN　　All the land knows that;
　However, yet there is no great breach. When it comes,
　Cranmer will find a friend will not shrink from him.
SECOND GENTLEMAN
　Who may that be, I pray you?
THIRD GENTLEMAN　　　Thomas Cromwell,
　A man in much esteem with th'King, and truly
　A worthy friend. The King has made him Master　　110
　O'th'Jewel House,
　And one, already, of the Privy Council.
SECOND GENTLEMAN
　He will deserve more.
THIRD GENTLEMAN　Yes, without all doubt.
　Come, gentlemen, ye shall go my way, which
　Is to th'court, and there ye shall be my guests:
　Something I can command. As I walk thither,
　I'll tell ye more.
SECOND *and* THIRD GENTLEMEN
　　　　　You may command us, sir.　　*Exeunt*

　Enter Katherine, Dowager, sick, led between　IV.2
　Griffith, her gentleman usher, and Patience, her
　woman
GRIFFITH
　How does your grace?

KATHERINE   O Griffith, sick to death.
My legs like loaden branches bow to th'earth,
Willing to leave their burden. Reach a chair.
So: now, methinks, I feel a little ease.
Didst thou not tell me, Griffith, as thou ledst me,
That the great child of honour, Cardinal Wolsey,
Was dead?

GRIFFITH   Yes, madam; but I think your grace,
Out of the pain you suffered, gave no ear to't.

KATHERINE
Prithee, good Griffith, tell me how he died.
10   If well, he stepped before me happily
For my example.

GRIFFITH   Well, the voice goes, madam;
For after the stout Earl Northumberland
Arrested him at York, and brought him forward,
As a man sorely tainted, to his answer,
He fell sick suddenly, and grew so ill
He could not sit his mule.

KATHERINE   Alas, poor man.

GRIFFITH
At last, with easy roads, he came to Leicester,
Lodged in the abbey, where the reverend abbot,
With all his covent, honourably received him;
20   To whom he gave these words: 'O father abbot,
An old man, broken with the storms of state,
Is come to lay his weary bones among ye;
Give him a little earth for charity.'
So went to bed, where eagerly his sickness
Pursued him still, and three nights after this,
About the hour of eight, which he himself
Foretold should be his last, full of repentance,
Continual meditations, tears, and sorrows,
He gave his honours to the world again,

His blessèd part to heaven, and slept in peace.

KATHERINE

So may he rest; his faults lie gently on him!
Yet thus far, Griffith, give me leave to speak him,
And yet with charity. He was a man
Of an unbounded stomach, ever ranking
Himself with princes; one that by suggestion
Tied all the kingdom. Simony was fair play;
His own opinion was his law. I'th'presence
He would say untruths, and be ever double
Both in his words and meaning. He was never,
But where he meant to ruin, pitiful.   40
His promises were as he then was, mighty,
But his performance as he is now, nothing.
Of his own body he was ill, and gave
The clergy ill example.

GRIFFITH   Noble madam,
Men's evil manners live in brass; their virtues
We write in water. May it please your highness
To hear me speak his good now?

KATHERINE   Yes, good Griffith,
I were malicious else.

GRIFFITH   This Cardinal,
Though from an humble stock, undoubtedly
Was fashioned to much honour. From his cradle   50
He was a scholar, and a ripe and good one,
Exceeding wise, fair-spoken, and persuading;
Lofty and sour to them that loved him not,
But, to those men that sought him, sweet as summer.
And though he were unsatisfied in getting –
Which was a sin – yet in bestowing, madam,
He was most princely: ever witness for him
Those twins of learning that he raised in you,
Ipswich and Oxford! – one of which fell with him,

60 Unwilling to outlive the good that did it;
The other, though unfinished, yet so famous,
So excellent in art, and still so rising,
That Christendom shall ever speak his virtue.
His overthrow heaped happiness upon him,
For then, and not till then, he felt himself,
And found the blessèdness of being little;
And, to add greater honours to his age
Than man could give him, he died fearing God.

KATHERINE
After my death I wish no other herald,
70 No other speaker of my living actions,
To keep mine honour from corruption
But such an honest chronicler as Griffith.
Whom I most hated living, thou hast made me,
With thy religious truth and modesty,
Now in his ashes honour. Peace be with him!
Patience, be near me still, and set me lower;
I have not long to trouble thee. Good Griffith,
Cause the musicians play me that sad note
I named my knell, whilst I sit meditating
80 On that celestial harmony I go to.
Sad and solemn music

GRIFFITH
She is asleep. Good wench, let's sit down quiet,
For fear we wake her. Softly, gentle Patience.
The Vision:
Enter, solemnly tripping one after another, six per-
sonages clad in white robes, wearing on their heads
garlands of bays, and golden vizards on their faces;
branches of bays or palm in their hands. They first
congee unto her, then dance; and, at certain changes,
the first two hold a spare garland over her head, at
which the other four make reverent curtsies. Then the

*two that held the garland deliver the same to the other
next two, who observe the same order in their changes,
and holding the garland over her head; which done,
they deliver the same garland to the last two, who
likewise observe the same order. At which, as it were
by inspiration, she makes in her sleep signs of rejoicing,
and holdeth up her hands to heaven; and so in their
dancing vanish, carrying the garland with them. The
music continues*

KATHERINE
Spirits of peace, where are ye? Are ye all gone,
And leave me here in wretchedness behind ye?

GRIFFITH
Madam, we are here.

KATHERINE   It is not you I call for.
Saw ye none enter since I slept?

GRIFFITH   None, madam.

KATHERINE
No? Saw you not even now a blessèd troop
Invite me to a banquet, whose bright faces
Cast thousand beams upon me, like the sun?
They promised me eternal happiness,   90
And brought me garlands, Griffith, which I feel
I am not worthy yet to wear; I shall, assuredly.

GRIFFITH
I am most joyful, madam, such good dreams
Possess your fancy.

KATHERINE   Bid the music leave,
They are harsh and heavy to me.

          Music ceases

PATIENCE   Do you note
How much her grace is altered on the sudden?
How long her face is drawn? How pale she looks?
And of an earthy colour? Mark her eyes.

GRIFFITH
  She is going, wench. Pray, pray.

PATIENCE   Heaven comfort her!
    Enter a Messenger

MESSENGER
100   An't like your grace –

KATHERINE   You are a saucy fellow!
  Deserve we no more reverence?

GRIFFITH (*to Messenger*)   You are to blame,
  Knowing she will not lose her wonted greatness,
  To use so rude behaviour. Go to, kneel.

MESSENGER
  I humbly do entreat your highness' pardon;
  My haste made me unmannerly. There is staying
  A gentleman sent from the King, to see you.

KATHERINE
  Admit him entrance, Griffith; but this fellow
  Let me ne'er see again.   *Exit Messenger*
    Enter Lord Capuchius

                If my sight fail not,
  You should be lord ambassador from the Emperor,
110   My royal nephew, and your name Capuchius.

CAPUCHIUS
  Madam, the same: your servant.

KATHERINE   O my lord,
  The times and titles now are altered strangely
  With me since first you knew me. But I pray you,
  What is your pleasure with me?

CAPUCHIUS   Noble lady,
  First, mine own service to your grace; the next,
  The King's request that I would visit you,
  Who grieves much for your weakness, and by me
  Sends you his princely commendations,
  And heartily entreats you take good comfort.

KATHERINE

O my good lord, that comfort comes too late, 120
'Tis like a pardon after execution.
That gentle physic, given in time, had cured me,
But now I am past all comforts here but prayers.
How does his highness?

CAPUCHIUS   Madam, in good health.

KATHERINE

So may he ever do, and ever flourish,
When I shall dwell with worms, and my poor name
Banished the kingdom. Patience, is that letter
I caused you write yet sent away?

PATIENCE   No, madam.

She gives it to Katherine

KATHERINE

Sir, I most humbly pray you to deliver
This to my lord the King.

CAPUCHIUS   Most willing, madam. 130

KATHERINE

In which I have commended to his goodness
The model of our chaste loves, his young daughter –
The dews of heaven fall thick in blessings on her! –
Beseeching him to give her virtuous breeding.
She is young, and of a noble modest nature;
I hope she will deserve well – and a little
To love her for her mother's sake, that loved him,
Heaven knows how dearly. My next poor petition
Is that his noble grace would have some pity
Upon my wretched women, that so long 140
Have followed both my fortunes faithfully;
Of which there is not one, I dare avow –
And now I should not lie – but will deserve,
For virtue and true beauty of the soul,
For honesty and decent carriage,

A right good husband, let him be a noble;
And sure those men are happy that shall have 'em.
The last is for my men – they are the poorest,
But poverty could never draw 'em from me –
150 That they may have their wages duly paid 'em,
And something over to remember me by.
If heaven had pleased to have given me longer life
And able means, we had not parted thus.
These are the whole contents; and, good my lord,
By that you love the dearest in this world,
As you wish Christian peace to souls departed,
Stand these poor people's friend, and urge the King
To do me this last right.

CAPUCHIUS   By heaven, I will,
Or let me lose the fashion of a man!

KATHERINE
160 I thank you, honest lord. Remember me
In all humility unto his highness.
Say his long trouble now is passing
Out of this world. Tell him in death I blessed him,
For so I will. Mine eyes grow dim. Farewell,
My lord. Griffith, farewell. Nay, Patience,
You must not leave me yet. I must to bed;
Call in more women. When I am dead, good wench,
Let me be used with honour; strew me over
With maiden flowers, that all the world may know
170 I was a chaste wife to my grave. Embalm me,
Then lay me forth; although unqueened, yet like
A queen, and daughter to a king, inter me.
I can no more.   *Exeunt, leading Katherine*

*

Enter Gardiner, Bishop of Winchester, a Page with a torch before him, met by Sir Thomas Lovell

GARDINER
  It's one o'clock, boy, is't not?

PAGE   It hath struck.

GARDINER
  These should be hours for necessities,
  Not for delights, times to repair our nature
  With comforting repose, and not for us
  To waste these times. Good hour of night, Sir Thomas!
  Whither so late?

LOVELL   Came you from the King, my lord?

GARDINER
  I did, Sir Thomas, and left him at primero
  With the Duke of Suffolk.

LOVELL   I must to him too,
  Before he go to bed. I'll take my leave.

GARDINER
  Not yet, Sir Thomas Lovell. What's the matter?   10
  It seems you are in haste. An if there be
  No great offence belongs to't, give your friend
  Some touch of your late business. Affairs that walk,
  As they say spirits do, at midnight, have
  In them a wilder nature than the business
  That seeks dispatch by day.

LOVELL   My lord, I love you,
  And durst commend a secret to your ear
  Much weightier than this work. The Queen's in labour,
  They say, in great extremity, and feared
  She'll with the labour end.

GARDINER   The fruit she goes with   20
  I pray for heartily, that it may find
  Good time, and live; but, for the stock, Sir Thomas,
  I wish it grubbed up now.

153

LOVELL   Methinks I could
Cry the amen, and yet my conscience says
She's a good creature and, sweet lady, does
Deserve our better wishes.

GARDINER   But, sir, sir,
Hear me, Sir Thomas. You're a gentleman
Of mine own way; I know you wise, religious;
And let me tell you, it will ne'er be well –
30   'Twill not, Sir Thomas Lovell, take't of me –
Till Cranmer, Cromwell – her two hands – and she
Sleep in their graves.

LOVELL   Now, sir, you speak of two
The most remarked i'th'kingdom. As for Cromwell,
Beside that of the Jewel House, is made Master
O'th'Rolls, and the King's secretary; further, sir,
Stands in the gap and trade of more preferments,
With which the time will load him. Th'Archbishop
Is the King's hand and tongue, and who dare speak
One syllable against him?

GARDINER   Yes, yes, Sir Thomas,
40   There are that dare, and I myself have ventured
To speak my mind of him; and indeed this day,
Sir – I may tell it you – I think I have
Incensed the lords o'th'Council that he is –
For so I know he is, they know he is –
A most arch heretic, a pestilence
That does infect the land; with which they, movèd,
Have broken with the King, who hath so far
Given ear to our complaint, of his great grace
And princely care, foreseeing those fell mischiefs
50   Our reasons laid before him, hath commanded
Tomorrow morning to the Council board
He be convented. He's a rank weed, Sir Thomas,
And we must root him out. From your affairs

I hinder you too long. Good night, Sir Thomas.

LOVELL

Many good nights, my lord; I rest your servant.

Exeunt Gardiner and Page

Enter the King and Suffolk

KING HENRY

Charles, I will play no more tonight.
My mind's not on't; you are too hard for me.

SUFFOLK

Sir, I did never win of you before.

KING HENRY

But little, Charles,
Nor shall not, when my fancy's on my play.   60
Now, Lovell, from the Queen what is the news?

LOVELL

I could not personally deliver to her
What you commanded me, but by her woman
I sent your message, who returned her thanks
In the great'st humbleness, and desired your highness
Most heartily to pray for her.

KING HENRY   What sayst thou, ha?
To pray for her? What, is she crying out?

LOVELL

So said her woman, and that her sufferance made
Almost each pang a death.

KING HENRY   Alas, good lady!

SUFFOLK

God safely quit her of her burden, and   70
With gentle travail, to the gladding of
Your highness with an heir!

KING HENRY   'Tis midnight, Charles;
Prithee to bed, and in thy prayers remember
Th'estate of my poor Queen. Leave me alone,
For I must think of that which company

Would not be friendly to.

SUFFOLK   I wish your highness
A quiet night, and my good mistress will
Remember in my prayers.

KING HENRY   Charles, good night.

Exit Suffolk

Enter Sir Anthony Denny

Well, sir, what follows?

DENNY

80   Sir, I have brought my lord the Archbishop,
As you commanded me.

KING HENRY   Ha? Canterbury?

DENNY

Ay, my good lord.

KING HENRY   'Tis true. Where is he, Denny?

DENNY

He attends your highness' pleasure.

KING HENRY   Bring him to us.

Exit Denny

LOVELL (*aside*)

This is about that which the Bishop spake;
I am happily come hither.

Enter Cranmer and Denny

KING HENRY

Avoid the gallery.

Lovell seems to stay

Ha! I have said. Be gone.

What?   *Exeunt Lovell and Denny*

CRANMER (*aside*)

I am fearful – wherefore frowns he thus?
'Tis his aspect of terror. All's not well.

KING HENRY

How now, my lord? You do desire to know

Wherefore I sent for you.

CRANMER (*kneeling*)   It is my duty   90
T'attend your highness' pleasure.

KING HENRY   Pray you, arise,
My good and gracious lord of Canterbury.
Come, you and I must walk a turn together;
I have news to tell you. Come, come, give me your hand.
Ah, my good lord, I grieve at what I speak,
And am right sorry to repeat what follows.
I have, and most unwillingly, of late
Heard many grievous – I do say, my lord,
Grievous – complaints of you; which, being considered,
Have moved us and our Council that you shall   100
This morning come before us, where I know
You cannot with such freedom purge yourself
But that, till further trial in those charges
Which will require your answer, you must take
Your patience to you and be well contented
To make your house our Tower. You a brother of us,
It fits we thus proceed, or else no witness
Would come against you.

CRANMER (*kneeling*)   I humbly thank your highness,
And am right glad to catch this good occasion
Most throughly to be winnowed, where my chaff   110
And corn shall fly asunder, for I know
There's none stands under more calumnious tongues
Than I myself, poor man.

KING HENRY   Stand up, good Canterbury;
Thy truth and thy integrity is rooted
In us, thy friend. Give me thy hand, stand up;
Prithee let's walk. Now, by my holidame,
What manner of man are you? My lord, I looked
You would have given me your petition that

I should have ta'en some pains to bring together
120   Yourself and your accusers, and to have heard you
Without indurance further.

CRANMER   Most dread liege,
The good I stand on is my truth and honesty.
If they shall fail, I with mine enemies
Will triumph o'er my person, which I weigh not,
Being of those virtues vacant. I fear nothing
What can be said against me.

KING HENRY   Know you not
How your state stands i'th'world, with the whole world?
Your enemies are many, and not small; their practices
Must bear the same proportion, and not ever
130   The justice and the truth o'th'question carries
The due o'th'verdict with it. At what ease
Might corrupt minds procure knaves as corrupt
To swear against you? Such things have been done.
You are potently opposed, and with a malice
Of as great size. Ween you of better luck,
I mean in perjured witness, than your Master,
Whose minister you are, whiles here He lived
Upon this naughty earth? Go to, go to;
You take a precipice for no leap of danger,
140   And woo your own destruction.

CRANMER   God and your majesty
Protect mine innocence, or I fall into
The trap is laid for me!

KING HENRY   Be of good cheer;
They shall no more prevail than we give way to.
Keep comfort to you, and this morning see
You do appear before them. If they shall chance,
In charging you with matters, to commit you,
The best persuasions to the contrary

Fail not to use, and with what vehemency
Th'occasion shall instruct you. If entreaties
Will render you no remedy, this ring   150
Deliver them, and your appeal to us
There make before them. Look, the good man weeps!
He's honest, on mine honour. God's blest mother!
I swear he is true-hearted, and a soul
None better in my kingdom. Get you gone,
And do as I have bid you.   *Exit Cranmer*
       He has strangled
His language in his tears.
  Enter Old Lady
LOVELL (*within*)   Come back! What mean you?
  Enter Lovell, following her

OLD LADY
 I'll not come back; the tidings that I bring
 Will make my boldness manners. Now good angels
 Fly o'er thy royal head, and shade thy person   160
 Under their blessèd wings!
KING HENRY   Now by thy looks
 I guess thy message. Is the Queen delivered?
 Say 'Ay, and of a boy'.
OLD LADY   Ay, ay, my liege,
 And of a lovely boy. The God of heaven
 Both now and ever bless her! 'Tis a girl
 Promises boys hereafter. Sir, your Queen
 Desires your visitation, and to be
 Acquainted with this stranger. 'Tis as like you
 As cherry is to cherry.
KING HENRY   Lovell!
LOVELL   Sir?
KING HENRY
 Give her an hundred marks. I'll to the Queen.   *Exit* 170

OLD LADY

    An hundred marks? By this light, I'll ha' more.
    An ordinary groom is for such payment.
    I will have more, or scold it out of him.
    Said I for this the girl was like to him? I'll
    Have more, or else unsay't; and now, while 'tis hot,
    I'll put it to the issue.   *Exeunt*

V.2   *Pursuivants, pages, and others, attending before the*
            Council Chamber
            Enter Cranmer, Archbishop of Canterbury

CRANMER

    I hope I am not too late, and yet the gentleman
    That was sent to me from the Council prayed me
    To make great haste. All fast? What means this? Ho!
    Who waits there?
        Enter Keeper

               Sure you know me?

KEEPER   Yes, my lord,
    But yet I cannot help you.

CRANMER   Why?
    Enter Doctor Butts

KEEPER   Your grace
    Must wait till you be called for.

CRANMER   So!

BUTTS (*aside*)

    This is a piece of malice. I am glad
    I came this way so happily; the King
    Shall understand it presently.   *Exit*

CRANMER (*aside*)   'Tis Butts,

10   The King's physician. As he passed along,
    How earnestly he cast his eyes upon me!

Pray heaven he sound not my disgrace! For certain
This is of purpose laid by some that hate me –
God turn their hearts! I never sought their malice –
To quench mine honour. They would shame to make
    me
Wait else at door, a fellow Councillor,
'Mong boys, grooms, and lackeys. But their pleasures
Must be fulfilled, and I attend with patience.

    Enter the King and Butts, at a window above

BUTTS
  I'll show your grace the strangest sight –
KING HENRY   What's that, Butts?
BUTTS
  I think your highness saw this many a day.   20
KING HENRY
  Body o'me, where is it?
BUTTS   There, my lord –
  The high promotion of his grace of Canterbury,
  Who holds his state at door, 'mongst pursuivants,
  Pages, and footboys.
KING HENRY   Ha? 'Tis he indeed.
  Is this the honour they do one another?
  'Tis well there's one above 'em yet. I had thought
  They had parted so much honesty among 'em –
  At least good manners – as not thus to suffer
  A man of his place, and so near our favour,
  To dance attendance on their lordships' pleasures,   30
  And at the door too, like a post with packets.
  By holy Mary, Butts, there's knavery!
  Let 'em alone, and draw the curtain close;
  We shall hear more anon.

    They partly close the curtain, but remain watching;
    Cranmer withdraws to wait without

A council-table brought in with chairs and stools, and
placed under the state. Enter Lord Chancellor, places
himself at the upper end of the table on the left hand,
a seat being left void above him, as for Canterbury's
seat. Duke of Suffolk, Duke of Norfolk, Surrey, Lord
Chamberlain, Gardiner, seat themselves in order on
each side; Cromwell at lower end, as secretary.
Keeper at the door

LORD CHANCELLOR
Speak to the business, master secretary:
Why are we met in council?

CROMWELL   Please your honours,
The chief cause concerns his grace of Canterbury.

GARDINER
Has he had knowledge of it?

CROMWELL   Yes.

NORFOLK   Who waits there?

KEEPER
Without, my noble lords?

GARDINER   Yes.

KEEPER   My lord Archbishop,
And has done half an hour, to know your pleasures.

LORD CHANCELLOR
Let him come in.

KEEPER   Your grace may enter now.
        Cranmer approaches the council-table

LORD CHANCELLOR
My good lord Archbishop, I'm very sorry
To sit here at this present and behold
10   That chair stand empty, but we all are men
In our own natures frail, and capable
Of our flesh; few are angels; out of which frailty
And want of wisdom, you, that best should teach us,
Have misdemeaned yourself, and not a little,

Toward the King first, then his laws, in filling
The whole realm, by your teaching and your chaplains' –
For so we are informed – with new opinions,
Diverse and dangerous, which are heresies,
And, not reformed, may prove pernicious.

GARDINER

Which reformation must be sudden too, 20
My noble lords; for those that tame wild horses
Pace 'em not in their hands to make 'em gentle,
But stop their mouths with stubborn bits and spur
    'em
Till they obey the manage. If we suffer,
Out of our easiness and childish pity
To one man's honour, this contagious sickness,
Farewell all physic – and what follows then?
Commotions, uproars, with a general taint
Of the whole state, as of late days our neighbours,
The upper Germany, can dearly witness, 30
Yet freshly pitied in our memories.

CRANMER

My good lords, hitherto in all the progress
Both of my life and office, I have laboured,
And with no little study, that my teaching
And the strong course of my authority
Might go one way, and safely; and the end
Was ever to do well. Nor is there living –
I speak it with a single heart, my lords –
A man that more detests, more stirs against,
Both in his private conscience and his place, 40
Defacers of a public peace than I do.
Pray heaven the King may never find a heart
With less allegiance in it! Men that make
Envy and crookèd malice nourishment
Dare bite the best. I do beseech your lordships

That, in this case of justice, my accusers,
Be what they will, may stand forth face to face,
And freely urge against me.

SUFFOLK   Nay, my lord,
That cannot be; you are a Councillor,
50   And by that virtue no man dare accuse you.

GARDINER
My lord, because we have business of more moment,
We will be short with you. 'Tis his highness' pleasure
And our consent, for better trial of you,
From hence you be committed to the Tower;
Where, being but a private man again,
You shall know many dare accuse you boldly,
More than, I fear, you are provided for.

CRANMER
Ah, my good lord of Winchester, I thank you;
You are always my good friend. If your will pass,
60   I shall both find your lordship judge and juror,
You are so merciful. I see your end:
'Tis my undoing. Love and meekness, lord,
Become a churchman better than ambition.
Win straying souls with modesty again;
Cast none away. That I shall clear myself,
Lay all the weight ye can upon my patience,
I make as little doubt as you do conscience
In doing daily wrongs. I could say more,
But reverence to your calling makes me modest.

GARDINER
70   My lord, my lord, you are a sectary,
That's the plain truth. Your painted gloss discovers,
To men that understand you, words and weakness.

CROMWELL
My lord of Winchester, you are a little,

By your good favour, too sharp. Men so noble,
However faulty, yet should find respect
For what they have been. 'Tis a cruelty
To load a falling man.
GARDINER   Good master secretary,
  I cry your honour mercy; you may worst
  Of all this table say so.
CROMWELL   Why, my lord?
GARDINER
  Do not I know you for a favourer   80
  Of this new sect? Ye are not sound.
CROMWELL   Not sound?
GARDINER
  Not sound, I say.
CROMWELL   Would you were half so honest!
  Men's prayers then would seek you, not their fears.
GARDINER
  I shall remember this bold language.
CROMWELL   Do.
  Remember your bold life too.
LORD CHANCELLOR   This is too much;
  Forbear, for shame, my lords.
GARDINER   I have done.
CROMWELL   And I.
LORD CHANCELLOR
  Then thus for you, my lord: it stands agreed,
  I take it, by all voices, that forthwith
  You be conveyed to th'Tower a prisoner,
  There to remain till the King's further pleasure   90
  Be known unto us. Are you all agreed, lords?
ALL
  We are.
CRANMER Is there no other way of mercy,

But I must needs to th'Tower, my lords?

GARDINER   What other
Would you expect? You are strangely troublesome.
Let some o'th'guard be ready there.

Enter the Guard

CRANMER   For me?
Must I go like a traitor thither?

GARDINER   Receive him,
And see him safe i'th'Tower.

CRANMER   Stay, good my lords,
I have a little yet to say. Look there, my lords.
By virtue of that ring I take my cause
Out of the gripes of cruel men, and give it
To a most noble judge, the King my master.

LORD CHAMBERLAIN
This is the King's ring.

SURREY   'Tis no counterfeit.

SUFFOLK
'Tis the right ring, by heaven. I told ye all,
When we first put this dangerous stone a-rolling,
'Twould fall upon ourselves.

NORFOLK   Do you think, my lords,
The King will suffer but the little finger
Of this man to be vexed?

LORD CHAMBERLAIN   'Tis now too certain.
How much more is his life in value with him!
Would I were fairly out on't!   *Exit King above*

CROMWELL   My mind gave me,
In seeking tales and informations
Against this man, whose honesty the devil
And his disciples only envy at,
Ye blew the fire that burns ye. Now have at ye!

Enter the King frowning on them; takes his seat

GARDINER

    Dread sovereign, how much are we bound to heaven
    In daily thanks, that gave us such a prince,
    Not only good and wise, but most religious;
    One that in all obedience makes the church
    The chief aim of his honour, and, to strengthen
    That holy duty, out of dear respect,
    His royal self in judgement comes to hear   120
    The cause betwixt her and this great offender.

KING HENRY

    You were ever good at sudden commendations,
    Bishop of Winchester. But know I come not
    To hear such flattery now, and in my presence
    They are too thin and bare to hide offences;
    To me you cannot reach. You play the spaniel,
    And think with wagging of your tongue to win me;
    But whatsoe'er thou tak'st me for, I'm sure
    Thou hast a cruel nature and a bloody.
    (To Cranmer)
    Good man, sit down. Now let me see the proudest,   130
    He that dares most, but wag his finger at thee.
    By all that's holy, he had better starve
    Than but once think this place becomes thee not.

SURREY

    May it please your grace –

KING HENRY   No, sir, it does not please me.

    I had thought I had had men of some understanding
    And wisdom of my Council, but I find none.
    Was it discretion, lords, to let this man,
    This good man – few of you deserve that title –
    This honest man, wait like a lousy footboy
    At chamber door? – and one as great as you are?   140
    Why, what a shame was this! Did my commission

Bid ye so far forget yourselves? I gave ye
Power as he was a Councillor to try him,
Not as a groom. There's some of ye, I see,
More out of malice than integrity,
Would try him to the utmost, had ye mean;
Which ye shall never have while I live.

LORD CHANCELLOR   Thus far,
My most dread sovereign, may it like your grace
To let my tongue excuse all. What was purposed
150   Concerning his imprisonment was rather –
If there be faith in men – meant for his trial
And fair purgation to the world than malice,
I'm sure, in me.

KING HENRY   Well, well, my lords, respect him.
Take him and use him well; he's worthy of it.
I will say thus much for him: if a prince
May be beholding to a subject, I
Am, for his love and service, so to him.
Make me no more ado, but all embrace him;
Be friends, for shame, my lords! My lord of Canter-
       bury,
160   I have a suit which you must not deny me:
That is, a fair young maid that yet wants baptism;
You must be godfather, and answer for her.

CRANMER
The greatest monarch now alive may glory
In such an honour. How may I deserve it,
That am a poor and humble subject to you?

KING HENRY Come, come, my lord, you'd spare your
spoons. You shall have two noble partners with you, the
old Duchess of Norfolk and Lady Marquis Dorset.
Will these please you?
170   Once more, my lord of Winchester, I charge you
Embrace and love this man.

GARDINER　　　　　　　With a true heart
　And brother-love I do it.
CRANMER　　　　　　And let heaven
　Witness how dear I hold this confirmation.
KING HENRY
　Good man, those joyful tears show thy true heart.
　The common voice, I see, is verified
　Of thee, which says thus: 'Do my lord of Canterbury
　A shrewd turn and he's your friend for ever.'
　Come, lords, we trifle time away; I long
　To have this young one made a Christian.
　As I have made ye one, lords, one remain;　　　　　180
　So I grow stronger, you more honour gain.　　　*Exeunt*

　　　Noise and tumult within. Enter Porter and his Man　V.4
PORTER You'll leave your noise anon, ye rascals. Do you
　take the court for Parish Garden? Ye rude slaves, leave
　your gaping.
SERVANT (*within*) Good master porter, I belong to
　th'larder.
PORTER Belong to th'gallows, and be hanged, ye rogue!
　Is this a place to roar in? Fetch me a dozen crab-tree
　staves, and strong ones: these are but switches to 'em.
　I'll scratch your heads. You must be seeing christen-
　ings? Do you look for ale and cakes here, you rude　10
　rascals?
MAN
　Pray, sir, be patient. 'Tis as much impossible,
　Unless we sweep 'em from the door with cannons,
　To scatter 'em as 'tis to make 'em sleep
　On May-day morning; which will never be.
　We may as well push against Paul's as stir 'em.
PORTER How got they in, and be hanged?

MAN

    Alas, I know not. How gets the tide in?
    As much as one sound cudgel of four foot –
20   You see the poor remainder – could distribute,
    I made no spare, sir.

PORTER   You did nothing, sir.

MAN

    I am not Samson, nor Sir Guy, nor Colbrand,
    To mow 'em down before me; but if I spared any
    That had a head to hit, either young or old,
    He or she, cuckold or cuckold-maker,
    Let me ne'er hope to see a chine again –
    And that I would not for a cow, God save her!

SERVANT (*within*) Do you hear, master porter?

PORTER I shall be with you presently, good master
30   puppy. Keep the door close, sirrah.

MAN What would you have me do?

PORTER What should you do, but knock 'em down by
th'dozens? Is this Moorfields to muster in? Or have we
some strange Indian with the great tool come to court,
the women so besiege us? Bless me, what a fry of
fornication is at door! On my Christian conscience, this
one christening will beget a thousand: here will be
father, godfather, and all together.

MAN The spoons will be the bigger, sir. There is a fellow
40   somewhat near the door, he should be a brazier by his
face, for, o'my conscience, twenty of the dog-days now
reign in's nose; all that stand about him are under the
line, they need no other penance. That fire-drake did I
hit three times on the head, and three times was his
nose discharged against me; he stands there like a
mortar-piece, to blow us. There was a haberdasher's
wife of small wit near him, that railed upon me till her

pinked porringer fell off her head, for kindling such a
combustion in the state. I missed the meteor once, and
hit that woman, who cried out 'Clubs!', when I might 50
see from far some forty truncheoners draw to her
succour, which were the hope o'th'Strand, where she
was quartered. They fell on; I made good my place. At
length they came to th'broomstaff to me; I defied 'em
still; when suddenly a file of boys behind 'em, loose
shot, delivered such a shower of pebbles that I was fain
to draw mine honour in, and let 'em win the work. The
devil was amongst 'em, I think, surely.

PORTER These are the youths that thunder at a playhouse,
and fight for bitten apples, that no audience but the 60
tribulation of Tower Hill or the limbs of Limehouse,
their dear brothers, are able to endure. I have some of
'em in *Limbo Patrum*, and there they are like to dance
these three days, besides the running banquet of two
beadles that is to come.

Enter the Lord Chamberlain

LORD CHAMBERLAIN
Mercy o'me, what a multitude are here!
They grow still, too; from all parts they are coming,
As if we kept a fair here! Where are these porters,
These lazy knaves? You've made a fine hand, fellows!
There's a trim rabble let in: are all these 70
Your faithful friends o'th'suburbs? We shall have
Great store of room, no doubt, left for the ladies,
When they pass back from the christening.

PORTER   An't please your honour,
We are but men, and what so many may do,
Not being torn a-pieces, we have done.
An army cannot rule 'em.

LORD CHAMBERLAIN   As I live,

If the King blame me for't, I'll lay ye all
By th'heels, and suddenly; and on your heads
Clap round fines for neglect. You're lazy knaves,
80 And here ye lie baiting of bombards, when
Ye should do service.

Trumpets

                 Hark! The trumpets sound;
They're come already from the christening.
Go break among the press, and find a way out
To let the troop pass fairly, or I'll find
A Marshalsea shall hold ye play these two months.

PORTER
Make way there for the Princess!

MAN   You great fellow,
Stand close up, or I'll make your head ache.

PORTER
You i'th'camlet, get up o'th'rail;
I'll peck you o'er the pales else.   *Exeunt*

V.5   *Enter trumpets, sounding; then two Aldermen, Lord
Mayor, Garter, Cranmer, Duke of Norfolk with his
marshal's staff, Duke of Suffolk, two noblemen
bearing great standing bowls for the christening gifts;
then four noblemen bearing a canopy, under which the
Duchess of Norfolk, godmother, bearing the child
richly habited in a mantle, etc., train borne by a lady;
then follows the Marchioness Dorset, the other godmother, and ladies. The troop pass once about the
stage, and Garter speaks*

GARTER Heaven, from thy endless goodness, send prosperous life, long, and ever happy, to the high and
mighty Princess of England, Elizabeth!

Flourish. Enter the King and Guard

CRANMER (*kneeling*)
And to your royal grace, and the good Queen!
My noble partners and myself thus pray
All comfort, joy, in this most gracious lady,
Heaven ever laid up to make parents happy,
May hourly fall upon ye!

KING HENRY   Thank you, good lord Archbishop.
What is her name?

CRANMER   Elizabeth.

KING HENRY   Stand up, lord.

The King kisses the child
With this kiss take my blessing: God protect thee!   10
Into Whose hand I give thy life.

CRANMER   Amen.

KING HENRY
My noble gossips, you've been too prodigal;
I thank ye heartily. So shall this lady
When she has so much English.

CRANMER   Let me speak, sir,
For heaven now bids me, and the words I utter
Let none think flattery, for they'll find 'em truth.
This royal infant – heaven still move about her! –
Though in her cradle, yet now promises
Upon this land a thousand thousand blessings,
Which time shall bring to ripeness. She shall be –   20
But few now living can behold that goodness –
A pattern to all princes living with her,
And all that shall succeed. Saba was never
More covetous of wisdom and fair virtue
Than this pure soul shall be. All princely graces
That mould up such a mighty piece as this is,
With all the virtues that attend the good,
Shall still be doubled on her. Truth shall nurse her,

Holy and heavenly thoughts still counsel her;
30 She shall be loved and feared. Her own shall bless her;
Her foes shake like a field of beaten corn,
And hang their heads with sorrow. Good grows with her;
In her days every man shall eat in safety
Under his own vine what he plants, and sing
The merry songs of peace to all his neighbours.
God shall be truly known, and those about her
From her shall read the perfect ways of honour,
And by those claim their greatness, not by blood.
Nor shall this peace sleep with her; but as when
40 The bird of wonder dies, the maiden phoenix,
Her ashes new-create another heir
As great in admiration as herself,
So shall she leave her blessèdness to one –
When heaven shall call her from this cloud of darkness –
Who from the sacred ashes of her honour
Shall star-like rise, as great in fame as she was,
And so stand fixed. Peace, plenty, love, truth, terror,
That were the servants to this chosen infant,
Shall then be his, and like a vine grow to him.
50 Wherever the bright sun of heaven shall shine,
His honour and the greatness of his name
Shall be, and make new nations. He shall flourish,
And like a mountain cedar reach his branches
To all the plains about him; our children's children
Shall see this, and bless heaven.

KING HENRY   Thou speakest wonders.

CRANMER
She shall be, to the happiness of England,
An agèd princess; many days shall see her,
And yet no day without a deed to crown it.
Would I had known no more! But she must die –
60 She must, the saints must have her – yet a virgin;

A most unspotted lily shall she pass
To th'ground, and all the world shall mourn her.

KING HENRY

O lord Archbishop,
Thou hast made me now a man; never before
This happy child did I get anything.
This oracle of comfort has so pleased me
That when I am in heaven I shall desire
To see what this child does, and praise my Maker.
I thank ye all. To you, my good Lord Mayor,
And you, good brethren, I am much beholding:
I have received much honour by your presence,
And ye shall find me thankful. Lead the way, lords;
Ye must all see the Queen, and she must thank ye;
She will be sick else. This day, no man think
'Has business at his house, for all shall stay:
This little one shall make it holiday.   *Exeunt*

THE EPILOGUE

'Tis ten to one this play can never please
All that are here. Some come to take their ease,
And sleep an act or two; but those, we fear,
We've frighted with our trumpets; so, 'tis clear,
They'll say 'tis naught. Others to hear the city
Abused extremely, and to cry 'That's witty!' –
Which we have not done neither; that, I fear,
All the expected good we're like to hear
For this play at this time is only in
The merciful construction of good women,
For such a one we showed 'em. If they smile,
And say 'twill do, I know within a while
All the best men are ours; for 'tis ill hap
If they hold when their ladies bid 'em clap.

COMMENTARY

References and Quotations

THE spelling and punctuation of quotations from sixteenth-
and seventeenth-century texts have usually been modernized.

Bishops' Bible	Translation of the Bible (1568), the standard Elizabethan version, from which all Biblical quotations are given unless they are otherwise attributed
F	The Folio edition of Shakespeare's plays (1623), the first collected edition
Foakes	*Henry VIII*, revised Arden edition (1957), edited by R. A. Foakes
Foxe	John Foxe, *Acts and Monuments*, edition of 1596
Holinshed	Raphael Holinshed, *Chronicles of England* (second edition, 1587). References are to the edition by Henry Ellis (1807–8)
Rowley	Samuel Rowley, *When You See Me You Know Me* (1605). References are to the Malone Society Reprint (1952), edited by F. P. Wilson and John Crow
Tilley	M. P. Tilley, *Dictionary of the Proverbs in England in the Sixteenth and Seventeenth Centuries* (1950)

The Characters in the Play

No list of these is provided in F. Editions differ somewhat in
the number of very brief parts they include (for instance,
servants or messengers with a few words only). The attempt
has been made here to mention all speaking or singing parts,

and to group them approximately according to function – King, courtiers, churchmen and their entourage, miscellaneous functionaries, Queen Katherine and her household, Anne Bullen and her Old Lady. 'Lord Sands' appears in the II.1.54 stage direction as 'Sir Walter Sands'; see the note at that point. It is Griffith who in the trial scene speaks to the Queen (II.4.127): F attributes the speech to the Queen's Gentleman Usher, but that he and Griffith are identical is clear from the entry direction of IV.2.

The Setting

70 The action takes place in London, Westminster, and Kimbolton.

Prologue

The style of the Prologue (which Dr Johnson thought un-Shakespearian, and tentatively ascribed to Ben Jonson) certainly lacks the Shakespearian idiosyncrasy. It has something of Jonson's derisive challenge, and something of Fletcher's relaxed persuasiveness, as in the Prologue and Epilogue of *The Two Noble Kinsmen* (to which, however, it is superior, though not so pre-eminently so as to make Fletcher's authorship unlikely). True Shakespearian Prologues, as in *2 Henry IV*, *Henry V*, *Romeo and Juliet*, and *Troilus and Cressida*, engage very closely with their plays, whereas this one deals vaguely with the play's contents, and indeed gives a misleading impression of its end. In its favour, however, is the fact that it offers the speaker the chance to attract the attention of the audience sympathetically and seriously to *our chosen truth* (line 18).

10   1   *I come no more to make you laugh.* The first performance, or early performances, must have followed some comedy to which audiences would catch the reference, though which one is unknown. The allusion in lines 14–16 may well be to Samuel Rowley's chronicle drama, *When You See Me You Know Me. Or*

the famous Chronicle History of King Henry the Eighth (written in 1603–5, published in 1605 and 1613; see Introduction, pages 9–11).

3   *Sad, high, and working* serious, lofty, and moving
     state stateliness

9   *May here find truth.* This is possibly an allusion to an earlier or alternative title to the play, *All is True*, as in Sir Henry Wotton's letter; see Introduction, page 7. The Prologue repeatedly stresses the historical reality conveyed in the play – see lines 18, 21, 25–7.

10   *show* spectacle. (The play is unusually elaborate in ceremonial.)

12   *their shilling.* Admission to prominent seats near the stage, in which gallants might display themselves, cost one shilling or more by the date of the play. Dekker advises his gull in *The Gull's Hornbook* (1609; page 2) 'When at a new play you take up the twelvepenny room, next the stage (because the lords and you may seem to be hail-fellow-well-met)'; and Overbury writes of 'The Proud Man' in *Characters* (1614) 'If he have but twelvepence in's purse, he will give it for the best room in a playhouse.' Playhouse prices are discussed in detail by E. K. Chambers in *The Elizabethan Stage*, Volume 2, page 534, note 1.

13   *two short hours.* This period bears little relationship to the play itself, though two hours is often mentioned, conventionally, as the time taken by play performances; compare 'the two hours' traffic of our stage' (*Romeo and Juliet*, Prologue, 12), 'these two short hours' (*The Alchemist*, Prologue, 1), and 'scenes ... worth two hours' travel' (*The Two Noble Kinsmen*, Prologue, 28). The actual time taken must often have been longer; the Induction to Jonson's *Bartholomew Fair* refers to 'the space of two hours and an half, and somewhat more'. *Henry VIII* is among the longest of Shakespeare's history plays, and the elaborate ceremonials would in themselves take a considerable time.

14–16   *a merry, bawdy play ... guarded with yellow*. This refers probably to Rowley's *When You See Me You Know Me*, which contains two fools, Patch and Will Summers, attached respectively to Wolsey and Henry VIII. It includes a sword-and-buckler fight (compare *A noise of targets*, line 15) between Henry himself, in disguise, and Black Will, a thief, which ends in their both being seized by the watch. It is certainly (among other things) *merry*, and, in regard to Will Summers's witticisms, tolerably *bawdy*.

15   *targets* bucklers, shields

16   *a long motley coat guarded with yellow*. Professional fools wore long coats of 'motley', a greenish-yellow stuff, trimmed (*guarded*) with yellow strips.

17   *deceived* disappointed

19–21   *forfeiting | Our own brains, and the opinion that we bring | To make that only true we now intend* giving up any claim we have to intelligence and our reputation for presenting truthfully what we are to show

22   *an understanding friend*. This is probably a quibbling allusion to the groundlings who stood below the stage; compare Jonson, *Bartholomew Fair*, Induction, 49: 'the understanding gentlemen o'the ground there asked my judgement.' E. K. Chambers, in *The Elizabethan Stage*, Volume 2, page 527, note 6, gives several examples of this playhouse jest.

23   *for goodness' sake* out of your good nature (not the modern colloquial sense)

24   *The first and happiest hearers* the leading and best qualified audience

25   *sad* serious

25–30   *Think ye see ... mightiness meets misery*. The fact that this appeal to the audience sketchily resembles that in the Prologue of *Henry V* –

    Suppose within the girdle of these walls
    Are now confined two mighty monarchies ...

> Think, when we talk of horses, that you see them
> Printing their proud hoofs i'th'receiving earth –

has sometimes been offered as evidence that Shakespeare wrote this Prologue. It could more properly be offered as evidence to the contrary, the difference in vividness and dramatic quality being so striking.

25–6   *ye see* | . . . *story* (an example of 'laxity in versification', as Dr Johnson calls it, not infrequent in drama; compare Epilogue, 9–10).

I.1   Most of Shakespeare's history plays begin their action in the first scene without any prefatory material, and four of them (*King John*, *Richard II*, *1 Henry IV*, and *Richard III*) open with the titular character. The argument that the unifying and organizing centre of *Henry VIII* is Henry himself would be stronger were this the case here; instead, one's attention is first drawn to Wolsey. Nevertheless, the scene gives valuable information and suggests viewpoints and themes essential to the play.

   J. R. Sutherland, in 'The Language of the Last Plays' (*More Talking of Shakespeare*, edited by J. Garrett, 1959, page 154), suggests that the elliptical and tricky style shows Shakespeare 'putting forth a mighty effort in the opening scene' (as also in *Cymbeline*) and galvanizing himself into a high style – 'The old eagle is soaring with his mighty spread of wing, but he is toiling upwards where once he sailed along the wind'. Yet there is a vivacious energy in the strain of style that seems the outcome of nearly uncontrolled exuberance rather than of willed effort.

(stage direction) *one door* . . . *the other*. Stage directions often refer to the doors, on each side of the stage rear in Elizabethan theatres, for entrances and exits.

2   *saw* saw each other, met (compare *Cymbeline*, I.1.124, 'When shall we see again?')

4–5   *An untimely ague | Stayed me a prisoner.* Henry VIII of England and Francis I of France met on 7 June 1520, and meetings continued until 24 June. Their meeting-place was called the Field of the Cloth of Gold, so splendid was the panoply of the two monarchs and their followers. Buckingham was in fact present for at least part of the ceremonies: Holinshed (III.654) records that 'The Lord Cardinal in stately attire, accompanied with the Duke of Buckingham, and other great lords, conducted forward the French King, and in their way they encountered and met the King of England and his company right in the valley of Andren.' Norfolk, for his part, was in England. Presumably Shakespeare's reversal of this is meant to dissociate Buckingham from Wolsey's extravagant *vanities* as displayed at the Field of the Cloth of Gold.

6   *Those suns of glory.* The sun metaphor is common for royalty; compare lines 33 and 56. There may also be a quibble on 'sons'.

7   *Andren ... Guynes and Arde.* Guynes, held by the English, and Arde (modern Ardres), held by the French, lie each side of the valley of Andren in Picardy.

9   *lighted* alighted

10   *as* as if

11   *Which had they* had they done so
         weighed equalled

15–16   *Till this time pomp was single, but now married | To one above itself* pomp has reached a higher pitch in this conjoined splendour of the two Kings than each ever had singly

15   *single* (1) unmarried; (2) insignificant (compare *Macbeth*, I.6.16, 'poor and single business')

16–18   *Each following day ... Made former wonders its* each successive day taught its lesson (of glory) to the next one, till the last summed up all the wonders that had preceded it

19   *clinquant* glittering. Cotgrave's *Dictionary* (1611) defines the noun as 'Thin plate-lace of gold or silver'.

like heathen gods (perhaps a reminiscence of Psalm 115.4, 'their idols are silver and gold, even the work of men's hands')

21–2   *India . . . Showed like a mine.* The idea of India itself as a source of untold wealth was reinforced by the gold mines of the New World (South America and the West Indies); compare *1 Henry IV*, III.1.162–3, 'as bounti-ful | As mines of India', and Donne, 'The Sun Rising', line 17, 'both th'Indias of spice and mine'.

23   *madams* ladies of rank

24–5   *sweat to bear | The pride upon them.* The theme of overweening extravagance runs throughout this ac-count, leading to the attack upon Wolsey as exploiter and ruiner of the country. Pride is a fault not only socially ruinous but theologically fatal.

25   *that* so that

26   *Was to them as a painting* coloured them as if they were rouged

26–8   *Now this masque . . . a fool and beggar.* Holinshed has several accounts of brilliant masques presented by both French and English courts.

30–31   *him in eye | Still him in praise* the one seen was ever the one praised

33   *in censure* in judging which was the better. *Censure* bears no sense of condemnation here, as it does at III.1.64.

36   *that* so that

former fabulous story old stories hitherto thought fabulous

38   *Bevis* (a Saxon knight and medieval romance hero, said to have been made Earl of Southampton by William the Conqueror)

39–40   *As I belong to worship, and affect | In honour honesty* as I am a nobleman and honourably cherish truth

40– 42   *the tract of everything . . . Which action's self was tongue to* 'the course of these triumphs and pleasures, however well related, must lose in the description part of that spirit and energy which were expressed in the real action' (Dr Johnson)

42–7   *All was royal . . . as you guess?* F starts Buckingham's speech at 'All was Royall', and ends it at 'Of this great Sport together?' (line 47); it gives 'As you guesse:' (line 47) to Norfolk, as if Buckingham showed signs of guessing the answer. But it is unlikely that Buckingham would comment so decisively (*All was royal . . . full function*) on an event seen by Norfolk but not by himself, or that he would be credited with a guess he has not made. The alteration, first made by Theobald in the eighteenth century, has been adopted by most editors since then.

44–5   *Order gave each thing view; the office did | Distinctly his full function* the whole affair was so well ordered as to be easily seen; those in charge carried everything through clearly and properly

47   *sport* entertainment

48   *certes* certainly (here one syllable, though sometimes two, as in *The Tempest*, III.3.31, 'For certes, these are people of the island')

       promises no element seems no proper constituent

51   *Cardinal of York.* Wolsey was appointed Archbishop of York in 1514 and a Cardinal in 1515.

52   *The devil speed him!* may the devil (not God) look after him!

52–3   *No man's pie is freed | From his ambitious finger.* 'To have a finger in the pie' was proverbial; Tilley, F 228.

54   *fierce vanities* wild follies

55   *keech* animal fat rolled up into a lump for tallow-making. Wolsey was reputedly a butcher's son (compare line 120, *This butcher's cur*), though his father was

in fact a grazier and wool merchant. In *2 Henry IV*,
II.1.89, a butcher's wife is 'goodwife Keech' and in *1
Henry IV*, II.4.224, Prince Hal calls Falstaff 'greasy
tallow-catch', probably a variant of the same word.

56 *Take up the rays o'th'beneficial sun* absorb in himself all
the King's favour

58 *stuff* qualities

59–60 *whose grace | Chalks successors their way* whose virtue
marks out the way for those who follow

61 *high feats* great services

61–2 *allied | To eminent assistants* connected with ministers
of state

63 *self-drawing web* web spun from his own resources.
Since spiders were thought poisonous and sinister,
the analogy reflects damagingly upon Wolsey.

'a gives us note he lets us know. The F reading, 'O gives
us note', has been defended as an exclamation of
passion or as meaning that Wolsey is, by himself, a
mere cipher. But it is far more likely to be a misprint of
the colloquial ''a' meaning 'he'.

65 *A gift that heaven gives for him* his merits he considers as heaven-sent gifts bestowed on his behalf

70–72 *If not from hell ... A new hell in himself* if his pride
come not from hell, the devil must, unexpectedly, be
tight-fisted – or has already given away all the pride he
owned, and Wolsey now originates a new hell of his
own, as Lucifer's pride originated the first one.
(Throughout the play Wolsey's pride and ambition
are condemned on theological grounds; similarly,
Thomas Churchyard's poem on Wolsey in *A Mirror
for Magistrates* (1559) associates his pride with
Lucifer's: 'Your fault not half so great as was my
pride, | For which offence fell Lucifer from skies'.)

73 *going out* expedition

74 *privity* participation (in secret business)

75 *file* list

77–8 *To whom as great a charge as little honour | He meant to lay upon* on whom he meant to impose expenses as great as the honour intended to them is little

78–80   *his own letter . . . he papers.* This is a striking instance of Shakespeare's late, eccentric, style. The F reading – 'his owne Letter | The Honourable Boord of Councell, out | Must fetch him in, he Papers.' – verges on the incomprehensible, though A. P. Rossiter argued that it means 'The Cardinal's mere letter, that distinguished and impudent mockery of the whole Council whose rights it usurps, once sent out, had the power to call up and fetch in whomsoever he was pleased to put down on paper' (*The Times Literary Supplement*, 15 July 1949, page 459). But this more-than-telegraphese use of *out*, and the jolting antithesis of *out* and *in*, are syntactically too far-fetched even for late Shakespeare.

79   *The honourable board of Council out* 'without consent of the whole board of the Council' (Holinshed, III.644)

80   *Must fetch him in he papers* must involve whomever he puts on his list

84   *Have broke their backs with laying manors on 'em* have ruined themselves by pawning or selling their estates so as to dress extravagantly. The idea of breaking one's back financially, or bearing one's birthright on one's back, was proverbial; Tilley, B 16, L 452.

85   *vanity* futile extravagance

86–7   *minister communication of | A most poor issue* bring about the disclosure of a fruitless result. This clumsy phrase goes back to Holinshed (III.644): 'he knew not for what cause so much money should be spent . . . and communication to be ministered of things of no importance.'

88   *not values* is not worth

90   *the hideous storm.* The storm – a historical fact – figures appropriately also as a dramatic portent of conflict: Holinshed writes 'On Monday, the eighteenth of June, was such an hideous storm of wind and weather that

many conjectured it did prognosticate trouble and
hatred shortly after to follow between princes'
(III.654).

91	*not consulting* without pausing to consult others
93	*aboded* boded, foreboded
95	*flawed* cracked, broken
	attached seized by legal process. (The seizure of English goods at Bordeaux in fact took place in March 1523, but is here anticipated for dramatic effect.)
96	*therefore* for that reason
97	*Th'ambassador is silenced.* This detail is probably taken from Edward Hall, who writes 'The ambassador was commanded to keep his house in silence' (*The Union of the Two Noble Families of Lancaster and York* (1548), edited by Henry Ellis, 1809, page 634), rather than Holinshed, who has 'The ambassador . . . was commanded to keep his house' (III.676).
98	*A proper title of a peace* a fine thing to call a peace
99	*superfluous rate* excessive price
100	*Like it* may it please
101	*difference* quarrel
104	*read* reckon
105	*potency* power (to harm)
108	*A minister in his power* an agent to effect it
109–12	*I know his sword . . . Thither he darts it* (a variant on the proverb 'Kings have long arms'; Tilley, K 87)
111–12	*where 'twill not extend,*	*Thither he darts it* he makes it wound even though at a distance
114	(stage direction) *the purse* the bag containing the great seal (carried before the Lord Chancellor as an emblem of his office)
115	*surveyor* overseer of estates. Buckingham's surveyor was his cousin, Charles Knevet.
116	*examination* testimony
120	*butcher's cur.* See note on line 55. 'As surly as a butcher's cur' was a proverbial phrase; Tilley, B 764.
121–2	*best*	*Not wake him* (that is, let sleeping dogs lie)

122–3   *A beggar's book | Outworths a noble's blood* a beggar's learning has more power than a nobleman's high birth. 'This is a contemptuous exclamation very naturally put into the mouth of one of the ancient, unlettered, martial nobility' (Dr Johnson).

124   *temperance* self-control
   appliance only sole remedy

125   *in's* in his

127   *abject object* object of contempt

128   *bores* fools, cheats. The exact sense is uncertain; editors have suggested 'undermines', 'stabs', 'wounds', or, by connexion with the French *bourder*, 'mocks', 'cheats'. 'To bore the nose' or 'bore the nostrils' is found in the sense 'outwit' or 'lead by the nose', and *bore* may derive thence; compare the anonymous *Thomas Lord Cromwell* (reprinted in *The Shakespeare Apocrypha*, edited by C. F. Tucker Brooke, 1908), III.2.167, 'I am no earl but a smith, sir, one Hodge, a smith at Putney, sir; one that hath gulled you, that hath bored you, sir', and Beaumont and Fletcher, *The Spanish Curate*, IV.5.149–50, 'I am abused, betrayed! I am laughed at, scorned, | Baffled, and bored, it seems!'

131–45   *To climb steep hills ... wastes it.* Norfolk delivers a string of proverbial or gnomic phrases; for example, lines 131–2, 132–4, 140–41, 141–3, 143–5.

133   *full hot* high-spirited

134   *Self-mettle* his own ardour

137   *from a mouth of honour* with the voice of a nobleman

138   *Ipswich* (Wolsey's birthplace)

139   *There's difference in no persons* distinctions of rank count for nothing
   Be advised take heed

140–41   *Heat not a furnace ... singe yourself* (an allusion to Daniel 3.22, 'Therefore because the King's command was strait, and the furnace was exceeding hot, the

men that put in Sidrach, Misach, and Abednego, the
flame of the fire destroyed them')

144   *mounts the liquor* makes the liquid rise

147   *More stronger* (an instance of the double comparative or
superlative form common in Elizabethan English)

149   *allay* moderate

151   *top-proud* proud in the highest degree

152-3   *Whom from the flow of gall I name not, but | From
sincere motions* whom I speak of not from personal
rancour but from honest motives. By the medieval
doctrine of the 'humours', the gall-bladder was held
to produce 'choler', the origin of anger and bitterness.

153   *intelligence* information

154-5   *proofs as clear . . . gravel.* This resembles a passage in
one of the scenes attributed to Shakespeare in *The
Two Noble Kinsmen*, I.1.112-13, 'Like wrinkled
pebbles in a glassy stream | You may behold 'em'.

157   *vouch* assertion

161   *his mind and place* his intentions and high position

164   *suggests* prompts (in a bad sense)

167   *wrenching* (1) rinsing; (2) twisting. Compare likewise
Gerard Manley Hopkins's poem 'Spring': 'thrush |
Through the echoing timber does so rinse and wring |
The ear'.

169   *articles o'th'combination* terms of the treaty or league

172   *Count-Cardinal.* Pope's emendation to 'court-cardinal',
that is, Cardinal engrossed in court policy, may be
right ('r' being easily misread as 'n'). The F reading
indicates Wolsey's assumption of lordly rank – the
very grounds of Buckingham's hatred.

174-90   *Now this follows . . . the foresaid peace.* This is closely
derived from Holinshed's account of the connivance
between Wolsey and Charles V, who landed in
England in May 1520.

176-7   *Charles the Emperor . . . the Queen his aunt.* Katherine
of Aragon was sister of Joanna, mother of Charles,

Emperor of the Holy Roman Empire and King of Spain.

178   *colour* pretext

179   *whisper* speak secretly with

184-7   *as I trow ... the way was made.* The syntax is erratic, but the sense is clear.

184   *trow* believe

192   *buy and sell* traffic in (a proverbial phrase, often with implications of ignoble dealing; compare *Richard III*, V.3.306, 'Dickon thy master is bought and sold', and *Coriolanus*, III.2.9-10, 'woollen vassals, things created | To buy and sell with groats')

195   *mistaken* misrepresented

197   (stage direction) *Brandon.* The Duke of Suffolk's family name was Brandon, but there is no sign that Suffolk is intended here; the name may have occurred to Shakespeare haphazardly. The arrest was actually effected by Sir Henry Marney, captain of the King's guard, on 16 April 1521, as Holinshed relates (III.658). *Sergeant-at-Arms.* The monarch is attended by a body of sergeants-at-arms, of knightly rank, charged with his protection and the arrest of traitors.

200   *Hereford* (pronounced 'Herford'. F by a slip reads 'Hertford'.)

204   *device and practice* tricks and plots

204-6   *I am sorry ... The business present* 'I am sorry to see that you are taken prisoner, and to be an eye-witness of the event' (J. M. Berdan and C. T. Brooke, Yale edition, 1925)

207   *th'Tower* (of London, where traitors were, and are, imprisoned)

211   *Aberga'nny* Abergavenny (spelt 'Aburgany' in F, and so pronounced; 'Aburgauennie' in Holinshed)

216-21   *Here is a warrant ... Nicholas Hopkins.* 'There was also attached [arrested] the foresaid Chartreux monk [Nicholas Hopkins], master John de la Car *alias* de la Court, the Duke's confessor, and Sir Gilbert Perke,

priest, the Duke's chancellor. ... After the appre-
hension of the Duke, inquisitions were taken in diverse
shires of England of him; so that by the knights and
gentlemen he was indicted of high treason, for certain
words spoken ... by the same Duke at Blechingly, to
the Lord of Abergavenny; and therewith was the same
lord attached for concealment, and so likewise was the
Lord Montacute, and both led to the Tower' (Holinshed, III.658).

217   *Lord Montacute* (Henry Pole, Lord Montacute (1492–
1539), son-in-law of Abergavenny; he was pardoned on
this occasion but executed for treason in 1539)

219   *Gilbert Perk, his chancellor.* F has 'Gilbert Pecke, his
Councellour' for Holinshed's 'Sir Gilbert Perke, priest,
the Duke's chancellor', both changes being easy errors
of transcription or misreading. 'Perke' is probably a
mistake for 'clerk'; contemporary records refer to
'Robert Gilbert, clerk' as Buckingham's chancellor
(*Calendar of State Papers, Henry VIII*, Part I, 490–95).
Shortly after, Holinshed refers correctly to 'Robert
Gilbert, his chancellor' (III.660).

221   *Chartreux* Carthusian order (introduced into England
late in the twelfth century)
    Nicholas Hopkins. F has 'Michaell Hopkins' for
Holinshed's 'Nicholas Hopkins'; perhaps 'Nicholas'
was indicated by 'Nich.', misread 'Mich.'.

223–4   *My life is spanned ... I am the shadow* 'my time is
measured, the length of my life is now determined'
(Dr Johnson). This echoes Psalm 39.6–7 (Prayer Book
version): 'Behold, Thou hast made my days as it
were a span long. ... For man walketh in a vain
shadow.'

224–6   *I am the shadow ... darkening my clear sun* I am
reduced to the mere semblance of my substantial self,
whose form this sudden cloud of misfortune has taken,
eclipsing the sun of my life (my own glory, or the
King's favour). (It is impossible to get all the elements

of this complicated though expressive figure into focus at once, but the general sense is clear.)

226   *My lord.* F reads 'My Lords', but Norfolk is the only person of whom Buckingham can take farewell, since Abergavenny accompanies him off, with Brandon.

I.2   (stage direction) *under the King's feet* at the King's feet (the King's seat or 'state' being raised up)

1   *best heart* very essence

2   *level* aim, line of fire

3   *full-charged* fully loaded

4   *choked* suppressed. The word could be used for blotting out a battery of cannon, and so carries on the artillery metaphor of lines 2–3; compare Beaumont and Fletcher, *The Mad Lover*, I.1.96–7, 'If he mount at me, | I may chance choke his battery.'

5   *That gentleman of Buckingham's* (the surveyor referred to at I.1.222–3)

8   (stage direction) *state* canopied throne, chair of state

12   *moiety* half

13   *Repeat your will, and take it* say what you desire and it is yours (no sense of repetition is involved)

20–29   *There have been commissions ... In loud rebellion.* 'By the Cardinal there was devised strange commissions, and sent in the end of March into every shire ... that the sixth part of every man's substance should be paid in money or plate to the King without delay. ... Hereof followed such cursing, weeping, and exclamation against both King and Cardinal that pity it was to hear' (Holinshed, III.708–9). The date of these events was 1525, but they are predated here so that Katherine can plead for the oppressed and for Buckingham, and stand out at once as an opponent of Wolsey. This is a foretaste of Shakespeare's sympathetic development of Katherine, far beyond the indications Holinshed gave him.

20–21   *commissions . . . which hath flawed.* The use of a singular verb with a plural subject, and vice versa, is common in Elizabethan English.

24   *putter-on* instigator

27–8   *breaks | The sides of loyalty* is more than loyalty can bear. Shakespeare often presents a violent inner anguish as bursting through the body; compare *King Lear*, II.4.196–7, 'O sides, you are too tough! | Will you yet hold?', and *Antony and Cleopatra*, I.3.16–17, 'the sides of nature | Will not sustain it'.

31–7   *The clothiers all . . . serves among them.* 'The Duke of Suffolk, sitting in commission about this subsidy in Suffolk, persuaded by courteous means the rich clothiers to assent thereto: but when they came home, and went about to discharge and put from them their spinners, carders, fullers, weavers, and other artificers, which they kept in work aforetime, the people began to assemble in companies. . . . The Duke . . . commanded the constables that every man's harness should be taken from him. . . . Then the rage of the people increased, railing openly on the Duke and Sir Robert Drury, and threatening them with death, and the Cardinal also. And herewith there assembled together after the manner of rebels four thousand men . . . which put themselves in harness, and rang the bells' alarm, and began still to assemble in great number' (Holinshed, III.709).

32   *'longing* belonging

33   *spinsters, carders, fullers* spinners, combers (those who remove impurities from wool by combing it), cleansers (those who beat wool to clean or thicken it)

37   *danger serves among them* danger is welcomed as a comrade in arms. The personification may have been derived from the answer made by the rebels to the Duke of Norfolk: 'Poverty was their captain, the which with his cousin Necessity had brought them to that doing' (Holinshed, III.709).

41-2   *I know but of a single part in aught | Pertains to th'state*
I know only an individual's share in state matters

42-3   *and front but in that file | Where others tell steps with me*
and merely march in the front rank with others who
step in pace with me (that is, all the Council are
jointly responsible)

44-7   *you frame | Things that are known alike ... their
acquaintance* all members of the Council equally know
what measures are taken, but it is you who frame these
measures, which, however harmful, are then imposed
on those who would wish to evade them but cannot

50   *The back is sacrifice to th'load* the back must suffer
under its burden

52   *exclamation* protest

56   *subject's.* F's 'Subiects' might be singular or plural:
it is taken here, after *The*, as a generic singular.
grief grievance

57   *commissions, which compels.* See the note on lines 20–21.

59   *pretence* pretext

62   *Allegiance* (four syllables)

64-5   *This tractable obedience is a slave | To each incensèd will*
their willingness to be obedient is mastered by their
anger

67   *primer* more urgent
business. F reads 'basenesse', which some editors
retain: 'no primer baseness' would mean 'no more
pressing example of wickedness', but the expression
would be awkward. The Queen's point seems to
be the urgent need of attending to this matter of
concern.

70   *A single voice* my individual vote

71   *approbation of the judges.* Wolsey claims that he supported only measures whose legality the judges had
justified. 'The Cardinal excused himself and said that
when it was moved in Council how to levy money to the
King's use, the King's Council, and namely the judges,
said that he might lawfully demand any sum by com-

mission, and that by consent of the whole Council it was done' (Holinshed, III.710).

73   *faculties* qualities

73–4   *will be | The chronicles of my doing* presume to expound all that I do

75   *place* high office

78   *cope* encounter (compare *As You Like It*, II.1.67, 'I love to cope him in these sullen fits')

80   *new-trimmed* newly fitted out (as a seaworthy vessel is immune from sharks, so honest men are immune from slanderers who try to harm them)

82   *sick interpreters, once weak ones* unsound, distorted, commentators, in a word, weak-witted ones. For this sense of *once*, compare *Much Ado About Nothing*, I.1.297, 'Look what will serve is fit. 'Tis once, thou lovest'; *Coriolanus*, II.3.1–2, 'Once, if he do require our voices, we ought not to deny him.'

83   *Not ours, or not allowed* not acknowledged as our act, or not approved

83–4   *as oft | Hitting a grosser quality* appealing just as often to cruder minds

86   *our motion* whatever move we make

88   *state-statues* effigies of statesmen

90   *example* precedent
        issue outcome

93–4   *We must not rend our subjects from our laws, | And stick them in our will* we must not rend our subjects away from the rule of law and fix them under our arbitrary wills

95   *trembling* fearful

95–8   *we take ... drink the sap* if we do this it is like lopping off branches, bark, and part of the main timber; even though the root is left, the life-blood (*sap*) of a tree so hacked will dry up

96   *lop* small branches, loppings

99   *questioned* disputed

104–7   *The grievèd commons ... pardon comes.* 'The Cardinal,

195

to deliver himself of the evil will of the commons, purchased by procuring and advancing of this demand, affirmed, and caused it to be bruited abroad, that through his intercession the King had pardoned ·and released all things' (Holinshed, III.710).

105   *Hardly conceive* think harshly
          noised reported

106   *our* (Wolsey uses the royal plural)

110   *Is run in* has incurred

110–28   *It grieves many . . . hear too much.* Closely though much of this scene follows Holinshed, the King's impressive eulogy does not derive from the source, where Wolsey alone examines Buckingham's surveyor. Shakespeare probably wishes to strengthen the King's dramatic role at this point, in keeping with the power of command Henry has just shown in reproving Wolsey. In each successive crisis the King displays more initiative. Here he follows up and completes the action Wolsey initiated against Buckingham. In the trial of Queen Katherine he exonerates Wolsey from the charge of being the chief mover, and attributes the action to his own scruples of conscience and concern for his realm. In the fall of Wolsey he reveals his independence of his great chancellor. And in favouring Cranmer he acts as the unquestioned and unrivalled ruler.

111   *learned* (one syllable, as also at line 142, and II.4.206 and 238; elsewhere two syllables)

112   *bound* indebted

114   *out of himself* beyond his own powers

116   *disposed* applied

118   *complete* (accented on the first syllable)

120   *with ravished listening* ravished with listening. The word order is eccentric or erroneous.

122   *monstrous habits* hideous garments

130   *Most like a careful subject.* Wolsey's Machiavellianism is evident, since far from being a *careful subject* the surveyor is his own bribed ally.

130–31   *collected | Out of* gathered from

139   *This dangerous conception in this point* 'this particular part of this dangerous design' (Dr Johnson)

140   *Not friended by his wish* not successful in his wish (that you should die without issue)

142   *learned* (one syllable; see note on line 111)

145   *fail* (1) death; but also probably (2) failure to beget an heir (see lines 133–4 and 168–9, and II.4.198, *By this my issue's fail*)

147   *Nicholas Henton* (the *Nicholas Hopkins* of I.1.221, the confusion arising from Holinshed's sentence 'Nicholas Hopkins, a monk of an house of the Chartreux order beside Bristow, called Henton, sometime his confessor')

150   *of sovereignty* about the gaining of the crown

151   *sped to* made your expedition to

152–71   *The Duke being at the Rose ... Shall govern England.* 'The same Duke, the tenth of May [1520], in the twelfth year of the King's reign, at London in a place called the Rose, within the parish of Saint Lawrence Poultney, ... demanded of the said Charles Knevet esquire what was the talk amongst the Londoners concerning the King's journey beyond the seas? And the said Charles told him that many stood in doubt of that journey, lest the Frenchmen meant some deceit towards the King. Whereto the Duke answered that it was to be feared lest it would come to pass according to the words of a certain holy monk. "For there is," saith he, "a Chartreux monk, that diverse times hath sent to me, willing me to send unto him my chancellor; and I did send unto him John de la Court, my chaplain, unto whom he would not declare anything till de la Court had sworn unto him to keep all things secret, and to tell no creature living what he should hear of him, except it were to me. And then the said monk told de la Court that neither the King nor his heirs should prosper, and that I should endeavour myself to purchase the good wills of the commonalty of England; for I the same Duke and my blood should prosper, and have the rule of the realm of England"' (Holinshed, III.660–61).

152 *the Rose* (a manor of Buckingham's, converted in 1561 into the Merchant Taylors' School)

157 *Presently* at once

158 *doubted* feared

164 *confession's.* F has 'Commissions', but the relevant passage in Holinshed reads 'he had done very well to bind his chaplain John de la Court under the seal of confession to keep secret such matter' (III.659).

167 *with demure confidence* in solemn trust

170 *To win the love o'th'commonalty.* The first Folio reads 'To the loue o'th'Commonalty'. The unauthoritative fourth Folio inserted 'gain' between 'To' and 'the loue'. The present emendation is based on Holinshed, who in the relevant passages has 'to win the favour of the people' (III.658), 'to win their favour and friendships' (III.659), and 'to purchase the good wills of the commonalty' (III.661); these may have coalesced and produced *To win the love o'th'commonalty.*

172–3 *lost your office | On the complaint o'th'tenants.* 'Now it chanced that the Duke ... went before into Kent unto a manor place which he had there. And whilst he stayed in that country ... grievous complaints were exhibited to him by his farmers and tenants against Charles Knevet his surveyor, for such bribing as he had used there amongst them. Whereupon the Duke took such displeasure against him that he deprived him of his office, not knowing how that in so doing he procured his own destruction, as after appeared' (Holinshed, III.645).

174 *spleen* malice (the spleen being supposedly the source of strong passions)

175 *spoil your nobler soul* blot your soul, which is of greater value than any human rank

178–86 *I told my lord ... Should have gone off.* 'Then said
Charles Knevet, "The monk may be deceived through
the devil's illusion", and that it was evil to meddle
with such matters. "Well," said the Duke, "it cannot
hurt me", and so (saith the indictment) the Duke
seemed to rejoice in the monk's words. And further, at
the same time, the Duke told the said Charles that if
the King had miscarried now in his last sickness, he
would have chopped off the heads of the Cardinal,
of Sir Thomas Lovell, knight, and of others' (Holinshed, III.661).

180 *For him to ruminate on this.* F reads 'For this to ruminate on this'. Shakespeare does not elsewhere use the
phrase 'to ruminate on', and the intended reading
may be 'For him to ruminate this'.

181 *forged him* caused him to fashion

186 *Ha!* This exclamation, frequent in Henry's mouth,
may derive from Rowley's *When You See Me You
Know Me*, where the King so repeatedly uses it that
it is recognized almost as his slogan; for example:

> KING Am I not Harry, am I not England's king, ha?
> WILL SUMMERS So la, now, the watchword's given,
> nay, and he once cry 'Ha!', ne'er a man in the court
> dare for his head speak again.   (lines 657–60)

This trait, together with a threatening countenance,
seems to have been part of the received portrait of
Henry. Foxe's *Acts and Monuments* (page 1025) reports
that when Henry examined the martyr John Lambert
he turned to him 'with his brows bent, as it were
threatening some grievous thing unto him, [and] said
these words, "Ho, good fellow, what is thy name?"'
See also the Roman Catholic life of Saint John
Fisher (Harleian MSS. 6382, edited by R. Bayne,
1921, page 62), '"No, ah!" quoth the King, and
therewith looking upon my lord of Rochester with a
frowning countenance'.

so rank (1) so gross, corrupt; (2) grown so high (with reference to Buckingham's plotting)

188–209   *Being at Greenwich . . . an irresolute purpose.* 'The same Duke on the fourth of November [1519], in the eleventh year of the King's reign, at east Greenwich in the county of Kent, said unto one Charles Knevet esquire, after that the King had reproved the Duke for retaining William Bulmer, knight, into his service, that if he had perceived that he should have been committed to the Tower (as he doubted he should have been) he would so have wrought that the principal doers therein should not have had cause of great rejoicing; for he would have played the part which his father intended to have put in practice against King Richard the Third at Salisbury, who made earnest suit to have come unto the presence of the said King Richard; which suit if he might have obtained, he, having a knife secretly about him, would have thrust it into the body of King Richard, as he had made semblance to kneel down before him. And, in speaking these words, he maliciously laid his hand upon his dagger; and said that if he were so evil used he would do his best to accomplish his pretended purpose, swearing to confirm his word by the blood of our Lord' (Holinshed, III.660).

190–91   *remember | Of* have memory of (a usage not found elsewhere in Shakespeare)

191   *sworn* (two syllables)

195   *my father.* Henry Stafford, Duke of Buckingham, figures in *Richard III*, first as Richard's ally, then as his foe, captured and executed.

198   *semblance of his duty* a show of dutifully kneeling

199   *A giant traitor!* Maxwell (in the New Cambridge edition, 1962) suggests that this phrase, and *Hamlet*, IV.5.118, 'That thy rebellion looks so giant-like', may glance at the Titans' rebellion against the gods in Greek mythology.

201   *And this man out of prison* while this man is at liberty

204   *stretched him* raised himself to his full height
209   *irresolute* unaccomplished
       his period the end he aims at
210   *attached* arrested

I.3.2 *strange mysteries* outlandish freaks
    6 *the late voyage.* Elizabethan dramatists often satirize
       gallants who affect foreign fashions: for example,
       Chapman, *Bussy D'Ambois* (1607), I.2.42-50:

       Never were men so weary of their skins,
       And apt to leap out of themselves as they;
       Who, when they travel to bring forth rare men,
       Come home, delivered of a fine French suit.
       Their brains lie with their tailors.
               . . . he's sole heir
       To all the moral virtues that first greets
       The light with a new fashion, which becomes them
       Like apes, disfigured with the attires of men.

       Holinshed's account (III.635) of foolish antics on a
       mission in February 1520, some months before the
       Field of the Cloth of Gold, has been adapted here to
       make them a consequence of that extravagant episode:
       'During this time remained in the French court diverse
       young gentlemen of England, and they with the
       French King rode daily disguised through Paris,
       throwing eggs, stones, and other foolish trifles at the
       people. . . . And when these young gentlemen came
       again into England, they were all French in eating,
       drinking, and apparel, yea, and in French vices and
       brags, so that all the estates in England were by them
       laughed at, the ladies and gentlewomen were dis-
       praised, but if it were after the French turn'.
    7 *A fit or two o'th'face* a grimace or two
       shrewd acute
   10 *Pepin or Clotharius* (early Frankish kings, of the eighth

and sixth centuries respectively; the implication is of
French affectations, but grotesque and barbarous ones)
keep state affect (an awkward) grandeur

11 *new legs* new ways of walking and bowing

12 *see.* Pope altered to 'saw' and most editors follow, but
see was not infrequent as a past tense, and still can
be so in dialect or popular idiom.

spavin (disease of horses, making the hock swell and
causing lameness)

13 *Or.* F reads 'A', which most editors change to 'Or'
or 'And'.

springhalt (nervous twitching of the hind-legs in horses;
from 'stringhalt', 'an unnatural binding of the
sinews' as Gervase Markham's *Cheap and Good
Husbandry* (1614), F3ʳ, describes it)

Death by God's death (an oath)

14 *to't* as well

15 *worn out Christendom* exhausted every Christian fashion

17 *the new proclamation.* After describing the travellers'
follies (see note on line 6), Holinshed writes (III.640),
'The King's Council caused the Lord Chamberlain
to call before them diverse of the privy chamber,
which had been in the French court, and banished
them the court for diverse considerations. . . . Which
discharge out of court grieved sore the hearts of these
young men'.

18 *court gate.* In Ralph Agas's map of London (*c.* 1560),
one of the gates of Whitehall is so named, probably
the one designed by Holbein facing Charing Cross to
the south of the banqueting house.

23 *the Louvre* (the seat of the French court)

25 *fool and feather* folly and foppery (apparently a set
phrase for fashionable gallants: extravagant plumes
worn in headgear were often satirized)

26 *honourable points of ignorance* points of empty-headed
etiquette

27 *as* such as

fireworks (as well as the usual sense there is probably a quibble on whores, the source of venereal disease, so often referred to in terms of burning etc.)

28–9   *Abusing better men than they can be | Out of a foreign wisdom* mocking better men than themselves, through the 'wisdom' they have gained abroad. (The sense continues from *points of ignorance*.)

29–31   *renouncing clean ... types of travel.* The grammatical construction goes back to *leave those remnants | Of fool and feather.*

30   *tennis* (a French game, known in England from the thirteenth century; it was popular with Henry VIII, who built the tennis court at Hampton Court, and with the courtiers of James I)

30–31   *tall stockings, | Short blistered breeches.* Long stockings, coming high up the thigh, went with the fashion of short puffed breeches, slashed like blisters to show the satin lining. In *A Tale of a Tub* (*Works*, edited by Herford and Simpson, Volume 3) Jonson satirizes 'long sausage hose' (I.4.11) and 'pinned-up breeches, like pudding bags' (II.2.125).

31   *types* marks, signs

32   *understand* (1) use their minds; (2) use their legs (compare *Twelfth Night*, III.1.77–8, 'My legs do better understand me, sir, than I understand what you mean')

34   *cum privilegio* by special licence (the phrase applied to the privilege granted for the publishing of books)
      'oui' talk French. The first Folio reads 'wee'; the second Folio alters to 'wear', and some editors follow.

35   *lag end* latter end

38   *trim vanities* spruce fops
      marry by the Virgin Mary (an oath)

40   *speeding* successful

41   *fiddle.* Here, and in some other cases, there may be an equivoque; compare Heywood, *The Fair Maid of the Exchange* (*Dramatic Works*, edited by R. H. Shepherd,

1874, II.21), 'Ne'er a wench in all the town but will
scorn to dance after my fiddle'; and Fletcher, *The
Honest Man's Fortune*, V.1.37-9:

LAMIRA You two will make a pretty handsome con-
sort.
MONTAGUE Yes, madam, if my fiddle fail me not.
LAMIRA Your fiddle? Why your fiddle? I warrant
thou meanest madly.

44-5   *beaten ... out of play* outdone in (amorous) play
(compare *The Winter's Tale*, I.2.187-8, 'thy mother
plays, and I | Play too')

45   *plainsong* simple melody, without frills

47   *Held current music* be accepted as good music

48   *colt's tooth* youthful wildness (especially in older men;
compare the proverb 'He has a colt's tooth in his head';
Tilley, C 525)

49   *stump* (ostensibly 'stump of a tooth', but with a bawdy
double meaning)

58   *He had a black mouth* he would have a wicked tongue

59   *has wherewithal* he has what he needs to be liberal

61   *Men of his way should be most liberal* (probably echoing
1 Timothy 3.2, 'A bishop ... must be ... a lover of
hospitality')

63   *stays* is waiting

67   *comptrollers* stewards, or masters of ceremonies
(comptrollers were the officers regulating expenditure
in great households; the old spelling still survives)

I.4   (stage direction) *Hautboys* oboes
state canopy (with a 'chair of state' below it)

7   (stage direction) *Lord Chamberlain, Lord Sands*. At the
actual time of Wolsey's entertainment (3 January
1527) the Lord Chamberlain was Lord Sands himself,
who succeeded in 1526. But at the time assumed in

the play, before Buckingham's trial in 1521, the Lord
Chamberlain was the Earl of Worcester.

11   *lay* unclerical

12   *running banquet* quick refreshment, appetizer (implying
'amorous pursuit followed by a feast of love-making':
Eric Partridge, *Shakespeare's Bawdy*). Another sense,
at V.4.64, is a whipping at the cart's tail.

20   *Place you* arrange the guests

30   *kiss you twenty* kiss twenty ladies (or, perhaps, kiss
twenty times over). The *you* is virtually superfluous;
this usage, the 'ethic dative', is frequent in Elizabethan
English for a person addressed but only 'indirectly
interested in the fact stated' (*Concise Oxford Dictionary*).

    with a breath in the space of a breath

    Well said that's right (spoken of something said or done,
in this case probably the seating of the guests)

33   *cure* (1) charge, group of parishioners (joking on the
phrase 'cure of souls'; compare the mocking ecclesiastical reference at line 32); (2) remedy (for preventing
the ladies' frowns)

41   *beholding* indebted

43–4   *The red wine first must rise | In their fair cheeks.* The
flushing of the skin with drinking was thought to
result from extra blood into which wine was supposed
quickly to transmute itself; compare Marlowe,
Tamburlaine, Part 2, III.2.107–8, 'airy wine, | That,
being concocted, turns to crimson blood' (cited by
Foakes).

46   *make my play* win what I play for (with an equivoque
on 'amorous play'; compare I.3.45)

49   (stage direction) *Chambers* small cannon (for salutes, or
theatre use. The firing at this point set the Globe
Theatre on fire on 29 June 1613.)

50   *Look out there.* Cavendish in his *Life of Wolsey* writes
that by Wolsey's order the Lord Chamberlain and Sir
Henry Guilford 'were sent to look': Holinshed,

following Stow, writes that they 'sent to look'. It is evidently Holinshed who is followed here.

53–86   *A noble troop . . . Ye have found him, Cardinal.* This whole episode follows very closely Holinshed's long account of the masque, save for two points: Anne Bullen was not present, and Wolsey failed to identify the King, selecting instead Sir Edward Neville.

53   *strangers* foreigners

55   *make* are coming

75   *The fairest hand I ever touched!* There is no reference in any of the chronicles to so early a meeting between Henry and Anne as the dramatic date of this scene (1521), though there is some evidence that they met the next year. According to Holinshed (III.740), Wolsey learnt of the King's attachment only in 1529, long after Buckingham's fall in 1521, and at the time of the trial of Queen Katherine. The quite unhistorical introduction of Anne to the banquet looks like dramatic confusion, since Henry is bound to appear deceitful when he later insists that only conscientious scruples separate him from Katherine.

84   *take it* (that is, take his place under the 'state')

89   *unhappily* unfavourably

90   *pleasant* merry

92   *An't* if it

93   *Rochford.* Sir Thomas Bullen became Viscount Rochford in June 1525, later than the dramatic date of this scene (1521) but earlier than its historical date (1527).

95   *take you out* dance with you

96   *to kiss you* (as was customary after a dance, the lady replying with a curtsy; compare *The Tempest*, I.2.377, 'Curtsied when you have and kissed')

106   *a measure* a stately dance

108   *best in favour* best-looking

         knock it strike up

II.1	(stage direction) *several* different
2	*the Hall* (Westminster Hall, the great hall of the royal palace of Westminster, founded by William Rufus and reconstructed by Richard II to be the banqueting hall of the palace; it was the scene of many great state trials – those of Sir Thomas More and Anne Bullen, as well as Buckingham, and later of Charles I, Strafford, and Warren Hastings)
11	*in a little* in brief
11–36	*The great Duke ... a most noble patience.* 'The Duke was brought to the bar, and, upon his arraignment, pleaded not guilty, and put himself upon his peers. Then was his indictment read, which the Duke denied to be true, and (as he was an eloquent man) alleged reasons to falsify the indictment, pleading the matter for his own justification very pithily and earnestly. The King's attorney against the Duke's reasons alleged the examinations, confessions, and proofs of witnesses.

'The Duke desired that the witnesses might be brought forth. And then came before him Charles Knevet, Perk, de la Court, and Hopkins the monk of the priory of the Charterhouse beside Bath, which like a false hypocrite had induced the Duke to the treason with his false forged prophecies. Diverse presumptions and accusations were laid unto him by Charles Knevet, which he would fain have covered. . . . Thus was this prince Duke of Buckingham found guilty of high treason, by a duke, a marquis, seven earls, and twelve barons. The Duke was brought to the bar sore chafed, and sweat marvellously; and after he had made his reverence he paused a while. The Duke of Norfolk as judge said, "Sir Edward, you have heard how you be indicted of high treason . . ." The Duke of Buckingham said, "My lord of Norfolk, you have said as a traitor should be said unto, but I was never any; but, my lords, I nothing malign for that you have done to

me, but the eternal God forgive you my death, and I
do; I shall never sue to the King for life, howbeit he is
a gracious prince, and more grace may come from him
than I desire. I desire you, my lords, and all my
fellows, to pray for me' (Holinshed, III.661–2).

13   *allegèd* brought forward

14   *defeat the law* refute the case brought against him

16   *proofs* testimonies

20   *Sir* (a frequent courtesy title for a priest)

29   *Was either pitied in him or forgotten* produced merely
   pity for him or had no lasting effect at all

40   *the end of this* at the bottom of this

41–9   *Kildare's attainder ... from court too.* In order to
prosecute his schemes against Buckingham, Wolsey
had to remove the Earl of Surrey, Buckingham's son-
in-law, to a distance. He did so in 1520 by bringing
charges against Kildare, Lord Deputy of Ireland, and
having Surrey appointed in his place (Holinshed,
III.645).

44   *father* father-in-law

45   *envious* malicious

50   *perniciously* with deadly loathing

53   *The mirror of all courtesy.* 'He is termed in the books
of the law in the said thirteenth year of Henry the
Eighth (where his arraignment is liberally set down)
to be the flower and mirror of all courtesy' (Holinshed, III.671).

54   (stage direction) *tipstaves* officers of the law (charged
with taking prisoners into custody; their staves were
metal-tipped)
   the axe with the edge towards him (a sign of execution)
   halberds (long-shafted weapons topped by a spearpoint
and a blade at right angles)
   Sir Walter Sands (an error for Holinshed's Sir William
Sands, the Lord Sands of I.3–4, by the date of which –
1527 – he had been ennobled)

55   *close* (1) out of sight; (2) silent

57   *lose* forget

60   *sink me* (that is, to hell)

63   *'T has done ... but justice.* 'Buckingham is made to
        appear sufficiently the innocent victim for Wolsey to
        appear his cruel tormentor, while he is made to
        appear sufficiently guilty to keep the audience from
        blaming the King, or even from regarding him as
        merely Wolsey's dupe' (Paul Bertram, in *In Defense of
        Reading*, edited by R. A. Brower and R. Poirier, 1962,
        page 161).
        premises evidence

67   *build their evils on the graves* forward their crimes by
        destroying the lives. There may be an ambiguity in
        evils, possibly for a building of gross use (jakes?
        brothel?); *Measure for Measure*, II.2.171–2, has a
        similar implication of unholy ignominy: 'Shall we
        desire to raze the sanctuary | And pitch our evils there?'

74   *only bitter to him, only dying* the only bitter thing, the
        only real sense of death

77   *Make of your prayers one sweet sacrifice* (an apparent
        echo of Psalm 141.2: 'Let my prayer be directed before
        thy face as an incense; let the lifting up of mine hands
        be an evening sacrifice')
        sacrifice holy offering

78   *a* in

80–81   *If ever any malice ... forgive me frankly.* See I.2.185–6
        for an assertion that Buckingham had threatened
        Lovell's death.

82–3   *I as free forgive you | As I would be forgiven.* This
        echoes the Lord's Prayer: 'Forgive us our trespasses as
        we forgive them that trespass against us'. The falls of
        Buckingham, Katherine, and Wolsey alike prompt
        speeches of Christian resignation and forgiveness;
        compare III.1.175–81, III.2.440–49, and IV.2 *passim*.

85   *take* make
        envy ill-will

88–90   *My vows and prayers ... blessings on him.* There are

209

similar prayers for the King's safety in *Henry V*, II.2, from the nobles condemned for plotting his death.

89   *forsake* leave (my body)

91   *tell* count

94   *monument* tomb (with the sense, doubtless, of a memorial to future times)

97   *undertakes* takes charge of

97–103   *Prepare there . . . Edward Bohun.* 'Then was the edge of the axe turned towards him, and he led into a barge. Sir Thomas Lovell desired him to sit on the cushions and carpet ordained for him. He said "Nay, for when I went to Westminster I was Duke of Buckingham; now I am but Edward Bohun, the most caitiff of the world." Thus they landed at the Temple, where received him Sir Nicholas Vaux and Sir William Sands, baronets, and led him through the city, who desired ever the people to pray for him' (Holinshed, III.662).

99   *furniture* furnishings

103   *Bohun.* His family name was Stafford, but he descended in the female line from the Bohuns, Earls of Hereford, and held the office of Lord High Constable, which was hereditary in that family.

105–6   *I now seal it,* | *And with that blood will make 'em one day groan for't* 'I now seal my truth and loyalty with blood, which blood shall one day make them groan' (Dr Johnson)

107–14   *My noble father . . . Restored me to my honours.* 'Henry Stafford . . . was son to Humphrey, Earl Stafford, and was High Constable of England and Duke of Buckingham. This man, raising war against Richard the Third usurping the crown, was in the first year of the reign of the said Richard . . . betrayed by his man Humphrey Banister (to whom being in distress he fled for succour) and brought to Richard the Third . . . where the said Duke . . . was beheaded without arraignment or judgement. . . . Edward Stafford, son to Henry, Duke of Buckingham . . . was by Henry the Seventh restored to his father's inheritance' (Holinshed, III.671).

108   *raised head* raised an armed force

124   *end* purpose

125   *This from a dying man receive as certain.* The last words of the dying were proverbially held to be truthful; compare Tilley, M 514, 'Dying men speak true (prophesy)'; *Richard II*, II.1.5–6, 'the tongues of dying men | Enforce attention like deep harmony'; and *Cymbeline*, V.5.41–2, 'And but she spoke it dying, I would not | Believe her lips in opening it.'

127   *loose* careless

129   *rub* check

129–30   *fall away | Like water* (an apparent echo of Psalm 58.6, 'Let them fall away like water that runneth apace')

133   *my long weary life.* Buckingham was in fact only forty-three.

140–53   *I can give you inkling . . . That durst disperse it.* 'This is the first direct hint at the main action of the play. It is exceptional for it to be given so late as the second Act' (D. Nichol Smith, in the Warwick edition, 1899). 'There rose a secret bruit in London that the King's confessor Doctor Longland and diverse other great clerks had told the King that the marriage between him and the lady Katherine, late wife to his brother Prince Arthur, was not lawful; whereupon the King should sue a divorce and marry the Duchess of Alençon, sister to the French King. . . . The King was offended with those tales, and sent for Sir Thomas Seymour, Mayor of the city of London, secretly charging him to see that the people ceased from such talk' (Holinshed, III.719–20).

143   *faith* trustworthiness

146   *confident* (that is, of your discretion)

147   *You shall* (that is, you shall have it)

       of late days. Time is much abridged; the events of

1527–8 are made to follow immediately upon those of 1521. Campeius, reported *lately* arrived (line 160), landed in 1528.

153–4   *that slander, sir,* | *Is found a truth.* 'It may be a slander but it is no lie' was proverbial; Tilley, S 520.

156–7   *Either the Cardinal* | *Or some about him.* The first man Holinshed mentions as instigating the King's scruples is Doctor Longland, his confessor (see note on lines 140–53). Later, Holinshed is uncertain whether Longland or Wolsey was the initiator (III.736) but attributes to Wolsey rather than to others the idea that the King should marry the Duchess of Alençon so as to strengthen the French alliance (see III.2.85–6). Divorcing Katherine would conduce to this end and also shame Charles V, who (Holinshed reports, though there seems no truth in the allegation) had refused Wolsey the archbishopric of Toledo; see lines 162–4 and Holinshed, III.736. Actually, the Duchess married Henry of Navarre early in 1527, before any such scheme, if it ever existed, could have been promoted.

160   *Cardinal Campeius.* Lorenzo Campeggio (Campeius) reached London in October 1528.

168   *open* public

II.2.1–8   *My lord . . . our mouths, sir.* The germ of this letter may lie in Rowley's *When You See Me You Know Me*, lines 1268–9, where a citizen complains that one of Wolsey's emissaries 'hath taken up | Commodities valued at a thousand pound' for Wolsey's advantage.

2   *ridden* broken in for riding

6   *main power* sheer force

14   *sad* grave

16–17   *No, his conscience . . . another lady.* See Introduction, page 19.

17   *'Tis so* (replying to the Lord Chamberlain, Suffolk's comment being spoken to himself)

19   *blind* (1) blind to the general opinion, or general
welfare; (2) blindfold, like Fortune, arbitrarily controlling men's fates; compare *Henry V*, III.6.29–34,
'Fortune is painted blind, with a muffler afore her
eyes . . . and . . . with a wheel, to signify . . . that she is
turning, and inconstant, and mutability, and variation'.
eldest son privileged offspring

30–31   *like a jewel . . . About his neck*. Precious stones were
often worn as pendants around the neck. In *Twelfth
Night*, II.5.59–60, Malvolio will 'wind up my watch,
or play with my – some rich jewel'.

35   *Will bless the King* (as in fact she does, at IV.2.163–4)

37   *These news are*. 'News' was commonly, and ought to
be, plural.

40   *The French King's sister* (as at III.2.85–6)

42   *This bold bad man* (probably an accepted phrase; it is
found in Spenser, *The Faerie Queene*, I.1.37, Fletcher,
The Loyal Subject, IV.5.91, and Massinger, *A New
Way to Pay Old Debts*, IV.1.160)

46   *From princes into pages*. Holinshed relates that when
saying Mass Wolsey 'made dukes and earls to serve
him of wine . . . and to hold to him the basin at the
lavatory' (III.631).

46–8   *All men's honours . . . what pitch he pleases*. This
probably alludes to Romans 9.21 : 'Hath not the potter
power over the clay, even of the same lump to make
one vessel unto honour, and another unto dishonour?'

48   *pitch* height

60   (stage direction) *The King draws the curtain*. He is
disclosed already sitting in the curtained recess at the
rear of the stage.

68   *business of estate* state business

71   (stage direction) *Enter Wolsey and Campeius*. 'But how-
soever it came about that the King was thus troubled
in conscience concerning his marriage, this followed
that like a wise and sage prince, to have the doubt
clearly removed, he called together the best learned of

213

the realm, which were of several opinions. Wherefore he thought to know the truth by indifferent judges, lest peradventure the Spaniards, and other also in favour of the Queen, would say that his own subjects were not indifferent judges in this behalf. And therefore he wrote his cause to Rome, and also sent to all the universities in Italy and France, and to the great clerks of all Christendom, to know their opinions, and desired the court of Rome to send into his realm a legate, which should be indifferent and of a great and profound judgement, to hear the cause debated. At whose request the whole consistory of the College of Rome sent thither Laurence Campeius, a priest cardinal, a man of great wit and experience, which was sent thither before in the tenth year of this King . . . and with him was joined in commission the Cardinal of York and legate of England' (Holinshed, III.736).

76–7   *have great care | I be not found a talker* see to it that what I have said is put into effect. 'Talkers are no good doers' was proverbial; Tilley, T 64.

81   *so sick though for his place* so diseased with pride even to gain his eminence

83   *have-at-him* thrust. 'Have at you!' signalled an attack; see III.2.309 and V.3.113.

87   *envy* malice

90   *clerks* scholars

94   *One general tongue* one to speak for all

98   *the holy conclave* (the College of Cardinals)

100   *strangers* visiting foreigners

105   *unpartial* impartial

106   *equal* just

114   *my new secretary.* Gardiner was appointed the King's secretary on 28 July 1529; the time-scale is again abridged. 'About this time the King received into his favour Doctor Stephen Gardiner, whose service he used in matters of great secrecy and weight, admitting him in the room of Doctor Pace [see lines 120–28], the

which being continually abroad in ambassages, and the same not much necessary, by the Cardinal's appointment, at length he took such grief therewith that he fell out of his right wits' (Holinshed, III.737).

120–34   *My lord of York . . . meaner persons.* 'Note the strong dramatic effect of this somewhat grim conversation. After loud protestations of justice, Wolsey unblushingly scoffs at virtue, and shows himself indifferent to having caused the death of one who would not be his tool' (D. Nichol Smith, in the Warwick edition, 1899).

120   *Doctor Pace.* Richard Pace (1482?–1536), Dean of St Paul's, Exeter, and Salisbury, was feared by Wolsey as a rival in the King's service. 'He was sent to Switzerland to hire the Swiss against Francis I, to Germany to promote the election of Henry VIII to the empire, and to Italy to secure the Papal chair for Wolsey. When abroad he was subjected to exactions and imprisonment, and his insanity may have been brought on by his sufferings. Wolsey can hardly be held responsible, certainly not for his death, for Wolsey died in 1530 and Pace in 1536' (C. K. Pooler, in the original Arden edition, 1915).

127   *a foreign man still* always abroad

132   *appointment* direction

134   *griped* laid hold on, fastened on

135   *Deliver this with modesty* make this known gently

137   *receipt of learning* reception of learned opinion, or learned men

      Blackfriars. This was the Dominican monastery of the Black Friars. 'The place where the Cardinals should sit to hear the cause of matrimony betwixt the King and Queen was ordained to be at the Black Friars in London, where in the great hall was preparation made of seats, tables, and other furniture, according to such a solemn session and royal appearance' (Holinshed, III.737).

140   *able* vigorous

II.3.9   *process* course of events

10   *give her the avaunt* bid her begone. This is the only use
            in Shakespeare of 'avaunt' as a noun, but the *Oxford
            English Dictionary* records 'the Devil tempted him,
            but he gave him the avaunt with the sword of the
            spirit', from William Barlow's *Three Christian Sermons*
            (1596), III.132.

13   *temporal* merely a thing of this world

14   *quarrel* quarreller. The use of abstract for concrete, or
            act for agent, is frequent in Shakespeare, and Johnson's
            suggestion that *quarrel* be so taken here is the simplest
            of many efforts to explain or emend this line.

15   *sufferance panging* anguish as acute. Compare V.1.68–9,
            and the similar idea in *Antony and Cleopatra*, IV.13.5–6,
            'The soul and body rive not more in parting | Than
            greatness going off'. 'Pang' is used verbally in
            Cymbeline, III.4.93–4, 'how thy memory | Will then be
            panged by me', and in a Shakespeare scene of *The Two
            Noble Kinsmen*, I.1.167–9, 'when could grief | Call
            forth, as unpanged judgement can, fitt'st time | For
            best solicitation?'

17   *a stranger* an alien

21   *to be perked up in a glistering grief* to mourn, decked
            out in the shining robes of high station

23   *our best having* the best thing we have

24   *Beshrew me* may evil befall me

29   *Affected* aspired to

31   *Saving your mincing* despite your affectation

32   *cheveril* elastic, pliant. The phrase 'cheveril conscience'
            was quasi-proverbial; Tilley, C 608. 'Cheveril' is
            kidskin leather, stretching and flexible; compare
            Twelfth Night, III.1.11–12, 'A sentence is but a
            cheveril glove to a good wit', and *Romeo and Juliet*,
            II.4.82–3, 'O, here's a wit of cheveril, that stretches
            from an inch narrow to an ell broad!'

36   *bowed* bent

hire (two syllables)

37   *queen it* (possibly quibbling on 'quean it', play the whore)

40   *Pluck off a little* come down a little in rank

41   *count* (one rank lower than a duke, and equivalent to an earl. A bawdy quibble has been suspected in *count* – pronounced 'coont', more or less – and would not be out of character with the speaker; compare the quibble on 'le count' in *Henry V*, III.4.48–50. Anne herself has invited ribaldry by her rather unexpected oath at line 23, *By my troth and maidenhead*.)

in your way (1) in your path; (2) (following the possible quibble on *count*) in your (virginal) condition

42   *For more than blushing comes to.* The general drift is apparent, though the precise connexion of ideas is elusive. Anne is blushing at the quibbles; the Old Lady says, in effect, 'For all your blushes, and more, and your affected modesty, I would not give much for the chances of a young count you came across (or for your own precarious virginity).'

42–3   *If your back | Cannot vouchsafe this burden* if your strength of body (and sexual power) cannot support the weight of a husband

44   *get* conceive

46   *little England* (1) England itself (often so called, affectionately, in contrast with larger countries); but perhaps also, by subconscious anticipation, (2) Pembrokeshire (of which Anne is to be Marchioness; see line 63. It was known as 'little England beyond Wales' – 'Concerning Pembrokeshire, the people do speak English in it almost generally, and therefore they call it little England beyond Wales'; John Taylor the Water Poet, *A Short Relation of a Long Journey*, Spenser Society reprint, page 19.)

47   *emballing* investment with the ball, as emblem of royalty. It signified the earth, and sovereignty;

compare *Henry V*, IV.i.253, 'the balm, the sceptre, and the ball'. A bawdy quibble is implied by the Old Lady's previous indelicacies.

48   *Caernarvonshire* (a wild, mountainous Welsh county, and so relatively undesirable)

52   *Not your demand* it is not worth the trouble of your inquiring

61   *Commends his good opinion* expresses his high regard

62   *flowing* abundant

63   *Marchioness of Pembroke.* 'On the first of September [1532] being Sunday, the King being come to Windsor created the Lady Anne Bullen Marchioness of Pembroke, and gave to her one thousand pounds land by the year' (Holinshed, III.776).

67–9   *More than my all is nothing . . . empty vanities* could I do more than my utmost it would still be as nothing, my prayers not holy enough, my wishes no more than worthless, ineffectual words

67–8   *nor . . . not* (the frequent double negative, for emphasis)

74   *approve the fair conceit* confirm the high opinion

77–9   *and who knows yet . . . all this isle?* (an anticipation of the accession of Queen Elizabeth in 1558)

78–9   *a gem | To lighten.* Jewels, particularly carbuncles, were supposed to shine with their own light in dark places; compare *Titus Andronicus*, II.3.227, 'A precious ring that lightens all this hole'.

85   *suit of pounds* petition for money

87   *compelled* (accented on the first syllable)

      compelled fortune fortune thrust upon you

89   *Forty pence* (a proverbial phrase for a small sum or wager)

92   *mud* (the source of Egypt's fertility and wealth)

93   *pleasant* merry

97–8   *honour's train | Is longer than his foreskirt* what will follow in the way of distinction will outdo these first signs of it

103   *salute my blood* exhilarate me

II.4

(stage direction) This elaborate stage direction closely follows Holinshed's description of the assembly in Blackfriars together with details from his retrospective account of Wolsey's love of pomp and pageantry (III.762–3).

sennet elaborate fanfare

habit of doctors (long furred gown and flat cap of Doctors of Law)

purse ... silver pillars. 'Then had he his two great crosses of silver, the one of his archbishopric, the other of his legacy, borne before him whithersoever he went or rode, by two of the tallest priests that he could get within the realm ... Before him was borne first the broad seal of England, and his cardinal's hat, by a lord, or some gentleman of worship, right solemnly; and as soon as he was entered into his chamber of presence, his two great crosses were there attending to be borne before him: ... Thus went he down through the hall with a sergeant of arms before him, bearing a great mace of silver, and two gentlemen carrying two great pillars of silver' (Holinshed, III.760).

Griffith. F does not give his name here, or in the speech heading at line 127, but that it was Griffith is clear from the entry direction of IV.2 and from Holinshed, III.738: 'With that, quoth Master Griffith, "Madam, you be called again." '

cloth of state canopy

consistory ecclesiastical court

3   *It hath already publicly been read.* A first session of the court, at which the legates received the papal bull of commission, had been held, according to Hall, three weeks earlier than the main trial, which took place on 21 June 1529. Holinshed does not mention this first session, but says that 'before the King and the judges within the court sat the Archbishop of Canterbury [William] Warham', that when the court had gathered 'the judges commanded silence whilst their commission

was read', and that the crier then called the King
and the Queen to come into the court (III.737). This
might be understood as meaning that the commission
was read before the King appeared (and so before this
scene begins); or Shakespeare may have decided that
the preliminaries to the trial had been long enough
already.

13–57 *Sir, I desire you ... Your pleasure be fulfilled.* This is
strikingly close to Holinshed (III.737): ' "Sir," quoth
she, "I desire you to do me justice and right, and take
some pity upon me, for I am a poor woman, and a
stranger, born out of your dominion, having here no
indifferent counsel, and less assurance of friendship.
Alas, sir, what have I offended you, or what occasion
of displeasure have I showed you, intending thus to put
me from you after this sort? I take God to my judge,
I have been to you a true and humble wife, ever conformable to your will and pleasure, that never con-
traried or gainsaid anything thereof; and being always
contented with all things wherein you had any delight,
whether little or much, without grudge or displeasure,
I loved for your sake all them whom you loved,
whether they were my friends or enemies.

' "I have been your wife these twenty years and
more, and you have had by me diverse children. If
there be any just cause that you can allege against me,
either of dishonesty or matter lawful to put me from
you, I am content to depart to my shame and rebuke;
and if there be none, then I pray you to let me have
justice at your hand. The King your father was in his
time of excellent wit, and the King of Spain my father
Ferdinando was reckoned one of the wisest princes that
reigned in Spain many years before. It is not to be
doubted but that they had gathered as wise counsellors
unto them of every realm as to their wisdoms they
thought meet, who deemed the marriage between you
and me good and lawful, etc. Wherefore I humbly

desire you to spare me, until I may know what counsel
my friends in Spain will advertise me to take, and if
you will not, then your pleasure be fulfilled".'

15   *stranger* foreigner

17   *indifferent* impartial

32   *to him derived* drawn upon himself

33   *gave notice.* One expects a negative ('did not I give
notice?') but this may be implied in *nay.* Or *gave
notice . . . discharged* may be an affirmation, not a
question ('I gave him notice . . .').

36   *Upward of twenty years* (1509 to 1529)

41   *Against your sacred person* owed to, directed towards,
your sacred person. Some editors insert a comma after
love and duty; the phrase would then mean '[*aught*]
directed against your sacred person'.

48-9   *one | The wisest* the very wisest

58   *of your choice.* Katherine chose the Archbishop of
Canterbury and the Bishops of Ely, Rochester, and
Saint Asaph 'and many other doctors and well learned
men' (Holinshed, III.737).

61   *bootless* useless

62   *That longer you desire the court* that you urge the court
to delay its business

70-73   *I am about to weep . . . sparks of fire.* Hermione speaks
comparably in *The Winter's Tale*, II.1.108-12:

> I am not prone to weeping, as our sex
> Commonly are . . . but I have
> That honourable grief lodged here which burns
> Worse than tears drown.

74   *before* before you are humble (for you will never be
so)

77   *challenge* objection (a legal term for rejecting a jury-
man)

79   *blown this coal* (a proverbial phrase; Tilley, C 465)

81   *abhor* protest against, reject (a canon law term)

86   *stood to* stood up for

92   *consistory* (College of Cardinals)

96   *gainsay my deed* deny something I have in fact done

98–100   *If he know . . . of your wrong* if he knows me innocent of your charges, he knows too that I am not immune from the wrong of your accusations

108   *sign* display

            in full seeming with a convincing show

112   *slightly* easily

113–15   *Where powers are your retainers . . . pronounce their office* where those in power (or 'the powers you wield') are at your beck and call, and your words, as obedient servants, effect your will in any way you direct them

116   *tender* cherish

121   (stage direction) *offers* shows her intention

122   *Stubborn* resistant

            apt to accuse it prompt to object to it

127   GRIFFITH. See the fifth note on the opening stage direction of this scene.

138   *government* control (of self and others)

139–40   *thy parts | Sovereign and pious else* your other excellent and faithful qualities (compare *Hamlet*, I.4.33, 'His virtues else', that is, his other virtues)

140   *speak thee out* describe you fully

144   *require* request

153   *one the least* the very least (compare lines 48–9 and note)

154–5   *Be to the . . . touch of her good person* sully her good character

157   *You are not to be taught* you need no telling

159–60   *like to village curs, | Bark when their fellows do* (a form of the proverb 'Like dogs, if one barks all bark'; Tilley, D 539)

161–93   *You're excused . . . This world had aired them.* ' "My lord Cardinal," quoth the King, "I can well excuse you in this matter . . . you have been rather against me in the tempting thereof than a setter forward or mover of the same. The special cause that moved me

unto this matter was a certain scrupulosity that
pricked my conscience, upon certain words spoken at
a time when it was, by the Bishop of Bayonne the
French ambassador, who had been hither sent upon
the debating of a marriage to be concluded between
our daughter the Lady Mary and the Duke of Orleans,
second son to the King of France.

'"Upon the resolution and determination whereof,
he desired respite to advertise the King his master
thereof, whether our daughter Mary should be
legitimate in respect of my marriage with this woman,
being sometimes [*sic*] my brother's wife. Which words
once conceived within the secret bottom of my
conscience engendered such a scrupulous doubt that
my conscience was incontinently accumbered, vexed,
and disquieted; whereby I thought myself to be
greatly in danger of God's indignation. Which appeared to me (as me seemed) the rather for that He
sent us no issue male: and all such issues male as my
said wife had by me died incontinent after they
came into the world, so that I doubted the great
displeasure of God in that behalf"' (Holinshed,
III.738).

165 *passages* proceedings

166 *speak* bear witness for

167– *Now, what moved me to't . . . When I first moved you.*
209 Muriel St Clare Byrne, describing Tyrone Guthrie's
production at Stratford-upon-Avon in 1949, comments
as follows: 'this is the key passage in the play.
Anthony Quayle rendered it with sincerity and conviction, beginning slowly as if thinking out this case of
conscience, warming up as he went on to speak of the
deaths of all his male heirs and of the danger to the
Tudor succession and the realm, finally turning with
vigorous appeal to the Bishop of Lincoln' (*Shakespeare Survey 3*, 1950, page 125).

178 *advertise* (accented on the second syllable) inform

181 *Sometimes* (Holinshed's word, too; see note on lines 161–93) sometime

183 *spitting* piercing

185 *mazed considerings* perplexed broodings

192 *Or ... or* either ... or

199– *Thus hulling in | The wild sea of my conscience.* 'Thus
200 my conscience being tossed in the waves of a scrupulous mind' (Holinshed, III.738).

199 *hulling* drifting at the mercy of waves and wind. 'To hull' is to drift with sails furled. A 'hulling' ship cannot be steered; either Shakespeare is writing loosely in line 200 – *I did steer* – or his mind has passed from the ship helpless before the storm to its later state when it can be directed towards safety.

204 *yet not well* even now not well

206 *learned* (one syllable; see note on I.2.111)

206–22 *First I began in private ... Under your hands and seals.* 'Wherein ... I moved it in confession to you, my lord of Lincoln, then ghostly father. And for so much as then you yourself were in some doubt, you moved me to ask the counsel of all these my lords: whereupon I moved you, my lord of Canterbury, first to have your licence ... to put this matter in question, and so I did of all you my lords; to which you granted under your seals' (Holinshed, III.738–9).

208 *reek* break into a sweat

213–14 *Bearing a state of mighty moment in't, | And consequence of dread* involving high state importance and consequences to be dreaded

214–15 *I committed | The daring'st counsel ... to doubt* I hesitated to urge the boldest plan

217 *moved you* opened this matter to you

225 *allegèd* proffered

229 *primest* most excellent

230 *paragoned* held up as a model of perfection

238 *learned* (one syllable; see note on I.2.111)

238–9   *Cranmer,* | *Prithee return.* This apostrophe to the
absent Cranmer (successor in 1532 to Warham as
Archbishop of Canterbury) marks the King's trans-
ference of trust away from Wolsey; compare III.2.400–
401.

II.1.3–14   *Orpheus, with his lute . . . or hearing die.* No contemporary musical setting of this lyric survives. The
words find a close parallel, interesting in view of
Fletcher's authorship of this scene, in Beaumont and
Fletcher's *The Captain,* III.1.31–8:

> Music,
> Such as old Orpheus made, that gave a soul
> To agèd mountains, and made rugged beasts
> Lay by their rages: and tall trees that knew
> No sound but tempests, to bow down their branches
> And hear, and wonder: and the sea, whose surges
> Shook their white heads in heaven, to be as midnight
> Still, and attentive.

3   *Orpheus* (son of the muse Calliope; Apollo presented
him with a lyre on which he played so enchantingly
that not living creatures only but rocks and streams
obeyed his music)
lute. This was an Elizabethan, not a Grecian, instru-
ment. In the early performances of the play the song
was probably sung by a boy acting as one of the
Queen's women, accompanying himself on the lute.

17   *presence* presence chamber
18   *willed* bade
18–19   *Pray their graces* | *To come near.* According to Holin-
shed, the Queen rose from her work and went into
the 'chamber of presence' to meet the Cardinals
formally. In the play she invites them in, and the tone
is more personal.

22   *as righteous* (that is, as they themselves should be good)

23 *all hoods make not monks* (proverbial; Tilley, H 586. Shakespeare quotes it in its Latin form – '*cucullus non facit monachum*' – in *Twelfth Night*, I.5.50–51, and *Measure for Measure*, V.1.261.)

24–46 *Your graces find me here ... Pray speak in English.* 'The Cardinals being in the Queen's chamber of presence, the gentleman usher advertised the Queen that the Cardinals were come to speak with her. With that she rose up, and with a skein of white thread about her neck came into her chamber of presence, where the Cardinals were attending. At whose coming, quoth she, "What is your pleasure with me?" "If it please your grace", quoth Cardinal Wolsey, "to go into your privy chamber, we will show you the cause of our coming." "My lord," quoth she, "if ye have anything to say, speak it openly before all these folk, for I fear nothing that ye can say against me, but that I would all the world should hear and see it, and therefore speak your mind." Then began the Cardinal to speak to her in Latin. "Nay, good my lord," quoth she, "speak to me in English"' (Holinshed, III.739).

24 *part of* in some measure

31 *corner* secrecy. ('Truth seeks no corners' was proverbial; Tilley, T 587.)

38 *that way I am wife in* how I behave as a wife

40–41 *Tanta ... serenissima* so great is the integrity of our purpose towards you, most noble Queen. (The phrase is the dramatist's own; Holinshed merely states 'Then began the Cardinal to speak to her in Latin.')

45 *more strange, suspicious* more strange, even suspicious

63 *still bore* has always borne

64 *censure* judgement (here in an unfavourable sense; contrast I.1.33)

68–91 *My lords ... In mine own country, lords.* ' "My lord," quoth she, "I thank you for your good will, but to make you answer in your request I cannot so suddenly, for I was set among my maids at work, thinking full little of any such matter, wherein there needeth a longer deliberation and a better head than mine to make answer; for I need counsel in this case which toucheth me so near, and for any counsel or friendship that I can find in England, they are not for my profit. What think you, my lords? Will any Englishman counsel me or be friend to me against the King's pleasure that is his subject? Nay, forsooth. And as for my counsel in whom I will put my trust, they be not here; they be in Spain in my own country" ' (Holinshed, III.739–40).

70   *suddenly* impromptu, extempore

74   *set* seated

78   *The last fit of my greatness* 'the last attack which she felt would end the "fitful fever" of her life of greatness' (W. A. Wright, in the Clarendon edition, 1895)

83   *But little for my profit* very little help to me

86   *so desperate to be honest* so reckless as to stand up for honesty

87   *live a subject* yet be allowed to live in England

88   *weigh out* outweigh, make amends for

97   *part away* depart

100   *Heaven is above all* (proverbial; Tilley, H 348)

103   *cardinal virtues* (a punning reference to the schoolmen's list of principal virtues, justice, prudence, temperance, and fortitude, to which faith, hope, and charity – the theological virtues – were added to parallel the seven deadly sins)

104   *cardinal sins* (a punning reference to the seven deadly sins. 'The distress of Katherine might have kept her from the quibble to which she is irresistibly tempted' – Dr Johnson; but 'A passion there is that carries off its own excess by plays on words as naturally, and, therefore, as appropriately to drama, as by gesticulations, looks, or tones' – Coleridge, on *Richard II*, in *Lectures and Notes on Shakespeare*.)

110   *at once* all at once

112   *mere* sheer (compare *Othello*, II.2.3, 'the mere per-
       dition of the Turkish fleet')

113   *envy* ill-will

115   *professors* (that is, of Christianity)

119   *'has* he has

120   *old* (actually, about forty)

123-4 *All your studies | Make me a curse like this!* let all
       your learning conceive me another such affliction, if
       it can

124   *worse* (that is, than the reality)

125   *speak* describe

131   *Been . . . superstitious to him* idolized him

145   *angels' faces . . . hearts.* This is a form of the proverb
       'Fair face, foul heart' (Tilley, F 3) and possibly a
       passing glance at the familiar story, told in Bede's
       History of the English People, that Saint Gregory,
       seeing English slaves in Rome and being told they
       were '*Angli*', replied '*Bene, nam et angelicam habent
       faciem*' ('They have the faces of angels'); compare
       Peele, *The Arraignment of Paris*, V.1.72-3, 'Her people
       [Queen Elizabeth's] are y-clepèd Angeli, | Or, if I
       miss, a letter is the most'; and Greene, *The Spanish
       Masquerado* (*Works*, edited by Grosart, V.275),
       'England, a little island, where, as Saint Augustine
       [really, Gregory] saith, there be people with angels'
       faces'.

151-2 *the lily . . . flourished* (similarly Spenser, *The Faerie
       Queene*, II.6.16, 'The lily, lady of the flowering field')

159   *For goodness' sake* out of your good nature (not the
       modern colloquial sense)

161   *carriage* conduct

174   *utmost studies* most diligent endeavours

176   *used myself* conducted myself

III.2.2 *force* urge

8   *the Duke* (Buckingham)

10   *uncontemned* unscorned

228

or at least or have at least not been (the negative may be implied in '*un*contemned')

11   *Strangely neglected* treated distantly and neglectfully

13   *Out of* besides

14   *What he deserves . . . I know.* The Lord Chamberlain has changed his view since he defended Wolsey at I.3.57–8, but still remains temperate, and at lines 332–6 speaks of his fall sympathetically.

16   *way* opportunity

22   *he's settled* (referring probably to Wolsey, though possibly to the King)

23   *his* (the King's)

26   *contrary proceedings* (1) deceptive schemes (as in lines 30–36); (2) opposition to the King's wishes

29   *practices* intrigues

30–36   *The Cardinal's letters . . . Lady Anne Bullen.* 'Whilst these things were thus in hand [1529], the Cardinal of York was advised that the King had set his affection upon a young gentlewoman named Anne, the daughter of Sir Thomas Bullen, Viscount Rochford, which did wait upon the Queen. This was a great grief unto the Cardinal, as he that perceived aforehand that the King would marry the said gentlewoman, if the divorce took place. Wherefore he began with all diligence to disappoint that match, which, by reason of the misliking that he had to the woman, he judged ought to be avoided more than present death. While the matter stood in this state, and that the cause of the Queen was to be heard and judged at Rome, by reason of the appeal which was by her put in, the Cardinal required the Pope by letters and secret messengers that in any wise he should defer the judgement of the divorce till he might frame the King's mind to his purpose. Howbeit he went about nothing so secretly but that the same came to the King's knowledge, who took so high displeasure with such his cloaked dissimulation that he determined to abase his degree, sith as an unthankful

person he forgot himself and his duty towards him
that had so highly advanced him to all honour and
dignity' (Holinshed, III.740).

36   *creature* dependant

38–9   *coasts | And hedges* slinks closely and furtively along

40–41   *brings his physic | After his patient's death* (alluding to
the proverb 'After death the doctor (physic)'; Tilley,
D 133)

45   *Trace the conjunction* follow the union

50–52   *I persuade me . . . In it be memorized* (a further anticipation, like that in II.3.77–9, of the play's happy outcome)

50   *I persuade me* I am convinced

52   *memorized* made memorable

53   *Digest* stomach

56–7   *Cardinal Campeius . . . hath ta'en no leave.* In Holinshed, Campeius 'took his leave of the King and
nobility' (III.740). Shakespeare's contrary account
presumably derives from Foxe (page 906), according to
whom Campeius 'craftily shifted himself out of the
realm before the day came appointed for determination,
leaving his subtle fellow behind him to weigh with the
King in the meantime, while the matter might be
brought up to the court of Rome'. Foxe later (page
959), in a passage referring also to Anne's Lutheranism
(see lines 98–9), has 'Cardinal Campeius dissembling
the matter conveyed himself home to Rome again',
with the marginal note 'Cardinal Campeius slippeth
from the King'.

59   *Is posted* has sped

64   *returned in his opinions* returned in as much as he has
sent his opinions in advance, though he has not yet
arrived himself. (Another interpretation is that Cranmer has returned, bringing opinions with him; but *in*
would be an odd preposition to use for this, and had
such been the meaning Suffolk would have answered
Norfolk's simple question *When returns Cranmer?*

more naturally. The fact that by line 400 Cranmer *is returned with welcome* – the return is news to Wolsey – does not affect the matter here.)

66–7   *all famous colleges | Almost* almost all the famous colleges

68   *published* proclaimed

74   *an archbishop.* Cranmer succeeded when Warham died in 1532 and was consecrated on 30 March 1533.

76   *packet* parcel of state dispatches

78   *Presently* immediately

85–90   *the Duchess of Alençon ... Marchioness of Pembroke.* Chronology is again telescoped: Wolsey's scheme for the Duchess of Alençon is attributed in Holinshed (III.719–20) to 1527 (but for its doubtful authenticity see note on II.1.156–7); Katherine's trial began in 1529 and her divorce was effected in 1533; Wolsey died in 1530; and Anne became Marchioness of Pembroke in 1532. The play necessarily makes events more compact than they really were, and the sources – Holinshed interlaced with Foxe – are themselves far from straightforward in their sense of time.

96–7   *This candle burns not clear; 'tis I must snuff it, | Then out it goes* this intended marriage has snags which I am expected to remove (to snuff a candle being originally to trim its wick) – but instead I shall quash it

99   *spleeny* hot-headed

Lutheran. Anne's Lutheranism seems not to be mentioned in Hall or Holinshed, but Foxe writes 'the Cardinal of York perceived the King to cast favour on the Lady Anne, whom he knew to be a Lutheran' (page 959). In Rowley's *When You See Me You Know Me* Gardiner laments the favour Anne showed to Lutherans (lines 523–32), and Wolsey (quite unhistorically) mentions Katherine Parr as 'the hope of Luther's heresy', under whom 'the Protestants will swell'; he hopes to 'plot the downfall of these Lutherans' (lines 1490–95).

101   *hard-ruled* not easily managed

102–3   *one | Hath* one who has

105–6   *fret the string, | The master-cord* gnaw through the main
sinew. (The heart was thought to be controlled by vital
'strings' or nerves.)

106   *on's* of his
(stage direction) *reading of a schedule.* 'When the
nobles of the realm perceived the Cardinal to be in
displeasure, they began to accuse him of such offences
as they knew might be proved against him, and thereof
they made a book containing certain articles, to which
diverse of the King's Council set their hands. The
King, understanding more plainly by those articles the
great pride, presumption, and covetousness of the
Cardinal, was sore moved against him; but yet kept his
purpose secret for a while' (Holinshed, III.740).

124   *an inventory.* Shakespeare transfers to Wolsey a mis-
adventure suffered by Thomas Ruthall, Bishop of
Durham, who inadvertently delivered into the hands
of Wolsey himself, his enemy, an inventory of his own
excessive wealth (Holinshed, III.540–41).

127–8   *outspeaks | Possession of a subject* discloses more than a
subject should possess

134–5   *below the moon, not worth | His serious considering*
worldly, not the right subjects for his devotion

140   *spiritual leisure* the interim of your spiritual concerns

142   *husband* manager

143   *my companion.* It has been suggested that Henry
speaks of Wolsey and himself as companions in that
both are *ill husbands*, he in a marital sense, Wolsey in
an economic. Such an admission of fault from him is
unlikely, and what he would seem to mean is that,
ironically, he is glad to have as companion a man so
devoted to spiritual matters as to be neglectful of
worldly wealth.

154   *words are no deeds* (alluding to the proverb 'It is better
to do well than to say well'; Tilley, D 402)

155-6   *with his deed did crown | His word upon you.* Henry VII appointed Wolsey, his chaplain, Dean of Lincoln and ambassador to the Emperor Maximilian (Holinshed, III.757-8).

167-8   *than could | My studied purposes requite* than my most attentive efforts could repay

171   *filed with* kept pace with

172   *so that* only in the sense that

176   *allegiant* loyal

181-3   *The honour of it . . . the punishment* the honour loyalty earns is its own reward as, on the contrary, ill repute is the punishment of disloyalty

188   *notwithstanding that your bond of duty* over and above that general bond of duty you owe to be loyal

189   *in love's particular* for the special reason of love

192-6   *that am, have, and will be . . . yet my duty.* The syntax is irregular, conveying Wolsey's passion, but the sense is clear enough.

205-6   *He parted frowning . . . from his eyes.* Similarly in Rowley's *When You See Me You Know Me* the fool, Patch, reports 'I thought he would have killed my lord Cardinal, he looked so terribly' (lines 731-2). See note on I.2.186.

207   *galled* wounded (and so angered)

208   *makes him nothing* annihilates him

212   *mine own ends.* This shows up the hypocrisy of his professions at lines 171-4.
   to gain the popedom. In 1529 Wolsey heard a false report that Pope Clement VII had died, and ordered Gardiner 'to strike for no cost' to secure his election (Foxe, page 963).

214   *cross* perverse

215   *main* all-important

224   *meridian* highest altitude. There may be an echo of John Speed's *History of Great Britain* (1611), page 769: 'Cardinal Wolsey fell likewise in great displeasure of the King . . . but now his sun having passed the meridian

of his greatness began by degrees again to decline, till lastly it set under the cloud of his fatal eclipse' (cited by Foakes, who refers also to the cloud image in Buckingham's fall, I.1.224–6).

226   *exhalation* meteor. Meteors, lightning, and other aerial phenomena, whether fiery or cloudy, were thought to result from 'vapours drawn up [that is, exhaled] into the middle region of the air' (Florio, *New World of Words*). Compare Beaumont and Fletcher, *Thierry and Theodoret*, IV.1.105–6, 'kings, from height of all their painted glories, | Fall like spent exhalations'.

228–50   *Hear the King's pleasure ... who'll take it?* 'The King sent the two Dukes of Norfolk and Suffolk to the Cardinal's place at Westminster, who went as they were commanded and finding the Cardinal there they declared that the King's pleasure was that he should surrender up the great seal into their hands, and to depart simply unto Asher, which was an house situate nigh unto Hampton Court, belonging to the bishopric of Winchester. The Cardinal demanded of them their commission that gave them such authority, who answered again that they were sufficient commissioners, and had authority to do no less by the King's mouth. Notwithstanding, he would in no wise agree in that behalf, without further knowledge of their authority, saying that the great seal was delivered him by the King's person, to enjoy the ministration thereof, with the room of the chancellor for the term of his life, whereof for his surety he had the King's letters patents' (Holinshed, III.741).

231   *Asher* (Esher, near Hampton Court; *Asher* is an old form of the name)

    my lord of Winchester's. Wolsey was himself Bishop of Winchester; his successor as such, Stephen Gardiner, may be the man in the dramatist's mind. Holinshed says that Esher belonged to the 'bishopric of Winchester'. In being sent thither, therefore, Wolsey is being dismissed to one of his own residences.

236-7   *Till I find more than will or words to do it –* | *I mean your malice* till I find more reason for so doing (surrendering the great seal) than your mere verbal statement of the King's will – in fact, more reason than your malice

237   *officious* interfering. This is only the second instance of the modern sense recorded in the *Oxford English Dictionary*; the normal Elizabethan sense is 'zealous in duty'.

241   *sleek and wanton* unctuous and unprincipled

244   *warrant* justification (Wolsey is sarcastic)

250   *Tied it by letters patents* ratified it with an open (*patent*) authorization

253   *forty* (a conventional, not a precise, number)

255   *Thou scarlet sin* (alluding to the scarlet of the Cardinal's robes and the 'scarlet' sins of Isaiah 1.18: 'though your sins be as red as scarlet, they shall be as white as snow')

258   *parts* qualities

259   *policy* (a word then almost always of sinister sense) stratagems

260   *deputy for Ireland.* See note on II.1.41-9.
     Ireland (three syllables)

262   *gav'st him* falsely fixed upon him

272   *That* I that

274   *mate* match

280   *jaded* humiliated. The word carries a combined sense of 'cowed', 'treated with contempt', 'fooled', 'dispirited'.

282   *dare us with his cap, like larks* daze us, fascinated, with his scarlet cap. (Larks were caught by being 'dared' – dazzled or confused – by pieces of scarlet cloth, or small mirrors, or small hawks, which riveted their attention while the fowling-nets were dropped upon them.)

291   *issues* sons

295   *sacring bell* bell rung in the Mass at the elevation of the Host

       brown wench. There seems no specific ground for this jibe, but Wolsey was often accused of immorality; compare IV.2.43–4, *Of his own body he was ill, and gave | The clergy ill example.*

307   *dare* defy

310–30 *First . . . Of all the kingdom.* This is a close rendering of the six main charges against Wolsey as Holinshed records them.

311   *legate* the Pope's deputy

314–15 *'Ego et Rex meus' | Was still inscribed.* This charge, so expressed in Hall and Holinshed, has become famous, but it misrepresents the facts, which are that Wolsey was accused not of claiming priority over the King but of treating the King and himself as equals in state correspondence by using the Latin phrase quoted, the English equivalent of which is 'My King and I', not the presumptuous 'I and my King'.

315   *still* always

324   *mere* sheer

326   *innumerable substance* incalculable treasure (the words are Holinshed's)

339   *legatine* as papal legate. F reads 'Legatiue', but Holinshed regularly ends the word in 'ine', and 'iue' is the easiest of misreadings from manuscript.

340   *praemunire* (a writ, beginning *praemunire facias*, which charged a sheriff to summon anyone accused of maintaining papal jurisdiction in England and of appealing from the King's courts to those of the papacy. The penalties were forfeiture of goods, and outlawry; compare lines 342–4.)

343   *Chattels* movables. F reads 'Caſtles', presumably a transcription error for Holinshed's 'cattels'. 'Chattel' and 'cattle' are forms of the same word, meaning possessions.

353   *blossoms* (probably a verb)

354   *blushing* glowing

359   *wanton* sportive

359–61   *that swim on bladders . . . beyond my depth.* Foakes cites as a possible source John Speed's *History of Great Britain* (1611), page 769, where Wolsey 'being swollen so big by the blasts of promotion as the bladder, not being able to contain more greatness, suddenly burst, and vented forth the wind of all former favours'. But the idea is found elsewhere; for example, in Holinshed, III.613, where Wolsey is 'led with the like spirit of swelling ambition wherewith the rabble of popes have been bladder-like puffed and blown up'; and in Fletcher's *Wit at Several Weapons*, I.1.14–27:

> I rushed into the world, which is indeed
> Much like the art of swimming . . .
> For he that lies borne up with patrimonies
> Looks like a long great ass that swims with bladders,
> Come but one prick of adverse fortune to him
> He sinks.

In *A Mirror for Magistrates* (1559) the overweening Wolsey 'did swim, as dainty as a duck, | When water serves, to keep the body brave'.

363   *old.* Wolsey was approaching sixty.

364   *rude stream* rough torrent

365   *Vain pomp and glory of this world* (echoing the Book of Common Prayer baptismal service: 'Dost thou forsake the devil and all his works, the vain pomp and glory of the world?')

367   *that hangs on princes' favours* (possibly echoing Psalm 146.2 (3 in the Authorized Version), 'Put not your trust in princes', and Psalm 118.9, 'It is better to trust in God than to put any confidence in princes')

368–70   *There is . . . More pangs and fears.* See note on I.2.20–21.

371   *he falls like Lucifer.* This derives from Isaiah 14.12:

237

'How art thou fallen from heaven, O Lucifer'. Compare lines 440–41, and *Paradise Lost*, I.36–40:

> his pride
> Had cast him out from Heaven, with all his host
> Of rebel Angels; by whose aid, aspiring
> To set himself in glory above his peers,
> He trusted to have equalled the Most High.

For the parallel with *A Mirror for Magistrates*, see the note on I.1.70–72.

378   *I know myself* I realize my true nature. The idea of knowing oneself, and so living in true relationships, goes back to classical antiquity, and is much repeated in Elizabethan literature.

378–85   *I feel within me ... that hopes for heaven!* Holinshed (III.756) describes Wolsey as 'never happy till this his overthrow. Wherein he showed such moderation and ended so perfectly that the hour of his death did him more honour than all the pomp of his life past'.

393–
406   *Sir Thomas More ... her coronation.* Time is again abridged. More was chosen Chancellor in November 1529; Wolsey died in 1530; Cranmer was appointed to the see of Canterbury in 1532 and consecrated in 1533; Henry and Anne were married secretly in November 1532 or January 1533 and the marriage made public at Easter 1533; and Anne was crowned in June 1533.

399   *a tomb of orphans' tears.* 'The chancellor is the general guardian of orphans [or, rather, of "infants", persons under eighteen]. *A tomb of tears* is very harsh' (Dr Johnson). William Drummond of Hawthornden has a similar conceit in his elegy for Prince Henry, *Tears on the Death of Moeliades* (1614): 'The Muses, Phoebus, Love, have raisèd of their tears | A crystal tomb to him, wherethrough his worth appears' (*Works*, edited by Kastner, 1.84).

405   *voice* talk

411   *noble troops.* 'He had also a great number daily attending upon him, both of noblemen and worthy gentlemen, with no small number of the tallest yeomen that he could get in all the realm' (Holinshed, III.760).

420   *make use now* take the present opportunity

442   *The image of his Maker.* Compare Genesis 1.27: 'God created man in His own image, in the image of God created He him.'

443   *cherish those hearts that hate thee.* Compare Matthew 5.44: 'Love your enemies: . . . do good to them that hate you.'

445   *Still* always

448–9   *Then if thou fall'st . . . Thou fall'st a blessèd martyr.* Thomas Cromwell, Chancellor of the Exchequer in 1533, Lord Privy Seal in 1536, Lord Chamberlain in 1539, and Earl of Essex in 1540, was powerful and dreaded, but was accused of high treason and executed in 1540. The play of *Thomas Lord Cromwell* (1602) shows him as an able and generous man, rising high from a low estate, and brought to disgrace and execution by Gardiner's villainy.

451–2   *an inventory . . . 'tis the King's.* 'Then the Cardinal called all his officers before him, and took account of them for all such stuff whereof they had charge. . . . There was laid on every table books reporting the contents of the same, and so was there inventories of all things in order against the King's coming. . . . At Asher he and his family continued the space of three or four weeks, without either beds, sheets, table cloths, or dishes to eat their meat in or wherewith to buy any: the Cardinal was forced to borrow of the Bishop of Carlisle plate and dishes' (Holinshed, III.741).

452   *robe* cardinal's gown

455–7   *Had I but served . . . mine enemies.* 'If I had served God as diligently as I have done the King, He would not have given me over in my grey hairs' (Holinshed,

III.755). Wolsey's famous words were in fact addressed
not to Cromwell but to Sir William Kingston, Constable of the Tower, whom the King had sent to attend
upon him, and were uttered as he lay dying in Leicester
Abbey. Similar reflections are recorded from a variety
of fallen men; C. K. Pooler (in the original Arden
edition, 1915) gives instances from England, Scotland,
France, Spain, and Persia.

IV.1.1   *once again* (after meeting in II.1)

8   *royal minds* good will towards the King

9   *let 'em have their rights* to give them their due

    ever forward always eager to do

10–11   *shows, | Pageants, and sights of honour.* Holinshed's
account of Henry's reign is strikingly rich in accounts
of elaborate spectacles. The narration of Anne's
coronation proceedings (III.783–4) is particularly
splendid: 'First went gentlemen, then esquires, then
knights, then the aldermen of the city in their cloaks
of scarlet; after them the judges in their mantles of
scarlet and coifs. Then followed the Knights of the
Bath being no lords, every man having a white lace
on his left sleeve; then followed barons and viscounts
in their parliament robes of scarlet. After them came
earls, marquises, and dukes in their robes of estate of
crimson velvet furred with ermine. . . . After them
came the Lord Chancellor in a robe of scarlet . . . ;
after him came the King's chapel and the monks
solemnly singing with procession, then came abbots
and bishops mitred, then sergeants and officers of arms,
then after them went the Mayor of London with his
mace, and Garter in his coat of arms; then went the
Marquis Dorset in a robe of estate which bare the
sceptre of gold, and the Earl of Arundel which bare the
rod of ivory with the dove both together.

'Then went alone the Earl of Oxford, High Chamberlain of England, which bare the crown; after him went the Duke of Suffolk in his robe of estate also for that day being High Steward of England, having a long white rod in his hand, and the Lord William Howard with the rod of the marshalship, and every Knight of the Garter had on his collar of the order. Then proceeded forth the Queen in a circot and robe of purple velvet furred with ermine, in her hair coif and circlet as she had the Saturday [that is, the day of her progress through London, when "her hair hanged down, but on her head she had a coif with a circlet about it full of rich stones"], and over her was borne the canopy by four of the five ports, all crimson with points of blue and red hanging on their sleeves, and the Bishops of London and Winchester bare up the laps of the Queen's robe. The Queen's train, which was very long, was borne by the old Duchess of Norfolk; after her followed ladies being lords' wives, which had circots of scarlet with narrow sleeves. ... Then followed ladies being knights' wives, in gowns of scarlet, with narrow sleeves. ...

'When she was thus brought to the high place made in the midst of the church, between the choir and the high altar, she was set in a rich chair. And after that she had rested a while, she descended down to the high altar and there prostrate herself while the Archbishop of Canterbury said certain collects: then she rose, and the Bishop anointed her on the head and on the breast, and then she was led up again, where, after diverse orisons were said, the Archbishop set the crown of Saint Edward on her head, and then delivered her the sceptre of gold in her right hand, and the rod of ivory with the dove in the left hand, and then all the choir sung *Te Deum*. ... Then went she to Saint Edward's shrine and there offered, after which offering done she withdrew her into a little place made for the nonce on the one side of the choir. ... When the

Queen had a little reposed her, the company returned in the same order that they set forth; . . . then she was brought to Westminster Hall.'

21 *beholding* indebted

26 *order* rank (presumably the bishops mentioned by Holinshed as accompanying the Archbishop)

27 *a late court* a court lately

28 *Ampthill* (Ampthill Castle in Bedfordshire, forty-five miles north-west of London, made Crown property under Henry VII)

31 *main* strong

34 *Kimbolton* (Kimbolton Castle in Huntingdonshire, the residence of Katherine from her divorce until her death in 1536. F spells it 'Kymmalton', and presumably accents the first syllable.)

36 (stage direction) *flourish* fanfare

Garter Garter King-of-Arms (charged with proclaiming the sovereign's accession; see V.5.1–3)

he wore a gilt copper crown. The past tense is curious; the likeliest explanation is that the writer was so engrossed by closely following Holinshed's retrospective account as to slip into the past tense for his one finite verb. The *gilt copper crown* derives from Holinshed: 'every king-of-arms put on a crown of copper and gilt' (III.784).

demi-coronal narrow circlet or coronet

Earl of Surrey (in Holinshed Earl of Arundel; probably changed to save a stage part, Surrey having already appeared)

Collars of Esses chains formed of S-shaped links

robe of estate state robes

Duke of Norfolk (in Holinshed Lord William Howard, Norfolk's half-brother; probably changed to save a stage part)

four of the Cinque Ports. The barons of the Cinque Ports (originally Dover, Hastings, Sandwich, Hythe, and Romney, to which Rye and Winchelsea were later added) were entitled to carry the canopy over the sovereign at coronations.

in her hair with her hair hanging loose (the custom for brides; compare *The Two Noble Kinsmen*, IV.1.136, stage direction, '*Enter Emilia in white* [as a bride] *her hair about her shoulders*', and Webster, *The White Devil*, III.2.1–2, 'untie your folded thoughts, | And let them dangle loose as a bride's hair'). Foakes cites interesting parallels to this and other details, from Princess Elizabeth's marriage in February 1613, as described in *The Letters of John Chamberlain* (1939, I.424), 'in her hair that hung down long, with an exceeding rich coronet on her head', and in Henry Peacham's *The Period of Mourning* (1613), 'with a coronet on her head of pearl, and her hair dishevelled, and hanging down over her shoulders'. There is, Foakes observes, no mention of pearl in Holinshed.

45   *all the Indies.* See note on I.1.21–2.

46   *strains* embraces

47   *I cannot blame his conscience.* See note on I.4.75.

54   *Their coronets say so* ('Every countess a plain circlet of gold without flowers' (Holinshed, III.784); see section 10 of 'The Order of the Coronation')

55   *falling* (that is, falling from virtue. Foakes cites E.A., *Strange Foot-Post* (1613), B2ʳ: '*Cadentes*, that is, falling stars, whereunto wantons may be compared'.)

59   *rankness* (1) exuberance; (2) smelliness (compare *Coriolanus*, III.1.66, 'The mutable, rank-scented meiny')

61   *speak* describe

67   *opposing* displaying

72   *the shrouds* a ship's standing rigging

74   *Doublets* close jackets (sleeved or sleeveless)

91   *choicest music* finest musicians

94–7 *York Place ... Whitehall.* York Place, the London residence of the Archbishops of York, was annexed on Wolsey's fall to the King's palace of Westminster and known as Whitehall; Holinshed's marginal note reads 'York Place or White Hall now the palace of Westminster' (III.775).

101-3   *Stokesley and Gardiner ... London.* Gardiner, appointed the King's secretary in July 1529 (see note on II.2.114), became Bishop of Winchester in 1531 but continued as secretary until 1534. Stokesley was consecrated Bishop of London in November 1530.

102   *preferred from* promoted from being

110-11   *Master | O'th' Jewel House* (in charge of the royal plate and crown jewels; Cromwell was appointed in April 1532)

112   *one, already, of the Privy Council* (appointed in 1531)

IV.2   'This scene is above any other part of Shakespeare's tragedies, and perhaps above any scene of any other poet, tender and pathetic, without gods, or furies, or poisons, or precipices, without the help of romantic circumstances, without improbable sallies of poetical lamentation, and without any throes of tumultuous misery' (Dr Johnson); 'the crowning glory of the whole poem' (Swinburne, in *A Study of Shakespeare*). 'Tender and pathetic' as it is, and the more moving as it follows the public splendour of the coronation which ousts Katherine, it is less interesting in dramatic vitality than the scene of her trial, her challenge to Wolsey, and Henry's account of his scruples (II.4). With all its merits it does not support Swinburne's claim that no one but Shakespeare could have written it; its main distinction comes from the sensitive dignity with which it faithfully versifies Holinshed's own moving account.

6   *child* scion (a title tinged by chivalric romance, used normally for a young hero)

7   *dead.* Wolsey died on 29 November 1530, Katherine on 7 January 1536.

10   *happily* fittingly

11   *voice* talk

12   *stout* valiant

13   *Arrested him at York* (actually, at Cawood Castle, Yorkshire, on 4 November 1530; Holinshed, III.752)

14   *tainted* disgraced

17   *roads* stages

19   *covent* convent (a common form up to the end of the seventeenth century – for example, Covent Garden; used for religious companies of either sex)

21   *old man.* See note on III.2.363.

26-7   *the hour of eight, which he himself | Foretold should be his last.* 'Incontinent the clock struck eight, and then he gave up the ghost, and departed this present life: which caused some to call to remembrance how he said the day before that at eight of the clock they should lose their master' (Holinshed, III.755).

33-68   *He was a man ... he died fearing God.* These contrasting accounts closely follow two assessments in Holinshed, the earlier (III.756, drawn from Edmund Campion) stressing Wolsey's learning, affability, generosity, and final blessedness of spirit (compare lines 46-68), the later (III.765) his pride, craft, and vice (compare lines 33-44). It is fitting to the play's spirit of charity that the order should be reversed and the final mood, in Katherine's mind and the reader's, should be one of generosity.

34   *stomach* arrogance

35-6   *by suggestion | Tied all the kingdom* by intrigues brought the whole land into bondage. Holinshed writes that Wolsey 'by crafty suggestion gat into his hands innumerable treasure' (III.765). The play's words are less specific. For F's 'Ty'de' the reading 'Tyth'd' (tithed) has been suggested, for Holinshed mentions earlier that Wolsey proposed valuing all men's goods so that a tenth part might be taken for war expenses. Or 'tithed' might more loosely mean 'levied toll';

compare *King John*, III.1.153–4, 'no Italian priest |
Shall tithe or toll in our dominions'.

36   *Simony* trading in ecclesiastical appointments

37   *presence* royal presence chamber

38–9   *double | Both in his words and meaning* given to false-
hood and equivocation

43–4   *Of his own body ... ill example.* See note on
III.2.295.

43   *ill* vicious

45–6   *Men's evil manners live in brass; their virtues | We write
in water* (echoes of proverbial phrases: 'Injuries are
writ in brass', 'To write in water'; Tilley, I 71, W 114.
For the sentiment compare *Julius Caesar*, III.2.76–7,
'The evil that men do lives after them, | The good is
oft interrèd with their bones'.)

50   *honour. From his cradle* (often amended to 'honour
from his cradle.'. But compare Holinshed's stress on
Wolsey's precocity (III.756): 'being but a child, very
apt to be learned ... he was made bachelor of art,
when he passed not fifteen years of age, and was
called ... the boy bachelor'.)

58   *you* (apostrophizing Ipswich and Oxford)

59   *Ipswich and Oxford* (the college founded by Wolsey at
his birthplace, Ipswich, of which all that remains is a
brick gateway, and that at Oxford, Christ Church,
originally called Cardinal's College, whose crest, a
cardinal's cap, commemorates his munificence)

60   *good that did it* goodness that created it

62   *art* learning

64   *His overthrow heaped happiness upon him.* See note on
III.2.378–85.

74   *modesty* temperateness

80   *that celestial harmony I go to.* The soul, freed from the
body, was thought to hear the music of the spheres as
they circled round the earth; compare *The Merchant of
Venice*, V.1.60–65:

246

There's not the smallest orb which thou behold'st
But in his motion like an angel sings,
Still quiring to the young-eyed cherubins;
Such harmony is in immortal souls,
But whilst this muddy vesture of decay
Doth grossly close it in, we cannot hear it.

82   (stage direction) *The Vision.* The chronicles provide no
source for Katherine's vision, but other plays of the
time offer similar supernatural visitations; for example,
Cymbeline, V.4, *Pericles*, V.1, *The Tempest*, III.3 and
IV.1. In *The Winter's Tale* Antigonus reports his
vision of Hermione 'In pure white robes, | Like very
sanctity' (III.3.21-2). *The Two Noble Kinsmen* has
elegant pageant processions and ceremonies in the
first and last Acts. The dramatist may have heard
(though if so the means are unknown) of the funeral
oration in 1550 for Queen Marguerite of Navarre;
this describes her as seeing before her death 'a very
beautiful woman holding in her hand a crown which
she showed her saying that the Queen would be
crowned with it' (see E. E. Duncan-Jones in *Notes and
Queries*, April 1961, pages 142-3). Marguerite was the
wife Wolsey intended for Henry; see II.2.38-40 and
III.2.85-6.

    bays bay-leaves (traditional symbols of joyful triumph)
    congee curtsy reverently
    changes figures in the dance

94   *Bid the music leave* bid the musicians cease

98   *colour.* F reads 'cold', but Patience throughout is
describing Katherine's looks, and there seems no
reason for her to change to coldness, to the detriment
of the metre. 'Color' might easily be misread as
'cold'.

102   *lose* give up. Compare the similar sense at II.1.57.

105   *staying* waiting

132   *model* image
        his young daughter Mary Tudor (born in 1516, Queen
        of England from 1553 to 1558)
141   *both my fortunes* my fortunes good and bad
143   *now I should not lie.* See note on II.1.125.
145   *honesty and decent carriage* womanly honour and
        becoming conduct
146   *let him be a noble* let him be no less indeed than a noble
159   *fashion* making
169   *maiden flowers* flowers for chastity (compare Ophelia's
        'maiden strewments'; *Hamlet*, V.1.227)

V.1.2–3   *hours for necessities,* | *Not for delights.* 'Gardiner himself
           is not much delighted. The delights at which he hints
           seem to be the King's diversion, which keeps him in
           attendance' (Dr Johnson).
7   *primero* (a fashionable card game of the sixteenth and
           early seventeenth centuries, introduced from Spain or
           Italy)
13   *touch of your late business* hint of what you have just
           been doing, at this late hour
14   *As they say spirits do.* Spirits were creatures of the dark
           hours, like the ghost of Hamlet's father, 'Doomed for a
           certain term to walk the night' (I.5.10), and recalled
           to the other world at cockcrow.
22   *Good time* a good delivery. Compare *The Winter's Tale*,
           II.1.20, 'Good time encounter her!' (that is, Her-
           mione, in childbed).
28   *way* way of thinking (in religion)
34–6   *Master* | *O'th'Rolls . . . more preferments.* Having been
           made Master of the Jewel House (see note on
           IV.1.110–11) in 1532, Cromwell became Master of
           the Rolls in October 1534 and secretary to the King
           the same year; he later became a Knight of the Garter,
           Earl of Essex, and Lord High Chamberlain. The Mas-
           ter of the Rolls was keeper of the rolls, patents, and

grants made under the great seal, and records of the Court of Chancery.

36   *gap and trade* entrance and beaten path

40–156   *I myself have ventured ... do as I have bid you.*
'Certain of the Council ... by the enticement and provocation of his ancient enemy the Bishop of Winchester, and other of the same sect, attempted the King against him, declaring plainly that the realm was so infected with heresies and heretics that it was dangerous for his highness farther to permit it un-reformed. ... The King would needs know his accusers. They answered that for as much as he was a Councillor no man durst take upon him to accuse him; but if it would please his highness to commit him to the Tower for a time, there would be accusations and proofs enough against him, for otherwise just testimony and witness against him would not appear. ...

'The King perceiving their importune suit against the Archbishop (but yet not meaning to have him wronged ...) granted to them that they should the next day commit him to the Tower for his trial. When night came ... the Archbishop ... coming into the gallery where the King walked ... his highness said, "Ah, my lord of Canterbury, I can tell you news. For diverse weighty considerations it is determined by me and the Council that you tomorrow at nine of the clock shall be committed to the Tower, for that you and your chaplains (as information is given us) have taught and preached ... such a number of execrable heresies ...; and therefore the Council have requested me for the trial of this matter to suffer them to commit you to the Tower, or else no man dare come forth as witness in these matters, you being a Councillor."

'When the King had said his mind, the Archbishop kneeled down and said, "I am content, if it please your grace, with all my heart to go thither at your highness' commandment, and I most humbly thank your majesty that I may come to my trial, for there be that have many ways slandered me and this way I hope to try myself not worthy of such a report."

'The King perceiving the man's uprightness joined with such simplicity said, "O Lord, what manner a man be you? . . . I had thought you would rather have sued to us to have taken the pains to have heard you and your accusers together for your trial without any such indurance. Do not you know what state you be in with the whole world, and how many great enemies you have? Do you not consider what an easy thing it is to procure three or four false knaves to witness against you? Think you to have better luck that way than your master, Christ, had? I see by it, you will run headlong to your undoing, if I would suffer you. Your enemies shall not so prevail against you, for I have otherwise devised. . . . Yet notwithstanding, tomorrow when the Council shall sit and send for you, resort unto them, and if . . . they do commit you to the Tower, require of them . . . that you may have your accusers brought before them, and that you may answer their accusations without any further indurance, and use for yourself as good persuasions as you may devise, and if no entreaty or reasonable request will serve, then deliver unto them this my ring . . . and say unto them . . . "I . . . appeal to the King's own person."

'The Archbishop . . . had much ado to forbear tears. "Well," said the King, "go your ways, my lord, and do as I have bidden you" ' (Foxe, pages 1693–4).

43   *Incensed* stirred up. Some editors change to 'Insensed', that is, informed, a word found from the fifteenth to the seventeenth centuries. To a listener, either meaning might equally present itself, since the words sound alike. Either meaning would in fact suit here, as also in Rowley's *When You See Me You Know Me* (line 2528), where the Queen's enemies are said to have 'insenst' the King against her.

44   *so I know he is, they know he is.* If the text is correct, the sense is either (1) provided I know he is, they take my word for it; or (2) such I know him to be, and they know him to be too.

47   *broken with* broken the information to

50   *hath* and has

52   *convented* summoned

64   *who* and she (the Queen)

68   *sufferance.* See note on II.3.15.

69   *Almost each pang a death.* In Rowley's *When You See Me You Know Me* the Queen (Jane Seymour) gives birth to Prince Edward but dies in childbed. Holinshed says nothing about Queen Anne's labour.

72   *midnight.* The word could include the small hours; compare line 1, *It's one o'clock.*

74   *estate* condition

75–6   *company | Would not be friendly to* the presence of others would hinder

85   *happily* opportunely

86   *Avoid the gallery* leave the gallery. The 'gallery' is not the upper stage but the main stage where they all are – 'the gallery where the King walked' (Foxe, page 1694). In Rowley's *When You See Me You Know Me* the King is reported to be 'walking in the gallery | As sad and passionate as e'er he was' (line 550).

106   *You a brother of us* you being a fellow Councillor

110–11   *Most throughly ... shall fly asunder.* Compare *Troilus and Cressida*, I.3.27–30:

> Distinction, with a broad and powerful fan,
> Puffing at all, winnows the light away;
> And what hath mass or matter by itself
> Lies rich in virtue and unmingled.

114   *Thy truth and thy integrity is rooted.* See note on I.2.20–21.

116   *by my holidame.* See note on line 153. The sense is, virtually, 'by all that's holy'. 'As help me God and

halidom' originally referred to the 'holiness' of relics on which oaths were sworn. Condensed to 'by my halidom' it was also varied to 'by my holidame', by popular association with 'Our Lady', the Virgin Mary.

121 *indurance* duress (referring, presumably, to his proposed confinement in the Tower, line 106; Foxe uses the word twice, though in an unspecific sense: see the notes on lines 40–156 and V.3.147–58)

125 *Being of those virtues vacant* if it is devoid of truth and honesty

128–9 *their practices | Must bear the same proportion* their plots must be correspondingly many and great

131 *The due o'th'verdict* the merited verdict

135 *Ween you* do you reckon on

138 *naughty* wicked (compare *The Merchant of Venice*, V.1.91, 'So shines a good deed in a naughty world')

139 *precipice*. This was a recent word at the play's date; F's 'Precepit' may be what Shakespeare wrote, from French '*précépite*' (Foakes).

146 *commit you* sentence you to confinement

153 *God's blest mother!* In Rowley's *When You See Me You Know Me* such oaths are often in the King's mouth; for example, 'Mother of God' (lines 148, 754, 798, 1653), 'God-a-mercy' (line 168), 'God's holy mother' (line 262).

165–6 *bless her! 'Tis a girl | Promises boys hereafter*. The Old Lady is temporizing pretty well: *her* and *girl* ostensibly refer to the Queen, but *her* is ambiguous (the Queen or the baby) and *Promises boys hereafter* implies that no boy has yet arrived.

168–70 *as like you . . . an hundred marks*. In Rowley's *When You See Me You Know Me* the King says 'Who first brings word that Harry hath a son | Shall be rewarded well', and Will Summers adds 'Ay, I'll be his surety, but do you hear, wenches, she that brings the first tidings, howsoever it fall out, let her be sure to say the

child's like the father, or else she shall have nothing'
(lines 286–90).

170   *an hundred marks* (two thirds of £100, the mark being
the value – not a coin – of two thirds of £1)

V.2   (stage direction) *Pursuivants, pages, and others.* In F's
stage direction Cranmer is solitary; but see lines 17 and
23–4. Foxe writes that he 'was compelled there to wait
among the pages, lackeys, and serving men all alone'
(page 1694).
    Pursuivants junior officers of the heralds

8   *happily* luckily

9   *presently* at once

12   *sound* (probably) fathom (with an implication of the
physician's 'probe'; the alternative explanation, 'proclaim', 'make known', neglects the fact that the
disgrace is known to the King already and is not
apparently a matter of secrecy)

18   (stage direction) *above* on the upper stage (the gallery
over the rear of the stage)

21   *Body o'me* (an exclamation Henry uses also in Rowley's
When You See Me You Know Me, lines 2601, 2678,
etc.)

27   *parted so much honesty* shared so much honour

31   *post with packets* courier with letters

34   (stage direction) *They partly close . . . to wait without.*
F has no stage direction at all for the King, Butts, or
Cranmer, and apparently means the King and Butts to
be overlooking the Council's doings, and Cranmer to
be waiting at one side while the preparations go ahead
for the Council meeting, until he is summoned to the
centre of the stage at V.3.7. Such ambivalence of place
is not uncommon; for example, in *Julius Caesar*, III.1,
the scene changes from the outside to the inside of
the Capitol with no pause. Still, the position of Cranmer would be awkward, waiting on stage with the

company of lackeys while the preliminaries for his 'trial' take place, and it is better to arrange a new scene (though with the King and Butts still watching) and have Cranmer withdraw until called for.

V.3 (stage direction) *Lord Chancellor* (actually Sir Thomas More, as shown at III.2.393–4, but left unnamed 'perhaps to avoid the intrusion of a personality' (Foakes))

10–15 *we all are men ... Toward the King.* This is from an address made by Bishop Stokesley of London to his clergy in 1531, as given in Hall's *The Union of the Two Noble Families of Lancaster and York* (1809 edition, page 783), and reproduced exactly by Foxe (page 959) though, as Foakes notes, it is separated by more than 700 pages from the other Foxe material used: 'My friends all, you know well that we be men frail of condition and no angels, and by frailty and lack of wisdom we have misdemeaned ourself toward the King our sovereign lord and his laws.'

11–12 *capable | Of our flesh* subject to our fleshly weaknesses

19 *pernicious* deadly

20 *sudden* swift

22 *Pace 'em not in their hands* do not put them through their paces while leading them by hand

23 *stubborn* stiff

24 *manage* control (a term for the training of horses)

28 *taint* infection

30 *The upper Germany* inland Germany. The allusion is perhaps to the Peasants' Rising under Thomas Münzer in Saxony in 1524, or the Anabaptist rising in Münster in 1535. Foxe refers unspecifically to 'horrible commotions and uproars, like as in some parts of Germany' and 'no small contentions and commotions ... as of late days the like was in diverse parts of Germany' (page 1694). Similarly Rowley's *When You See Me You Know Me* (lines 2201–5):

Much bloodshed there is now in Germany,
About this difference in religion,
With Lutherans, Arians, and Anabaptists,
As half the province of Helvetia
Is with their tumults almost quite destroyed.

38   *with a single heart* (a Biblical echo, of Genesis 20.5: 'with a single heart and innocent hands have I done this')

64   *modesty* moderation, temperateness

66   *Lay all the weight ye can upon my patience* oppress my patience as much as you can

67   *I make as little doubt as you do conscience* I have no more doubt than you have conscience

69   *modest*. Compare line 64.

70   *you are a sectary* you follow a sect (rather than the Church)

71   *Your painted gloss discovers* your specious pretence discloses

72   *words and weakness* 'empty talk and false reasoning' (Dr Johnson)

78   *I cry your honour mercy* (ironical; Gardiner is as much at odds with Cromwell as with Cranmer – see V.1.29–32)

85, 87   LORD CHANCELLOR ('Cham.' (Chamberlain) in F; but the Lord Chancellor is presiding)

94   *strangely* uncommonly

104–5   *we first put this dangerous stone a-rolling, | 'Twould fall upon ourselves.* Compare Proverbs 26.27: 'he that rolleth up a stone, it will return upon him'. The idea became proverbial; Tilley, S 889.

109   *gave* told

112   *envy at* hate

113   *Ye blew the fire that burns ye* (proverbial; Tilley, C 465)

114–21   *Dread sovereign ... this great offender.* 'Gardiner's fulsome flattery of the King recalls Wolsey's (III.2.166–79). There is, indeed, a certain similarity between the

255

two ecclesiastics; but Gardiner has nothing of the strength and grandeur of Wolsey' (D. Nichol Smith, in the Warwick edition, 1899).

119   *dear respect* heartfelt regard

122   *sudden* extempore

126   *play the spaniel* (a frequent and proverbial analogy for obsequious flattery; Tilley, S 704. Compare *Julius Caesar*, III.1.43, 'curtsies and base spaniel fawning', and *Antony and Cleopatra*, IV.12.20–21, 'The hearts | That spanieled me at heels'.)

132   *starve* die

133   *this place* this seat I appoint you to occupy. F reads 'his place', and some editors follow, interpreting as 'a place like his, as a Councillor'. But this reads awkwardly, and it is more natural that the King should follow up his instruction *sit down* (line 130).

135–46   *I had thought ... had ye mean.* 'His highness with a severe countenance said unto them, "Ah, my lords, I thought I had wiser men of my Council than now I find you. What discretion was this in you, thus to make the Primate of the realm, and one of you in office, to wait at the Council chamber door amongst servingmen? You might have considered that he was a Councillor as well as you, and you had no such commission of me so to handle him. I was content that you should try him as a Councillor, and not as a mean subject. But now I well perceive that things be done against him maliciously, and if some of you might have had your minds you would have tried him to the uttermost"' (Foxe, page 1694).

146   *mean* means

147–58   *Thus far ... all embrace him.* 'One or two of the chiefest of the Council, making their excuse, declared that in requesting his indurance, it was rather meant for his trial and his purgation against the common fame and slander of the world than for any malice conceived against him. "Well, well, my lords," quoth

the King, "take him and well use him, as he is worthy
to be, and make no more ado" ' (Foxe, page 1694).

166-7   *spare your spoons* save the expense of christening spoons
(the traditional gift from godparents)

167   *partners* co-sponsors

176-7   *Do my lord of Canterbury | A shrewd turn and he's your
friend for ever*. 'It came into a common proverb: Do
unto my lord of Canterbury displeasure or a shrewd
turn, and then you may be sure to have him your
friend whiles he liveth' (Foxe, page 1691).

I.4.2   *Parish Garden* (a noisy bear- and bull-baiting resort on
the south bank of the Thames, near the Globe Theatre.
The name probably meant what it said, but the place
was often called Paris Garden, supposedly 'from
Robert de Paris, who had a house there in Richard
II's time' (Thomas Blount, *Glossographia*, fourth
edition, 1674) or, by popular mythology, from the
Homeric hero (John Taylor, *The Carrier's Cosmo-
graphy*, 1637).)

3   *gaping* bawling

4-5   *belong to th'larder* work in the pantry

7   *crab-tree* crab-apple (a very hard wood)

8   *switches* twigs

10   *ale and cakes* (traditionally served at christenings,
festivals, and so on; compare *Twelfth Night*, II.3.111-
12, 'Dost thou think, because thou art virtuous, there
shall be no more cakes and ale?')

15   *May-day morning* (a holiday, begun before dawn, when
May-day dew was gathered for the complexion)

16   *Paul's* (St Paul's Cathedral)

22   *Samson ... Sir Guy ... Colbrand* (heroes famed for
superhuman strength; Sir Guy of Warwick was renowned in medieval romance for slaying the Danish
giant Colbrand in a duel at Winchester before Athel-
stan)

257

26   *see a chine* look on meat (a chine is a backbone or a joint of meat from an animal's back)

27   *not for a cow, God save her.* This is a phrase of uncertain and perhaps garbled sense, meaning, more or less, 'not for anything at all, God bless it!' The phrase 'I would not do that for a cow, save her tail', was recorded from Devon in 1862. Foakes also quotes the anonymous play *The Tell-Tale* (Malone Society Reprint, from line 1052):

> VICTORIA ... rather than my beauty
>   Should play the villain ...
>   Thus would I mangle it.
> JULIO Not for a cow, God save her.

Hilda M. Hulme, in *Explorations in Shakespeare's Language* (1962), discusses *chine* and *not for a cow* in detail but provides no assured explanation.

33   *Moorfields* (the district outside Moorgate in London, made into a park in 1606 and frequented by holiday crowds)

34   *some strange Indian.* Indians from America were shown as curiosities; compare *The Tempest*, II.2.29–32, 'There [in England] would this monster make a man. ... When they will not give a doit to relieve a lame beggar, they will lay out ten to see a dead Indian.' The condition and inhabitants of Virginia (founded in 1608) were matters of particular interest.
    tool penis

35–6   *fry of fornication* (1) offspring of fornication; (2) swarm of fornicators

39   *spoons* christening spoons (compare note on V.3.166–7)

40   *brazier* brass-worker

41   *dog-days* (hottest days of the year, supposedly from early July to mid-August, when the Dog-star, Sirius, rises at about the same time as the sun)

42–3   *under the line* on the equator

43   *fire-drake* fiery phenomenon (compare *meteor* in line
      49)

46   *mortar-piece* (a short piece of ordnance with large
      bore; that is, 'gaping upwards' (Foakes))
      blow us blow us up

48   *pinked porringer* (bowl-shaped cap, pierced or scalloped
      for ornament; compare *The Taming of the Shrew*,
      IV.3.64–5, 'Why, this was moulded on a porringer –
      | A velvet dish')

50   *Clubs!* (the cry summoning London apprentices to
      intervene in a fight)

51   *truncheoners* (a nonce word) cudgel bearers

52   *the hope o'th'Strand* likely lads of the Strand (a street of
      fashionable merchants' shop-dwellings, with appren-
      tices living on the premises)

54   *to th'broomstaff* to close quarters

55–6 *loose shot* unattached marksmen

57   *work* fort

61   *tribulation* troublemakers, pests
      Tower Hill (a rough London district; the most famous
      scaffold in England was a permanent feature, and
      executions attracted crowds of brutal spectators)

63   *in Limbo Patrum* in durance vile, gaol. (*Limbus Patrum*
      was a place of departed spirits in medieval theology,
      the abode between Heaven and Hell of the just who
      died before Christ's coming, and of unbaptized
      infants.)

64   *running banquet* light refreshment (compare note on
      I.4.12; here, in fact, a whipping through the streets)

65   *beadles* (minor officers of the law, who administered
      whippings, took offenders into custody, and so on)

69   *made a fine hand* made a good job of it (ironical)

71   *suburbs* (rowdy districts outside the City's jurisdiction)

79   *round* heavy

80   *baiting of bombards* refreshing yourselves with drink.
      To 'bait' is to take refreshment; 'bombards' were
      leather jugs for liquor, so-called because in shape and

colour they resembled cannon. Falstaff is 'that huge bombard of sack' in *1 Henry IV*, II.4.439.

85   *Marshalsea* (the famous prison, near Saint George's, Southwark)

88   *camlet* fine cloth (of silk or Angora goat's hair)

    get up o'th'rail. The meaning is not clear , though the *rail* may be the low one round the stage front. Who is to get upon or off it is uncertain. Unless the crowd addressed is off stage these remarks are presumably directed to the spectators – a theatrically entertaining effect – though picking out anyone dressed in camlet would be chancy unless an actor were planted there for the purpose. The matter is discussed by J. W. Saunders in 'Vaulting the Rails' (*Shakespeare Survey 7*, 1954, pages 69–81).

89   *peck you o'er the pales* pitch you over the railings. Which *pales* are intended is as uncertain as which *rail* in the previous line.

V.5   (stage direction) *Garter*. See note on IV.1.36 (stage direction).

    standing bowls bowls with legs

1–3   *Heaven . . . Elizabeth*. This closely follows the formula as pronounced by the Garter King-of-Arms in Holinshed (III.787): 'God of His infinite goodness send prosperous life and long to the high and mighty Princess of England, Elizabeth'. It would probably connect in spectators' minds with the marriage ceremonies of Princess Elizabeth and Prince Frederick in 1613, when the Garter King-of-Arms 'published the style of the Prince and Princess to this effect: "All health, happiness, and honour be to the high and mighty Princes, Frederick . . . and Elizabeth"' (quoted by Foakes from Henry Peacham's *The Period of Mourning*, 1613, H2ᵛ).

5   *partners* co-sponsors

12   *gossips* godparents (from 'God-sib', related in God)

      prodigal. 'The Archbishop of Canterbury gave to the Princess a standing cup of gold, the Duchess of Norfolk gave to her a standing cup of gold, fretted with pearl; the Marchioness of Dorset gave three standing bowls pounced [embossed], with a cover; and the Marchioness of Exeter gave three standing bowls graven, all gilt with a cover' (Holinshed, III.787).

17   *still* ever

23   *Saba* the Queen of Sheba (who, as related in 1 Kings 10, visited Solomon to prove him with hard questions and found that his wisdom and prosperity 'exceedeth the fame which I heard'. The spelling is that of bibles preceding the Authorized Version of 1611, save that the Geneva Bible (1560) has 'Sheba' in the text, though 'Saba' in chapter headings.)

26   *piece* person (probably in the sense of 'example'; compare *Pericles*, IV.6.110, 'Thou art a piece of virtue'; *The Winter's Tale*, IV.4.419–20, 'thou, fresh piece | Of excellent witchcraft'; and *The Tempest*, I.2.56, 'Thy mother was a piece of virtue')

33–5   *In her days ... all his neighbours* (Biblical echoes: 1 Kings 4.20, 'And Juda and Israel were many, even as the sand of the sea in number, eating, drinking, and making merry', and 4.25, 'And Juda and Israel dwelt without fear, every man under his vine, and under his fig-tree ... all the days of Solomon'; similarly 2 Kings 18.31, Isaiah 36.16, and Micah 4.4. Foakes points to frequent references to these visions of peace in sermons and other literature praising James I's reign.)

36   *God shall be truly known* true religion shall prevail

40   *maiden phoenix* (the fabulous Arabian bird, living unmated, and dying to give rise to a successor, a symbol often used for monarchs in respect both of their uniqueness and of their linking together precursors and successors; it was applied to Queen Elizabeth and to

261

Princess Elizabeth (Foakes). In Rowley's *When You See Me You Know Me* Henry marks the death of Queen Jane, giving birth to Prince Edward, with a Latin proverb translated as 'One phoenix dying gives another life' (line 491). In Dekker's *The Whore of Babylon*, III.3.235, King James is 'A second phoenix', arising after the death of Queen Elizabeth.)

42   *admiration* cause of wonder

43   *one* (James I)

44   *this cloud of darkness* this world where we live darkly

47   *fixed* as a fixed star

50–54   *Wherever the bright sun ... plains about him* (an echo, as Foakes observes, of God's promises to Abraham in Genesis 17.5–6: 'a father of many nations have I made thee. I will make thee exceeding fruitful, and will make nations of thee; yea, and kings shall spring out of thee'. The words were frequently alluded to in discourses on Princess Elizabeth's marriage to the Elector Palatine.)

52   *new nations* (probably alluding to the settlement of Virginia, which started in 1608)

53   *cedar* (echoing Psalm 92.12, 'The righteous shall flourish like a palm tree and shall spread abroad like a cedar in Libanus', and Ezekiel 17.22–3, 'Thus saith the Lord God, I will also take off the top of this high cedar ... and will plant it upon an high hill ... that it may bring forth boughs ... and be an excellent cedar; and under it shall remain all birds, and every fowl shall remain under the shadow of the branches thereof')

57   *An agèd princess* (Queen Elizabeth died in 1603, aged sixty-nine, having reigned since 1558)

65   *get* 'achieve, quibbling on "beget" ' (Foakes).

74   *sick* unhappy

75   *'Has* he has

76   *holiday* ('Holy-day' in F, a reminder of religious significance)

Epilogue

The Epilogue, in its commonplace banter and careless colloquialism, is very like that, by Fletcher, to *The Two Noble Kinsmen*.

5–6   *to hear the city | Abused.* Citizen life was often satirized in the drama as mercenary and illiberal.

9–10   *only in | . . . women.* For the 'rhyme', see note on Prologue, 25–6.

10   *construction* interpretation

'The historical dramas are now concluded, of which the two parts of *Henry the Fourth* and *Henry the Fifth* are among the happiest of our author's compositions; and *King John, Richard the Third*, and *Henry the Eighth* deservedly stand in the second class' (Dr Johnson).

AN ACCOUNT OF THE TEXT

THE earliest text is that in the first Folio (1623), *Mr. William Shakespeares Comedies, Histories, & Tragedies*. In the list of contents (or 'Catalogue of the seuerall Comedies, Histories, and Tragedies contained in this Volume') it is called *The Life of King Henry the Eight*; on its individual title-page it is *The Famous History of the Life of King Henry the Eight*.

The text is a good one, presenting only minor problems, and not many even of these. It is divided into acts and scenes at the points followed in modern editions, save that it runs together as the second scene of Act V what is now generally divided as scenes 2 and 3; consequently its subsequent scene numbers are one lower than in most modern editions.

The copy from which the text was set up was carefully prepared. Entrances and exits, except for a few self-evident ones, are duly marked and need little readjustment. Forms of speech prefixes show only unimportant variations, and indicate care to be fairly uniform: Queen Katherine appears as '*Queen*' (or abbreviations thereof) until, after her dethronement, she is '*Katherine Dowager*' in the entry direction for IV.2 and speaks as '*Kath.*'. The Lord Chamberlain appears in various abbreviations of his title; in V.3.85 and 87 the Folio reads '*Cham.*' where presumably '*Chan.*' (Lord Chancellor) is meant. But this is a very minor error.

The stage directions – which are retained in this edition except as indicated below (List 2) – offer interesting features. Some of them reflect stage terminology or the imperatives of practical instructions, and might seem to have originated in a prompt-book (for example, I.1.0, '*Enter the Duke of Norfolke at one doore. At the other, the Duke of Buckingham*'; or I.4.49, '*Drum and Trumpet, Chambers dischargd*'; see also, in the text, I.4.76, II.1.0, and II.2.119, and, in t he collations, I.4.74 and 81). Some express what looks like authorial imprecision rather than prompt-book specificity (for example, I.1.114, '*certaine of the Guard*'; I.1.197, '*two or theee* [*sic*] *of the Guard*'; I.4.0, '*diuers other Ladies, & Gentlemen*'). Some suggest the author indicating effects or situations (for example, I.1.114, '*The Cardinall in his passage, fixeth his eye on Buckingham, and Buckingham on him, both full of disdaine*'; I.4.63, '*They passe directly before the Cardinall, and gracefully salute him*'; II.2.0, '*. . . reading this Letter*'; IV.1.36 , '*A liuely Flourish . . .*'; see also II.1.54, II.2.60, III.2.203 and 372, and V.3.113). This kind of descriptive particularity includes a striking attention to details of behaviour or position (for example, I.2.0, '*Cornets. Enter King Henry, leaning on the Cardinals shoulder . . . the Cardinall places himselfe vnder the Kings feete on his right side*'; see also I.2.8, and such details as '*with some small distance*' in the entry direction for II.4). In the account of Katherine's vision (IV.2.82) there is an evident desire for interpretative description: '*. . . (as it were by inspiration) she makes (in her sleepe) signes of reioycing*'.

Particularly noticeable are the long descriptions of ceremonial arrangements, for the Queen's trial in II.4, the coronation procession in IV.1, the vision in IV.2, the Council assembly in V.3, and the christening in V.5. The curious past tense in section 5 of the coronation procession, where the Garter King-of-Arms '*wore a Gilt Copper Crowne*', suggests that the writer was influenced by Holinshed's past-tense narration, in which 'every king-of-arms put on a crown of copper and gilt, all which were worn till night'(III.784), rather than that he had his mind on the stage.

The reliability and uniformity of the text and speech prefixes might suggest that the Folio text was printed from a prompt-book; but the frequent narrative descriptions of actions and manners, and the graphic particularity with which processions and other spectacles are related, would be unusual in a prompt-book. These considerations together suggest that the Folio text was printed from a fair copy made by a scribe from an author's manuscript that had been carefully prepared as a text for reading rather than for stage production.

COLLATIONS

The following lists are selective, not comprehensive; they record significant variants, including variant punctuation where any change of sense is involved, but they do not include regularizations such as the correction of misprints or small changes in stage directions. 'F' indicates the first Folio (1623). Its readings are given here unmodernized, except that 'long s' (ʃ) is printed as 's'.

I

Accepted readings later than F

The following readings in the present text (given first, and terminating in a square bracket) originate in editions later than F; if proposed by a modern editor, they are identified. The rejected F reading follows.

I.i.	33	censure. When] censure, when
	42–7	All was royal; ... together,] *Buc.* All was Royall, ... together?
	45	function. BUCKINGHAM Who] Function: who
	47–8	as you guess? | NORFOLK One] *Nor.* As you guesse: | One
	63	web, 'a] (*G. L. Kittredge, 1936*); Web. O
	69–70	that? | If not from hell, the] that, | If not from Hell? The
	78–80	letter, | ... in he papers.] Letter | The Honourable Boord of Councell, out | Must fetch him in, he Papers.
	87	issue?] issue.
	120	venom-mouthed] venom'd-mouth'd

	123	chafed] chaff'd
	159–62	– for ... perform't, his ... reciprocally –] (for ... perform't) his ... reciprocally,
	183	him. He privily] him. Priuily
	200	Hereford] *Hertford*
	219	Perk] (*R. A. Foakes, 1957, from Holinshed's* Perke); *Pecke*
		chancellor] (*from Holinshed*); Councellour
	221	Nicholas] (*from Holinshed*); *Michaell*
	226	lord] Lords
I.2.	67	business] basenesse
	139–40	point:	... person,] point,	... person;
	156	feared] feare
	164	confession's] (*from Holinshed*); Commissions
	170	To win] (*C. J. Sisson, 1954*); To
	179–80	dangerous	For him] dangerous	For this
	190	Bulmer] (*from Holinshed*); *Blumer*
I.3.	13	Or] A
	34	'*oui*'] wee
	59	wherewithal: in him] wherewithall in him;
II.1.	18	have] him
	20	Perk] (*as at* I.1.219)
	42–3	who removed,	Earl Surrey was] who re-mou'd	Earle *Surrey*, was
	86	mark] make
II.2.	83	one have-at-him] one; haue at him
II.3.	14	quarrel, Fortune,] quarrell. Fortune,
	59	note's] notes
	61	of you,] of you, to you;
II.4.	127	GRIFFITH] *Gent. Vsh.*
	174	A] And
	219	summons. Unsolicited] Summons vnsolicited.
	239	return. With thy approach] returne, with thy approch:
III.1.	3	GENTLEWOMAN (*sings*)] SONG.
	61	your] our

III.1. 82–3 England | But little for my profit. Can] England, | But little for my profit can

175–7 forgive me | If . . . unmannerly. | You] forgiue me; | If . . . vnmannerly, | You

III.2. 171 filed] fill'd

209 I fear, the] I feare the

233 commission, lords? Words] Commission? Lords, words

292 Who] Whom

339 legatine] (*from Holinshed*); Legatiue

343 Chattels] Castles

351 Farewell, a long] Farewell? A long

IV.1. 9–10 forward – | In] forward | In

20 SECOND GENTLEMAN] I (*i.e.* FIRST GENTLEMAN)

34 Kimbolton] Kymmalton

54–5 indeed – | FIRST GENTLEMAN And] indeed, | And

101 Stokesley] (*from Holinshed's* Stokesleie); Stokeley

IV.2. 7 think] thanke

98 colour] cold

V.1. 1 PAGE] *Boy.*

37 time] Lime

140 woo] woe

157 LOVELL] *Gent.*

V.2. 7 piece] Peere

V.3. 0 *no fresh scene number in* F

85, 87 LORD CHANCELLOR] *Cham.*

125 bare] base

130–31 proudest, | He that] proudest | Hee, that

133 this] his

172 brother-love] Brother; loue

174 heart] hearts

V.4. 0 *scene numbered 'Scena Tertia' in* F

4, 28 SERVANT] *not in* F

V.5. 0 *scene numbered 'Scena Quarta' in* F

4 Queen!] Queen,
37 ways] way

2

Stage directions
The following list shows the more important amendments of
and additions to F's stage directions. F's reading follows the
square bracket. Additions such as 'aside' and indications of the
character to whom a speech is addressed are not listed.

I.2.	0	*Wolsey's Secretary in attendance*] not in F
	8	Queen!' *Enter the Queen, ushered by the Dukes of Norfolk and Suffolk*] *Queene, vsher'd by the Duke of Norfolke. Enter the Queene, Norfolke and Suffolke:*
I.3.	15	*Enter Sir Thomas Lovell*] *after* 'Lovell?', *line* 16
I.4.	30	*He kisses her*] not in F
	38	*He drinks*] not in F
	49	*Drum and trumpet. Chambers discharged*] *after line* 48
	50	*Exit a Servant*] not in F
	60	*Exit Lord Chamberlain, attended*] not in F
	74	*They choose ladies; the King chooses Anne Bullen*] *Choose Ladies, King and An Bullen.*
	81	*He whispers with the masquers*] *Whisper. (after* 'surrender it', *line* 81)
	84	*He comes from his state*] not in F
	86	*The King unmasks*] not in F
II.1.	54	*Enter . . . people, etc.*] *after* 'courtesy', *line* 53
II.2.	115	*Exit Wolsey*] not in F
		Enter Wolsey with Gardiner] *Enter Gardiner.*
II.3.	80	*Exit Lord Chamberlain*] *after* 'you', *line* 80
II.4.	0	*Archbishop*] *Bishop*
		then Griffith, a Gentleman Usher] *Then a Gentleman Vsher*
III.1.	19	*Exit Gentleman*] not in F

III.2.   106   *Enter . . . Lovell*] *Enter King, reading of a scedule. (after line* 104)

         201   *he gives him papers*] not in F

IV.1.   35   *Trumpets*] not in F

         36   (after the procession) *The procession passes over the stage in order and state*] Exeunt, *first passing ouer the Stage in Order and State, and then, A great Flourish of Trumpets.*

         42   *looking at the Queen*] not in F

         55   *The end of the procession leaves;*] not in F
                and then a great flourish of trumpets] after 'Order and State' (following section 10 of the Order of the Coronation)

IV.2.   128   *She gives it to Katherine*] not in F

V.1.   55   *Exeunt Gardiner and Page*] *Exit Gardiner and Page. (after line* 54)

         78   *Enter Sir Anthony Denny*] after line 79

         83   *Exit Denny*] not in F

         90   *kneeling*] not in F

        108   *kneeling*] not in F

        157   *Enter Lovell, following her*] not in F

        176   *Exeunt*] *Exit Ladie.*

V.2.   0   *Pursuivants . . . Chamber*] not in F

         4   *Enter Keeper*] after 'Sure you know me?'

         5   *Enter Doctor Butts*] after 'called for', *line* 6

         34   *They partly . . . wait without*] not in F

V.3.   0   *Keeper at the door*] not in F

        109   *Exit King above*] not in F

V.4.   81   *Trumpets*] not in F

V.5.   4   *kneeling*] not in F

         9   *The King kisses the child*] not in F

3

Rejected variants

The following list contains some of the more interesting variants proposed or accepted in editions after the first Folio but not accepted here. The readings of this edition are given first, followed by a square bracket. The rejected variants follow, separated by a semi-colon where there is more than one. The source is given of those that originate in modern editions. Where no source is named, the reading is one proposed by an earlier editor which has not gained general acceptance.

I.1.	63	web, 'a] Web. O!; web he; web, O,
	219	Perk] Peck; Parke
I.2.	43–4	lord? | You know no more than others?] lord, | You know no more than others:
	120	ravished listening] list'ning ravish'd
	139	This dangerous] His dangerous (*C. J. Sisson, 1954*)
	139–40	point: | Not friended . . . wish to . . . person,] point; | Not friended . . . wish, to . . . person
	147	Henton] Hopkins (*see* I.1.221 *and note to* I.2.147)
	170	To win] To gain
	179–80	dangerous | For him to] Dangerous | To; Dangerous for him | To
I.3.	12	see] saw
	13	Or] And
	34	'*oui*'] wear
I.4.	6	first, good] first-good; feast, good
	104–5	merry, | Good my lord Cardinal]: merry. Good my lord cardinal,
II.1.	20	Perk] Peck; Parke
	89	forsake] forsake me
II.2.	83	one have-at-him] one heave at him
II.3.	14	quarrel, Fortune,] quarr'lous Fortune; quarr'ler Fortune; cruel Fortune; fortune's quarrel

II.3.	61	of you,] to you,
II.4.	33	gave notice] gave not notice
	62	desire] defer
	148	At once] Atton'd
	182	bosom] bottom
	183	spitting] splitting
III.1.	21	coming. Now I think on't,] coming, now I think on't.
	124	a curse] accursed (*F. D. Hoeniger, 1969*)
III.2.	119–20	be, | There] be | There
	192	that am, have, and will be] that am I, have been, will be; that I am true and will be
	305	can blush] can, blush
IV.2.	36	Tied] Tyth'd
	50	honour. From his cradle] honour from his cradle.
	98	colour] coldness
V.1.	43	Incensed] Insensed
	122	good] ground
V.3.	11	frail, and capable] frail, incapable; frail, and culpable
	12	Of our flesh] Of frailty
	124	presence] presence;
	126	reach. You] reach, you
	172	brother-love] brother's love
V.5.	70	you, good] your good (F *has* 'you good')